WEAVING HOPE
MYSTERIOUS ARTS
BOOK FIVE

CELIA LAKE

Formatted with Vellum

CHAPTER I

"Do go have a look at the garden, Henny, and I'll put the kettle on." Eda brushed her hands off on her apron, considering the state of her loom, her shoulders, her feet, and her eyes. All of them could use a rest. She certainly wasn't getting any younger. It was time to pause, take a breath, and enjoy the moment without rushing. All things in their rhythm.

Henny, her second for the last three years, grinned and headed downstairs. Henny had anticipated the break, of course. It was coming up on half-two, a proper time for a cuppa before they got in another two or three hours for the day. Eda would be busy long after that, but that wasn't a bother.

Doing the bookkeeping reminded her how much she'd built here, and just how well they were doing. All told, the workshop right now supported six apprentices, four journeymen, an excellent second in Henny, and Eda herself. Not bad for a floor of looms and the people who worked magic with them. Henny had been with her for thirteen years next week. They'd have to get cakes in for tea to celebrate.

1

For the moment, she took in the state of the workshop. Only three of the looms were in use today. She and Henny had plans to warp the high-warp loom that reigned over the east side of the floor, beyond the stairs. But it would take ages, and they'd agreed to put it off for next week. Or possibly the week after. It wasn't as if they had a new commission for it. Eda had a plan, of course. She always had plans lying in wait that would do to use stocks of yarn they had or could get easily.

Right now, in this workshop at least, it was the more ordinary weaving, cloth for magical clothing that was selling well. Exceedingly well. She'd had more orders than she could entirely handle for wool twill, and also the wool and silk blend that many favoured for ritual robes. And, better yet, several of the orders wanted decorative work. It wasn't the same dull black for inch after inch. Black wool, woven with the proper charms, paid brilliantly, but it was nice to do something more interesting.

She'd have to find time to go out to the New Forest soon. Ferry had moved her own work there. She was working on her journeyman project, some substantial restoration of Ytene's tapestries. Eda had needed to nudge her into the confidence to take it on, but Lord Carillon had been delighted and convinced that Ferry would be the right person. He'd taken an interest in Ferry and her husband, his head of stables, some years ago. Better, he'd made it clear he'd pay Ferry's apprenticeship fees if her family decided to be difficult. Of course, he'd apparently been quite pointed at them, as well, and they hadn't dared.

From what Ferry said, her parents were cowed now. And adorable children had apparently eased some of the family tensions a tad, too. But Ferry was happy. She had a deft hand with the finest repairs. And Ferry had got better and more refined as she got more experience. And working at Ytene, whether on the repairs or on her own loom, meant she could be near her two little ones, who were both too small to leave for long without their mama handy.

There had been a time, back oh, thirty years ago, when she'd been young and optimistic, that Eda had thought that her path. Agreeable weaving to keep an income and use her skills. In that imagined future, small children grew bigger, like weaving grew on the loom. But while her marriage to Bert had been amiable enough in the main— well, until the last few years before the War— there had been no children. Now she was grateful for that. It had been enough of a challenge keeping the workshop steady through the War. More than enough.

That brought her back to the state of things. Alaine and Peggy had taken the week for a bit of a walking holiday with Peggy's brother. Eda had suspicions he was working up to courting Aliane, and Aliane was seeing how long it took him to be brave enough to ask her to walk out. The two women were testing a theory that one kind of walking might lead to the other. They were both far enough along in their apprenticeship that a pause was good, getting them ready to think about designing a journeyman project.

Rebecca and Caroline both had their own workshops as journeymen, their looms tucked into a room of their family home. Each had one of the remaining apprentices with them: Morry with Rebecca and Hester with Caroline. That was all plain weaving, not the tapestry work Eda had a reputation for, but plain work wore well and it was always in demand. They'd be in Trellech next week, for the fortnightly meeting and to bring in their finished cloth for sale through the Guild. That meant it would be properly certified for both the weaving quality and magical properties.

3

Even with half of them working elsewhere, the workshop took over the entire first floor of the house, and all the space that in any other home would be attic storage. The big tapestry loom stuck up, to get enough height for larger pieces. It was a good thing they had the large window to the back garden and courtyard available when they had to bring something large in or out. Once, it had been the main upstairs bedroom, but it was far more use as it was. And these days, mostly it was material going out, when there was a finished piece too large to easily bring down the twist in the stairs to the ground floor.

She heard Henny hit the loose step by the turn. Time for her to raise her voice, clapping twice loudly just out of step with the clacking thump of the looms, so the others would hear her.

"Break, Innis and Kay. Tea in a few."

Innis nodded, holding up her hand in the sign that meant she'd be down when they reached a good stopping point. Kay looked baffled, but Kay was still learning just about everything. He'd started an apprenticeship in March, when he'd turned sixteen. Eda wasn't sure he'd make a weaver, but she'd agreed to give him a try and see what he liked. It was a favour to a son of a guildmate of Bert, her late husband. It had been easier to give Kay a trial than argue. Kay was pleasant to deal with. He didn't sulk or pout. But he also found the maths confusing, and in some ways, weaving was far more about maths than about art.

Or it was also about art, but she couldn't teach the art. She could, with a bit of luck and skill, teach the maths. If someone could learn them.

For her part, Eda went downstairs, stopping to use the loo and wash her hands. Then she went in through the kitchen. She had enjoyed giving the entire house over to her workshop over the last few years. Oh, she had her own bedroom, tucked under the stairs, and a small study. But the sitting room and kitchen had chairs for their breaks. Everyone had a mug and a peg to hang it on in the kitchen. And just outside the kitchen was the garden. Mostly dye plants, of course, but some kitchen herbs as well. Carefully segregated, of course, one didn't want things mixing.

The kettle was going, and Henny had already set out their mugs, tea strainers at the ready. Eda stretched, feeling something in her neck click, before sinking into the old easy chair by the window that was her particular throne. "How's the new wool?" Henny had been working with yarn from a new spinning collective and sheep. It wasn't too different from what they'd been using, but the wool had a longer staple length, and it also took colour a little differently.

Henny held up her fingers, which were muddy with a mix of shades. "Coming off a bit in the work. I'll have a word with them about it. Do you have that rinse recipe handy, the one you taught the Groveshot folks, a couple of years ago?"

"Of course. Remind me and I'll copy it out for you." She considered. "It ought to be easier to get the dill for it now. I thought they'd done that yarn with madder. It ought to be colour-fast."

"Madder and something else, apparently. I'll ask. The weld was a lot better, thankfully. The madder should be fine once it's rinsed better, but they can do that before the next shipment. I'll get Kay to help me with this one. If the weather holds tomorrow, we should be able to get the tubs out and let it hang to dry overnight."

"I'll warn Lily." Eda's next-door neighbour was relatively tolerant of a number of things. But she did like to know when they were hanging out coloured items to dry, beyond the ordinary laundry. The shades distracted her if she wasn't prepared for it, apparently, and she'd look out the window for ages without getting about her own work. A little warning meant she set up in a different room for the day.

Once, it had been actual laundry hung up. But these days, Eda sent hers out to the laundry two blocks away. One person didn't make so much dirty linen as two. It wasn't that expensive, considering. Most importantly, it meant they could save clear days for washing and drying yarn and cloth and rugs. Sunny days could be at a premium in southern Wales, after all.

She was lucky to be tucked into the outer edge of Trellech. She was still inside the city walls, but with the green space that served as a buffer between the river and the magical community just over the wall. That meant she had room for the dye garden. She'd inherited the house from her grandmum, who'd used the garden for cooking ingredients for her shop down at the corner.

The kettle sang, Henny poured the water out, and then came back with her mug and Eda's. "Here. And— ah." It was always obvious when the looms stopped. Everything was charmed to be soundproof and to reduce the vibrations, but there was always a little telltale thump and shift. A moment later, they heard lighter steps on the stairs, then Innis's slower ones.

"Tea on the counter, Kay. And can you grab the biscuit tin?" Innis came in just behind Kay, guiding him. Once they were all settled, Henny nudged Eda's foot with hers. They were all in socks, of course, they'd had the floor looms in play. "What's next up to warp?"

"You're wanting to warp something else? Besides the duchess?" That was the pet name for the high-warp loom.

She sprawled like a great lady of the Georgian courts with panniers and skirts that wouldn't fit through a door straight on.

"You said you were thinking about whether we could take on an order for proper ritual silk. Black warp, colour for the weft, I thought we could do lengths in different colours, one of the elemental sets? All of one making, you know that sells well."

"I'd have to check our stocks. But you're right, that sells well. A simple border, maybe, something that plays with the black?"

"Oh, I was thinking suitable for the elements. I found a rather darling wave pattern in the guild library. I don't think anyone's done anything like that for years. Before the War, maybe."

"There's probably a reason for that. The delightful patterns to weave don't drop out of use that way." Eda had charged off at that particular target more than few times herself. "Draw up your patterns, do the maths on the sizes, and we'll talk about it, all right?"

"Grand." Henny beamed at her. "And you're getting on with the black."

"Another fortnight, maybe, to finish it up. But there's a nice length, indeed." She was getting along for yards, plenty of the same weaving to do something useful with. "And I should think about what I do next. Guild, tomorrow, once you've put out the washing to dry?"

Kay looked up at that, and Eda let Henny explain what they'd need to do, and how he could be helpful in doing it. She cupped her hands around her mug and settled back in her chair. In five minutes, they'd all go back to work, and it'd be too loud to chat.

CHAPTER 2
THE NEXT DAY AT EDA'S WORKSHOP

"Mistress Eda?" Henny was being formal, and that made Eda turn around, unsure of what she'd find. It was the end of their Friday, getting on towards five, and they were wrapping up for the week. Innis and Kay had just finished winding thread and yarn for next week's work. Eda's could be left until she picked up the shuttle again - likely after supper. And Henny had been downstairs checking on the supply lists.

"Yes?" Eda resisted the desire to smooth out her apron.

"There's a gentleman to see you, he asked, very polite, about making an appointment. Would you rather I take his particulars or would you prefer to come down?"

It was odd to have someone call, but she wasn't doing anything else. She waved a hand. "Show him through to the study, please." It was a better place for a guest, presumably with some sort of more private question, if he were asking for an appointment. "Innis, Kay, you head off now, please." She certainly didn't need them tromping down the stairs noisily. "I'll be down in a minute."

Henny disappeared back down the stairs, and Innis held

Kay back for a moment, time enough for Henny to escort whoever it was to the study. Then they went off. Eda took a breath before going downstairs. She ducked into her bedroom to tidy her hair, add a bit of lotion to her hands, and take off the apron and re-tuck her blouse. She washed her hands in the bathing room. The door of her study was ajar, though she couldn't hear any conversation. She knocked once, heard Henny's "Mistress Fellowes", and went in.

Henny had taken a seat on the bench under the window, but as soon as Eda entered, the man stood from one of the two chairs by the small fireplace. She took in his details automatically. She could see why Henny had defaulted to referring to him as a gentleman; his suit was tailored well and by someone who knew his work. But she thought the wool suiting was in the second tier of quality, not the first, and it was of a weight and weave that predated the War. It was still in good condition, and it had worn well. She thought it was the sort of worn well that suggested a man in some office job. He would be cautious with his income, rather than one of the gentry who wore old things out of habit.

The rest of him was nondescript. He had brown hair, short enough that he likely did little magical work of his own, blue eyes set behind copper-rimmed glasses. She guessed him to be perhaps five or six years younger than her own fifty and two. Not anyone she'd ever seen before to her knowledge. Though that was enough of a gap that even if he'd been at Alethorpe, they'd not have been there at the same time.

"Good afternoon. My second said you were hoping for an appointment?"

He offered his hand. "Mistress Fellowes. I am Jeremy

9

Royston. I would appreciate a consultation at your convenience. Of course, I am glad to pay your consulting fee. I gather you use the Ministry standard schedule, qualifying as Magistra?"

Eda inclined her head. Nothing he'd said had disabused her of the idea he spent his time in offices. Ministry offices, perhaps, since most people did not bring up the fee schedules. "I do. I would have time now if you don't expect it to take more than an hour. Or I would be glad to find a time next week." Henny made a small muffled noise, as if she'd been about to speak, but stifled herself so promptly she was sure the man hadn't noticed.

"If the present moment is convenient, Mistress. I realise it is the end of your week. Otherwise, I finish work at half-four." His voice, the more he heard of it, was precise, a pleasant sort of tenor. She suspected he'd worked hard to smooth out an accent to something appropriately professional. Certainly, his diction was unusually crisp.

"We've finished work for the week. Now is no bother. Thank you, Henny, we'll be fine."

"I'd be glad to finish up in the workshop, Mistress?" Henny offered it cautiously. It was the reasonable check of a woman considering a strange man. If this man wished her harm, Eda would eat all her most itchy and unpalatable wool yarn.

"Ah, no, I won't keep you. If you'd leave your notes for me, I'll look them over for Monday." Henny looked displeased, but she went. If she'd actually felt there was any real meaningful risk, she'd have stayed, or at least put up more of an argument. But there was plenty of light, and would be for hours yet. People were still coming and going in the street. And certainly Eda didn't worry much about scandal. She received business calls periodically at home, even if most of their business was done at the guildhall.

Henny closed the door behind her. Eda certainly might have liked a cup of tea, but she would not invite this man into the kitchen. That was a place to welcome friends and family, not strangers. And the sitting room was a trifle shabby on closer inspection, seeing as it was sorted for her use and those in the workshop. She settled in the chair facing him and folded her hands in her lap, glad she'd taken a moment to tidy up. "A consultation, then."

"Yes, Mistress." Master Royston drew out a small notebook from his jacket pocket, flipped it open, and peered at the paper. "I am a senior clerk at the Ministry of Materia. I am aware of the standard of work of all the weavers, including when it comes to magical restoration. Your name consistently tops our lists, and so it made sense to me to begin with you. I am hoping you will be able to recommend a course of action for a particular problem."

That made her raise an eyebrow. She was aware, of course, that she did excellent work, but she would not have pegged herself at the top of the list. Her cloth weaving was even and much in demand. The workshop's tapestry work normally went to private homes, either the demesne estates or the Great Families. Any of them might well accept praise of the work as their due, but they likely wouldn't mention the maker unless pressed in private for a referral. And, of course, the point of the restoration work Eda had done was in being invisible, returning an ancient and enchanted tapestry to its glory and proper magical purpose. "Do explain your situation, then."

Master Royston peered over his glasses at her, then looked down at his notepad. His voice changed, as if he had felt far more comfortable laying out the particulars of her standard of work. Now he wasn't sure of his footing or where his hands were. She kept her hands still, because her instinct was to check where she was in the pattern, touch the threads, and find her place that way. That would not help here.

"Two months ago, I inherited a home. A large manor house." He glanced up. "A series of deaths, before the War, during, and coming down to me."

"My condolences." Eda wasn't entirely sure what one said in this situation, and he hadn't named the deaths.

Master Royston nodded once, acknowledging it. "It came to me because of my father's death, five years ago. The others were distant cousins. It is entailed, and so it passed down to the son of a youngest son, of a younger son." That might well produce a number of distant cousins, indeed. And it explained why someone who worked in the Ministry, who was made to be a clerk, might inherit a significant property late in his life. Or at least a good way through his life.

"And, I presume, it has some weaving in it." Eda presumed tapestries, but it might be bed hangings or curtains or even rugs. Though she did not do rugs, other than items for her own use. For example, the one beside her bed, patterned from ends of yarn from other projects, in a jubilant explosion of private colour. She'd made it after Bert had died. Before that he'd have mocked her for the choice and refused to have it in the bedroom.

"Tapestries. A room of them, and they are not in the best condition, as I understand it. I do not know how to measure the amount of damage or deterioration." Master Royston leaned forward. "I would appreciate a great deal if you would consider an evaluation."

"At Ministry rates." Eda wouldn't do it for less than that.

"Ministry rates and your expenses. As well as the extra fee for travel time away from your work; the house is some seven miles from a portal. In return for the evaluation and a written proposal." He didn't need to consult his notes for that, and she liked he understood what he was offering to buy. "A day, in total, most likely."

She didn't answer him immediately. That sort of distance would be a bother, though it was not as if she had other pressing commissions at the moment. "Tell me a bit more about the house. And what you know of the tapestries." Her own voice came out crisp, more like his. "Please."

He cleared his throat. "It is a moated hall, with an open court in the interior, as I understand the terminology." He was awkward with it. But she'd already known he wasn't one of the sort who'd grown up with this sort of thing, like Lord Carillon or Lady Marrington, up north. "Built in the latter years of the Wars of the Roses, before the Pact. A family favoured under Edward IV, and then under the Woodvilles." That made it an interesting history indeed. "Later members of the family were Catholic recusants, favoured under Mary I. Followed by something of a fall under Elizabeth."

Albion did not, on the whole, care a great deal about the vagaries of Britain's royalty after 1484. That was when the Pact had ensured the transfer of the land magic from the king's line to the Lords and Ladies of the land and the Council. But she knew more than enough of her history to understand the brutal changes in religious regime. Many in Albion, within the magical communities, had been battered by it, of course. And many had, over the following decades, gone in directions other than Christianity.

"Your own faith?" She would ask it now. It would be terribly awkward if it were relevant later, and she didn't know.

Master Royston shook his head in the negative. "My great-uncle, yes. The two subsequent cousins, not so much, I gather. As I said, we were distant and not intimately acquainted. A name, in the family records, on both sides. It was more the solicitors who found me." He cleared his throat. "Obviously, there are a number of changes to the property. I gather there is documentation for most of it, but I have not had time to review all of it. I have not as yet found the sort of useful and informative summary sometimes provided by previous generations with a particularly antiquarian bent."

The phrasing of that made her smile, because he had a turn of phrase beyond that of other clerks she'd met. "We shall hope for one, then. They are often entertaining reading, at least in part. And the tapestries?"

"Made in one of the Norwich workshops not long after the Pact. Before, as I understand it, the primary weaving workshops had been set up here. During the height of the family's primacy, or rather begun during that time."

"Mmm. Pardon, let me get something for my own notes." She stood, and he bobbed upright as she did. That was a rather particular sort of manner. She gathered up a pencil and her working notebook. Sitting again, she smoothed out her skirt automatically, then jotted down a handful of phrases, enough to remind her. "A room full of tapestries. How big a room, and how many?"

"There are ten, in total. Four wider, along the two long walls, four narrower, on either side of the door along the shorter wall. The room is a rectangle, not a square. And two above the doors. They have been protected from most light, but they are frayed, faded, and I don't know what magical protections might or might not still be intact."

It was an interesting challenge, certainly.

CHAPTER 3
THAT AFTERNOON

J eremy was uncertain how to proceed. Nor was he clear on how to evaluate the woman before him. It turned out that there were many differences between a consultation in the usual line of his work and when it came to the manor. He kept discovering more of them, near every time he made what ought to be a step forward in getting something dealt with.

The file on Mistress Fellowes had been informative in some ways, but not all of them. He'd had a sense of her age, of course. It was easy for him to do the maths on that. She'd attended Alethorpe, apprenticed for seven years following, and there were notations about her apprentice work, her journeyman work, and her master work. He hadn't bothered to go round to the Weaver's Guild to view the items there. He knew he didn't have the experience to evaluate them.

But for all he'd known her age, six years his senior, she looked younger than that suggested. Her hair was still a pleasant dark brown, and she wore no glasses. Jeremy relied on his. She was dressed a touch informally, but weaving was presumably physical work. Her blouse was well-tended creamy white and her skirt was a simple but pleasant blue and white print. He'd noticed she wore no jewellery, nor even a visible pocket watch.

No, it wasn't youth. She had a sense of contentment to her that Jeremy didn't see all that often. Certainly, he didn't feel it himself. He had a good and respectable life. He did work that mattered and did it well. Jeremy was no magical specialist himself, but he knew the literature and could maintain the necessary standards for materia. He'd helped both his parents have a comfortable later life, as an only son ought. Jeremy wrote polite and appropriate cards to the extended family at both solstices, meeting the two cousins nearest his age for tea once a year. Beyond that, he followed the bohort, read the papers, and enjoyed a long ramble in the countryside when the weather allowed.

He might like to acquire a dog, if he could figure out how to make the manor a going concern. A dog to ramble with would be most pleasant. And dogs liked the countryside. Jeremy couldn't have one in his rooms in Trellech. There wasn't space. And his landlady had a cat who disapproved of any canine within several hundred feet of her realm.

Mistress Fellowes also seemed at ease in this room. It was small, but well-appointed, and he hadn't seen much else of the rest of the space. But two easy chairs suggested meetings with others. The desk was tidy but spacious, and she did not leave papers out, even when she had expected no one in her office. He certainly approved of that discipline and sensible precaution with private records.

Now, he waited for Mistress Fellowes to ask him whatever she needed to know. He didn't even know enough about tapestries to know what the relevant information might be. He'd attempted rough sketches. But he had had no artistic training beyond being able to draw straight lines in a book of accounts, and he had given up after three catastrophically blurred attempts.

Finally, she tapped her pencil on the notepad. "How big, an estimate will do for the moment. Are the narrower ones an arm's breadth, narrower, much wider?"

That, at least, he'd measured out. "The wider ones are seven feet wide, the narrower ones are three. Both seven feet in height. The ones over the doors are the width of the doors, six feet." He glanced at his notes. "They're double doors. The room itself is twenty-one by fourteen."

"Ah. I note the sevens involved. And the threes. And that means the entire wall covered, then, no gaps." There were little scratches of the pencil. "When you say they are in bad shape, faded and frayed, what do you mean by that? The proportion affected, what your impression of the damage is, and so on?" She held up a finger, though not abruptly. Or at least it did not disconcert him. "I understand you do not know the technical terminology or have a good sense of what it looked like new."

"Yes, Mistress." He hesitated. "Is there a sample of fabric I might use as a guide? An ordinary sort of piece?"

That made her tilt her head. She nodded once. "If you'd stay here, I'll be back shortly." He nodded in return and she stood, opening the door and going out. She was gone for two minutes, and came back with a piece of tapestry work hanging from a brass rod. It was much smaller than the tapestries at the manor, but the thing that struck him immediately was how bright the colours were. They were shining reds and blues and golds and greens. There were bits of black and deep purple for contrast. She hung it up on a hook on the mantlepiece, as if she sometimes hung things there for other reasons. When it stopped moving, he could see that it was a view out across the meadows toward the Wye, the river rolling in the distance, with flowers and the garden before the green of the meadows.

Jeremy did not move to touch it, but he took his time looking at it. That was a way to appreciate the work, and he was almost certain this was her work. Or if not hers, someone she cared about, her own apprentice mistress or a former apprentice. Finally, he spoke, choosing his words slowly. "For one thing, these colours are tremendously brighter. It's the difference between a living plant and a dried one, isn't it?"

Her mouth twitched up. "That's a fair way to put it. Fading is expected, in most cases, even if the materials aren't directly exposed to light. Many dyes aren't lightfast, not over centuries. Magic can be a help, and magic may certainly help brighten them up again, as part of the restoration, but the fading doesn't directly suggest damage. You mentioned fraying?"

"Yes, Mistress." Jeremy hesitated. "May I touch the piece? My hands are clean, or I'd be glad to wash them if you let me know where I might do so."

"Thank you for asking." She said it automatically, as if some people didn't. "Would you mind if I used a charm instead?"

He shook his head and offered his hands palms up. He supposed the bathing room or the water closet or whatever might be in more personal spaces in the home, and he wouldn't want to intrude there. She rubbed her palms together, then murmured the incantation before holding out her hands over his. He could feel the brush of the magic like a pleasant breeze, then it passed. "There." She nodded at the hanging. "It's sturdy enough for touching."

Jeremy stood, so he wouldn't overbalance and risk grabbing at it. First, he ran his fingers along the threads, feeling how they fit together, at least a bit. It had a texture he hadn't understood at first with the larger tapestries, threads diving down behind, at the colour shifts. "They have fraying in spots. None of the ones I could reach were much more than a hand span, but some of the higher ones looked like they might be larger."

"And the overall structure. Do you have a sense of that?" She nodded at the piece he was still touching. "Feel the back of that. Sometimes tapestries have a backing fabric. Restoration usually involves one. It helps reduce the weight the threads are supporting." He took his time, feeling the back, which in this case was as textured as the front. It was also remarkably tidy. He'd expected loose ends of thread, somehow.

When Jeremy took a step back toward his chair, he inclined his head. "Thank you for allowing me to touch. It's a pleasure to feel the threads. Is that silk, then?"

"Yes. Silk takes colour particularly well, rather a lot of it. It soaks dye up like a sponge. This was an indulgence, a few years ago. That's why it's relatively small." She hesitated for a minute pause, one he wasn't sure he was supposed to notice. "That is my work. The view over the wall, behind the cottage, of course. What I see from the workroom window, past the garden."

"A scene you know well, then, particularly tied to this place." Jeremy respected that. More to the point, it made him more certain he'd come to the right place, if she were willing to take the consultation proper. The thing he kept coming back to with the manor was trying to understand it as it was, rather than refusing to try, like his previous two cousins. "I had expected the back to feel more varied? More

20

threads. But that isn't the case at all." Jeremy offered it cautiously.

"Ah, that has tc do with how the weaving works. You don't need the treatise right now, but if you can feel threads, loose ends, on the back, then yes, things have been fraying. That can be damage from pests: moths, mice, depending on the materials. It can be damage from damp. Sword cuts or the like, more rarely, but they did happen."

"Thank you." Jeremy shivered at the thought of that. "Damaging something that took so much work seems like blasphemy. Tapestries of that size take a long time to make, don't they?"

Something in the question had surprised her, but he couldn't sort out what. She nodded, though she took a moment before answering. "It's tricky to do the math— it depends on the complexity of the pattern, the number of weavers, how much of the dye work they were involved with."

"Weavers, plural?" Jeremy had heard that, but he wanted to check.

"Oh, yes, especially for this kind of tapestry work. You need multiple hands to do everything needed, and from different places on the loom. Norwich often had a room of looms working on related works, pair and pair. It's important everyone can get on, or at least work smoothly, in a weaving workshop." That was an intriguing emphasis, and not a calculation Jeremy was used to including in his own professional maths. He wasn't sure how to sort that out, at least before you knew people. Then she was speaking again, and it caught him off guard. "What exactly are you hoping for, with the consultation?"

"I'd like someone, you or someone you recommend, by preference, come and look at them and make whatever measurements or evaluations are relevant. And then propose what it would take to restore them. Money is a concern, but—" He hesitated. "I need to weigh the relevant factors. And I can't do that without the proposals."

Mistress Fellowes considered. "You said seven miles from the portal. Let me consult with Henny, my second, and a few other people about scheduling. You were hoping soon, I presume?"

Jeremy nodded. "Next Friday, if it were convenient, or the following one. I am taking a little time from work to learn more about the estate. It's easier if I go out Friday to Sunday."

"Of course. Where shall I send a note round? I should have an answer for you by the Monday afternoon post." She stood, and Jeremy followed suit, reaching into his jacket pocket for his calling cards. He offered one with a slight bow. She glanced at it. "I'll write on Monday. May I show you out?"

"Of course. I've taken more than enough of your time. Would you prefer to add the fee for this consultation on to the rest, or should I arrange payment with the bank tomorrow morning?"

Again, there was the slight hesitation, just a fraction of a second. "Assuming we make arrangements for the further consultation promptly, I am glad to wait."

Jeremy nodded and then offered his hand. "I appreciate your time, Mistress Fellowes. I'll let you get back to your plans for your evening." She offered a slight smile at that, then showed him out. He found himself on the street, feeling pleasantly baffled by some of the conversation, but satisfied with the results.

CHAPTER 4

MAY 14TH AT OAKBURGH HALL, NORFOLK

"Mistress Summers."

The hall housekeeper let out a tiny sigh. She was, apparently, going to need to explain something to him again. She had been doling those out, patiently, with the most important points first. While Jeremy appreciated the spacing, he was beginning to dread that weighted pause. She'd seen the estate through the end of his great-uncle's life, continued through the cousins, and now she was responsible to him. Or rather, she was responsible for the house, and tolerated his presence until he proved he would not flee the estate and all it meant.

Jeremy had thought, from first meeting her, that she looked much like a housekeeper out of some literary novel. Her hair was pulled back in a neat bun. She wore a plain blue dress, tended well, and she had removed her apron for the walk around the manor to review what was needed.

"Properly, sir, it is Mrs Summers."

Jeremy stopped, about to take a step into the billiard room from the entrance arch. "Pardon?" He knew she'd never been married, and he'd always preferred the title

Albion used, the unabbreviated Mistress. Used that way, it denoted a completed apprenticeship or the equivalent skill and experience.

"We use the titles the non-magical prefer. It saves bother if we're greeted at a town market day or somewhat of the kind." She was not upset with him. Or at least he didn't think so. He often wasn't sure. More wondering how he'd grown to the age of forty-six without knowing such things.

Now Jeremy cleared his throat. "Thank you for that, Mrs Summers. As you prefer. And the same, for the other staff?"

"Yes, sir." There was a small approving nod. He might be the equivalent of a dim sort of dog, but apparently he could be taught, in her eyes. He was trying not to be stubborn about it, or resent each correction like a schoolboy.

"Right. Please remind me if I forget." Then he turned. "I hope we will have someone out next week to look at the tapestries. I expect it will be a day trip, she'll be coming from Trellech. But I think perhaps best if a room is ready, just in case she can't return that evening."

"Sir." Now he got a considering glance. "What sort of someone, sir? A lady of your acquaintance?"

"A weaver, to give an evaluation about what would be involved in repairs. Mistress Eda Fellowes. She's well respected for her skills by her guild, and she has a particular interest in tapestry restoration. A widow, I understand, so I'm sure she'd appreciate your presence." He wondered again, not for the first time in the last day, whether Mistress Fellowes made larger pieces herself, or even how one did that. The sheer width and breadth of something like those in the hall made the idea seem baffling.

"I'll make sure Douglas has the pony cart ready. Will you be coming with her in the morning, then, sir?" Mrs

Summers pulled out a little notebook from the reticule hung from her belt. Then she gestured them to go on, through the billiard room, down through the library, toward the tapestry room.

"Yes, please. I'll confirm the time with her on Monday, I hope, and send it along to you as soon as I know." There was twice daily post to the portal at Swaffham, but of course, someone had to get it from there to the house. Normally, that was Wednesday and Saturday, when someone went to the shops or market.

Jeremy could not yet justify the expense of one of the magical journals. Also, it would require Mrs Summers or Mr Haldane, the butler and estate steward, to have one. He might, however, consider a set that allowed communication between a handful of bound copies. Those were much more reasonable in cost.

Now he'd had the thought, he asked, "Would it be a help if I got one of the sets of journals, the three or four that allowed direct notes? I would keep one, one for you, one for Mr Haldane?"

She considered. "That might do, sir. The maids, they know their letters, but I can't say as they're entirely comfortable with writing. Reading is easier. Of course, we make sure they're taught properly."

That was another thing Jeremy knew nothing about. "Beg pardon?" He stopped one more time, because he was certain he couldn't think and talk at the same time.

Again, there was that little sigh and the preparation for elementary education. "You have met the staff, sir," Jeremy had. Mrs Summers, Mr Haldane, a cook, two maids, a kitchen maid, a man of all work, three gardeners, and a few others coming in for particular tasks at certain times of year on the grounds. It was, he gathered, tremendously understaffed for a house this size, even by the standards these days. On the other hand, he was only in residence two days in seven, and most of the rooms upstairs were under dust covers.

"Yes?" Jeremy tried to sound more certain than he felt.

"It is our duty, sir, to make sure they're properly educated. Alice and Margaret, now, they're good girls. And Ruth, in the kitchen. But they all came to us young, at thirteen. We're the ones responsible, the Ministry decrees say so, for making sure they have their letters and their numbers, as well as learning their duties."

It was a part of the Ministry he'd never given much thought to, after his own education. The younger members of his department had all generally come up through Dunwich, as he had, or they'd apprenticed in the Ministry. No one got into the Materia offices without a good head for lists, the necessary sums, and the multiplication, division, and proportions necessary for large quantities of materia. The most skilled went on to learn more detailed forms of accounting and balance sheets. "May I ask how that's done?"

"There's a set of lessons, sir, and they work through them, piece by piece. Most of them are marked by post, but once a month, someone from the Ministry comes by. Just for Ruth now, she's still under eighteen."

"But the others, they're expected to keep it up on their own." Jeremy wanted to make sure he had this right. "And that's true for the gardeners, as well?"

"Oh, I'm not as sure there. You'd have to ask Waters. But I believe they both went to school." He was the head gardener, who'd been in the place for decades. He was getting on for seventy. The other two were younger, one Waters' nephew, and the other a friend of his. They'd been in the War together and come back to the estate. He'd barely met the two younger men; Waters had made it clear they were shy of strangers.

"I'll have a word when I get a chance. I'd be glad to make sure there's, oh, suitable reading material, if they'd like to keep in better practice. Perhaps there are books about housekeeping they'd like, or local stories?" He offered it hesitantly.

Mrs Summers considered that, weighing it. "Perhaps I might put together a list of suitable titles next time I visit the lending library, for your approval. You can indicate which you'd like to order. I don't hold with young women reading some of the novels out there." She sniffed once, and then she added, "If they want to read those, they can improve their reading and borrow them themselves." That crack of humour suggested a number of new puzzling things about her. Jeremy knew if he quashed this, she'd never dare relax like that again. He knew little about people, but he knew that.

Now he spoke evenly. "You know the house and the household needs better than I do. Perhaps we might add a report on their reading to our weekly review, then? And I can look into getting some books once you get me a list." Browsing the bookshops in Trellech would not be a burden, at least, and he could do that without complicated travel.

When he'd found out he'd inherited the place, he'd thought that every single task involved would be new. As it turned out, he had a reasonable grasp of the account books. Mostly. And now, he could manage a bookshop. Two out of hundreds was not great odds, but it was slightly better than zero.

"Yes, sir. Now, the tapestries, you said? Will she be

wanting us to have them come down?" Mrs Summers led the way into the next room, and the tapestries.

"Ah." He hadn't asked about that. "I gather they can be delicate, and we don't really have space to lay them all out safely. I'll ask her on Monday, and add that to my notes. We won't need to move them, I presume, for the evaluation. She seems the sort who would have mentioned if that was involved." He looked at them, dubiously. They seemed even more faded than the last time he'd looked at them. Some of that was almost certainly dust, muddying the colours, but that wasn't all the fading.

"You know there's supposed to be a mystery to them, sir?" Mrs Summers spoke more cautiously now. "I don't know all that much about it. Master Royston, your great-uncle, he didn't talk about that sort of thing. There may be some notes in the muniments room, the old records. Mr Haldane might know where."

"What sort of mystery?" Surely they weren't hiding anything on the walls. He was sure they'd been moved enough for that over the centuries.

"Some say there's something hidden in the house. And there's a ghost who wanders, and you know the lore about ghosts." Mrs Summers brushed her hand on her skirt.

The lore was that ghosts, at least ghosts in Albion, often had something to do with a treasure or something hidden. "Where does the ghost wander?"

"Oh, out the front, sir, not any one place. The gate-house, some nights, but some nights she— there are long skirts, you see— comes through to the courtyard, some-times into the library. Though that wasn't the library always. Or into the tapestry room." She glanced back and forth, as if tracking the ghost.

"Have you seen, erm, her?" Jeremy wasn't at all sure what to make of this story.

"Once or twice, sir. Mostly when I was younger. She never scared me, though. She seemed like a sad ghost. Wanting something wistful. I can't say why I felt that." Then she cleared her throat. "At any rate, there's a legend that the tapestries hold some secret knowledge. I can't say that I've ever made sense of it, and I've looked at them plenty of times."

Jeremy certainly couldn't puzzle through that. He had looked at them for half an hour or so, last week. They were pleasant enough, each enumerating a virtue, the Latin word helpfully woven into the tapestry. It was a mix, neither sombre nor celebratory. The designs held a hint of seasonal progression, but nothing too obvious.

Some of them didn't make sense. Honour, for example, had a garden flowering and overflowing with greenery and plants. Certainly there were metaphors about abundance flowering, but that seemed not quite right. The other images also seemed scattered, unified by the colours they were woven in and the overall style of the pieces. And besides, they also had Abertas, abundance, in a different tapestry, why have the same basic theme twice?

But some were outdoors, joyful, like Gaudium, or the knight riding swiftly to battle in Alacritas. Others were inside, a great scene in Obedientia at what he thought was Queen Mary Tudor's court. Why that would be here, of all things, he wasn't sure. If one needed a court, surely one before the Pact would have been a more suitable image. One was far more explicitly religious, Ethicus held a number of obscure symbols he couldn't properly decipher.

Stabilitas made some sort of sense. It was an architectural detail of stairs made of lasting stone, climbing up toward some unknown destination, turning tightly around a central pillar. Tolerantia seemed like a scene out of a mediaeval metaphor. There was a crowd in a wide range of styles of dress and colours of skin, brought together in a large courtyard for some purpose. And the smallest ones, above the doors, those were both labelled Eloquentia, but they were books in a library, the titles too far away and blurred to be readable, even with his glasses.

Now he shook his head. "Let us go see if any of the damp has got in while we weren't looking. And then I'll see if I can catch Douglas about the cart."

CHAPTER 5

MAY 20TH IN NORFOLK

Eda felt that so far, the entire process was less than pleasant. The morning had begun with a light drizzle in Trellech, and a more insistent rain when she had emerged in Norfolk, at the Swaffham portal.

Master Royston had met her at the Trellech end, dressed in a country suit. She had her own umbrella. He did not offer space under his, and Eda could not decide if she approved of that or not. Proper manners would suggest the offer, but practicality made it awkward. She was carrying a carpetbag with her necessary tools, measuring tapes, her notebook, and a collection of other odds and ends. And, of course, an entire set of undyed wool threads to capture the shades needed in quantity.

He came through the portal a moment after her, and stepped to one side before glancing around. "Let me go see if someone is here with the cart. They'll be out in the street, just a moment." His precise language sounded a little flustered now, as if he weren't entirely sure someone would be there.

Eda nodded. "Of course." She was not terribly likely to

go wandering off. Besides, they were in a courtyard. The portal and the space around it were hidden from the road by some ancient boxwood. Or probably boxwood. Eda's plant identifications were focused on dye use or depictions in tapestry work or other weaving, where being flat rather than three-dimensional affected their looks.

Master Royston disappeared out onto the street beyond and he was gone for a good few minutes. Long enough that a bit of the damp crept through Eda's shoe; she'd need to see about getting it resoled or charm-mended. She rarely wore shoes for long, unless she was doing the shopping or being sociable. At home, she universally wore slippers with a thin leather sole, so she could shift onto and off the looms without changing shoes. Or warm socks, in the winter.

There was no one else in the courtyard. Of course, the place wasn't big enough, in terms of the magical community, for someone to be on duty during the day, as in Trellech or London. But she'd been to other out of the way portals. Usually there was someone with a shop or a workshop or something of the kind.

Finally, maybe ten minutes later, Master Royston appeared at the street entrance. He didn't wave her over or call out. He came over. "Beg pardon. There was something with some sheep. This way, if you please, Mistress?" He didn't offer his arm; perhaps he was a tad afraid of slipping on the slick paving stones. Once out in the street, she found a cart, a sturdy reddish horse flicking its tail, and a man in a cap and a well-worn waxed canvas rain cloak. The cart had some sacks in it, and a few boxes, but also a row of seats at the front.

"This way, may I help you up? This is Jack Douglas, our stableman." The man nodded, touching his cap once, but said nothing. Eda nodded back, set her bag on the edge of the cart, and accepted a hand up the steps at the back. She reclaimed her bag, found a seat on the bench, and tucked the bag in at her feet. Master Royston joined her.

It was not a quick trip. Her arm quickly became tired, holding the umbrella in place. It wasn't until they were well out of town that Master Royston cleared his throat. "I think we might now manage a charm against the rain. We're certainly damp enough. Keep the umbrella at the ready, on the off chance there's someone on the road."

"Ah." Eda wasn't used to thinking like that, but of course, they had to be careful about showing magic here. On the other hand, they hadn't passed anyone coming the other way on the road in at least twenty minutes. "Thank you." They bounced along, keeping a steady pace, and Eda let herself sink into feeling the rhythm of it. If she were weaving, it'd probably be a twill rather than a plain weave, the pattern off-set slightly each row. She could not have said why she felt that. The horse was going forward steadily and didn't seem lame. All the wheels of the cart seemed even enough.

Finally, ninety minutes after they'd left Swaffham, they could see more buildings. "Umbrella up, if you don't mind. We are nearly there."

She noticed he didn't say 'home'. They rolled through the village, turned down a long drive, past a small house on the main road and what looked like a chapel. Then the trees opened up, and she gasped. It was much larger than he'd implied, a huge moated manor, rising out of the mist. The red-brick was a vibrant contrast to the green of the trees and bushes and spring grass.

Eda glanced at him and thought Master Royston looked abashed. Certainly not proud or confident or whatever else. She'd been to a number of the great houses, on this kind of work, but the men who owned them didn't react like that. They were sure of themselves and what they had. Royston looked like a man who hadn't taken inventory of his thread stores in months and suspected he'd run out of at least a dozen essential shades without noticing.

The cart pulled up at the edge of the bridge over the moat, and Master Royston got out, holding out his hand to steady her down. Eda nearly tripped this time, as the last step was further than she expected. Then she took a breath. "Please. Lead on to your tapestries."

At least she had an idea what to expect now. They had left Trellech at quarter past eight. It was now half-ten. She would do ninety minutes of initial evaluation, there would be lunch, she would continue her evaluation. At four, she'd make a report. At five, she would be driven back to the portal. And Henny had promised to pick up supper for her. She should be back at home not long after seven.

Master Royston nodded, and then escorted her through into the courtyard, then across to a hallway. They took a turn into a large room, and yes, it was full of tapestries. They direly needed attention that she could feel in the magic, the sense of them, before she could get her eyes to adjust to the light. "Yes. I'll begin immediately."

"May we bring you tea, or anything else?" Master Royston looked a tad nervous, like a startled dog.

Eda took a breath. "Is there somewhere I might wash my hands? If not, a jug of water, a basin, and a bar of Castile soap if you have it. French milled or something equivalent if you don't, nothing harsh."

"I will consult with the housekeeper." He bowed slightly and left her to it. She made a slow circuit of the room, walking clockwise, getting an overall sense of what she was dealing with. Five minutes later, Master Royston returned, along with a maid, a small table, and another woman carrying a jug and basin.

"Castile soap, Mistress." That was the other mature woman. A moment later, her role was confirmed. "I am Mrs Summers, the housekeeper. Alice, here, will be working just down the hall, through the next door on the right, or the one after it, if you need anything this morning. The nearest water closet is the door on the left, the same hall, but I'm afraid the pipes there often bring a bit of rust. This water is from the good well. Is there anything else you need? A chair, perhaps?"

Naturally, they would not leave her entirely unsupervised. That was not sensible. "Oh. A chair and a small table to write at would be excellent, if it isn't a bother. Otherwise I'll make do. Beyond that, I understand there will be luncheon at noon?"

"Alice will come show you to the dining room. You'll hear the chime for it, a five-minute warning before the hour. I'll see about the table." She waited a bare moment for Master Royston to nod at her and disappeared.

From there, the rest of the morning went smoothly enough. She was left alone, with no one hovering over her, though twice she heard quiet voices down the hall from the room she was in. Eda was immersed in her evaluation. By luncheon she'd made note of the initial details, confirming the measurements, subjects, forms, and materials of the tapestries. None of that posed an immediate problem.

Most of it was of wool, and from the fraying threads, she suspected they could match the staple length well enough, though she'd need to see about commissioning some spinning and dyeing the thread to match. There might be something suitable in her stores, as well. If she agreed to take on the work, and if Master Royston agreed to the terms, she'd have to take some samples of the thread from the back to match.

Luncheon was quiet. Master Royston opened his mouth once or twice, as if to say something, but the conversation kept stuttering out. She was eager to get back to work. Making sketches of the tapestries sufficient to diagram the damage would take her quite a long time. That was true even with a bit of magic to help with the outlining and keep the proportions steady.

The day had not begun warm and it was still raining, but by the time she was finishing up at quarter to four, she could feel sweat in the small of her back, instead of damp from the rain. It made her want a bath, far sooner than she was going to get one. She had just finished making a clean copy of her notes with a final charm when she heard a cough from the door. "Mistress Fellowes?"

Eda looked up to find Master Royston hovering in the doorway. "Come in, please. I'm ready to walk you through the current situation." She began at the door he'd entered, working clockwise around the room. On each tapestry, she outlined the damaged portions, the ones that could be mended, the ones that would need to be recreated delicately by hand and charm. "We would need to remove each tapestry in turn, moving it onto a working frame. Each would be cleaned, then tended to. Once the tapestry was mended, we would attach a backing to reduce the weight the original threads have to hold up. Removable, of course, without damage to the original. There's a standard charm for that, used for centuries."

Master Royston blinked. "Oh. I suppose that makes sense. They're quite heavy, aren't they? Staff to take them down?"

"If you have a man or woman or two, ideally four

people total, with steady hands, two of whom can manage a ladder. Otherwise, there are day labourers with the Weaving Guild and the affiliated arts that hire out."

"And there was something about the colour?" Master Royston asked this hesitantly. "I saw you comparing something when I went by earlier." He looked embarrassed. "It's the easiest way to the muniments room, and I had to check some records."

"Ah." Eda considered which tapestry to use as an example. "Here, this one is easier to see it on." She picked one of the narrower tapestries, labelled Gaudium, with figures in different dresses and robes dancing. The front was muted reds and yellows and blues, but when she gently folded part of it back, she moved her charmlight to show the brighter colours. "Dye fades. It's different for each shade, each dye, sometimes the material. These were all woven from the same materials, at the same time, and largely the same dye lots, so it's been consistent across all of them." She gently replaced the tapestry.

"And the colour?"

"Some of it will brighten with cleaning. Once the fabric is mended, it is also possible to get an illusionist to enchant the whole so that the original colours show through. That takes collaboration with the tapestry weaver doing the repair. It is also an ongoing cost, because the tapestry needs to be checked, without the illusion, regularly, for any damage. Fortunately, once it's set up, it's much faster, and thus less expensive, to do again."

"Less expensive." Master Royston pursed his lips. "Which is not the same as low cost, I am sure."

Eda's mouth twitched, but she would be honest. "Skill doesn't come cheap, sir." Then she took a breath. "I would need to see if anyone from my workshop will take it on

Some of it will vary, depending on costs of materials, but I can give you a range for that, and where I think it is most likely to fall."

"Dyes?" Master Royston's fingers shifted, like he was holding a pen. "I know most of those."

"Wool, in this case. I'd want to match the type as closely as possible. Sheep have changed in four hundred years, but I think we can get close. But if that is a rarer breed, or it's more difficult to spin to the thickness— thinness is a better term— we want, that raises the cost. Again, paying for skill."

"Indeed." Master Royston took a breath. "Your proposal, then. The usual thing is to give me a chance to review it and consider, and let you know— it is Friday now, next Thursday, perhaps? I might call at your workshop to discuss, if I would like to go forward. Or let you know by letter if I do not wish to do so at this time?"

"As you wish. Should we take it on, I will need a fortnight to source materials, a deposit against them, and weekly payment for the labour. Those costs are all noted, along with related expenses. And of course, there's one rate if I do the work, versus one of the journeywomen."

"Ah." He took a breath. "I had heard you had someone in your workshop, finishing an apprenticeship, focusing on tapestries?"

Eda tilted her head. "Yes. But she is still engaged in her journeywork project, and that will take some months yet. And more to the point, she has two young children. I would not ask her to be away from them, particularly given how far you are from any portal. If you were within half an hour, she might make a daily trip, but here? It would need to be weekly, and that is no good for a young family. Bringing the tapestry to somewhere more convenient might be an option, but there are always some risks in that kind of transportation."

He took half a step back, then stopped. "You are protective of your people, Mistress. I respect that." He sounded uncertain again, but then pulled himself together. "I will go through your papers, and I appreciate your thorough explanations so far. I've the fee for your day's work, and when you're ready for the cart, we can get you back to the portal."

Five minutes later, she'd made one last use of the water closet and she was tucked into the cart. Master Royston came back to the portal with her, though he spoke little. He also, apparently, was staying at the house, because he left her at the portal with a brief, "I will be in touch."

Eda found herself back in Trellech about when she'd expected, but not at all sure whether she wanted him to accept her proposal for the work or not. She had not padded the estimate, but even at the lower end of the range, it would be a substantial investment in the tapestries. She was not at all sure the household could afford that.

CHAPTER 6
MAY 24TH AT OAKBURGH HALL

J eremy had spent the previous evening staring at the accounting. And he was still at it this morning, after a breakfast of toast and eggs. He was not, precisely, an accountant. Not primarily. His work, when he was at the Ministry, was oversight of Materia purchase and distribution. His office ensured that the quality controls were properly applied, oversaw the equitable distribution of limited resources, consulted with the growers of plants, and a dozen things more.

He also could run a budget, but the estate's budget was a morass. It had been sensibly documented until Great-Uncle Dennis's death. After that, though, it was chaos. He'd worked through some of it over the past months. Jeremy knew what was on account in the bank in Trellech. He knew what everyone got paid, and had gone through the ordinary expenses of the estate. And at least the bills had been paid. There was nothing in arrears.

What he couldn't figure out were the irregular ones. Or the incomes. So much had shifted between the War and the two brief inheritances of his cousins. Amounts came in dribs and drabs, at varied intervals, and most of them were not at all well documented. He had his own income from the Ministry, of course. But he could not be here and there at the same time. He could not live full time on the estate given the distance from the portal. And while he had some savings, they could sustain the necessary expenses for perhaps a year.

If they could figure out fixing up the place, perhaps they would discover art or sculpture or something else that could be sold off to appreciative buyers. Or perhaps nouveau riche, who wanted the trappings of history without being too particular about style, quality of construction, or materia. Jeremy was not sentimental about the art. It wasn't as if he had childhood memories of it, or amusing stories about a suit of armour in the corner that he'd imagined coming to life.

Come to think of it, he hadn't seen a suit of armour yet. Though he'd not gone through the second floor or the attics at all.

He was, perhaps, becoming attached to the tapestries. Certainly watching Mistress Fellowes had been interesting, the glimpses he'd got. Her explanation had been even more so. There was something in how she handled the tapestries, gently, with well-washed hands, but deliberately. They were fabric. They were meant to be touched in a way he couldn't quite understand. And it had been clear she found them intriguing. That had been under the surface, in her explanation, but far more explicit in her proposal.

Jeremy was almost certain he was going to agree to it. The tapestries were historic; the repairs were expensive, but worthwhile. And similar tapestries had sold for vast amounts, both within Albion and outside. There was that set that had been sold to someone in America a few years ago. Though he only remembered that because there had been an article about the depiction of the plants in one of the Materia journals he read. They were post-Pact, but made on the continent, and the article had argued they had been designed by someone with some substantial experience of the Fatae. Jeremy did not have the expertise to evaluate that entirely, but it seemed plausible.

He stared out the window of the muniments room. It was not currently raining. He might as well take a walk around the garden and see if he could spot Gerald Waters. He went upstairs to his bedroom and changed into what he had begun to call his country walking set. They were boots sturdy enough he wouldn't twist his ankle. They had enough of a tread he could walk more comfortably on slick surfaces, such as, for example, all that rain-washed paving stone.

Jeremy went out through the courtyard, across the bridge over the moat, then circled around clockwise, toward the more formal gardens and the greenhouses beyond. The gardens were flourishing. He did not know enough about plants or horticulture to be properly impressed, he was sure. But he could appreciate the effect.

From what he'd discovered in the notes, they'd kept the same basic planting schema for hundreds of years. Though, of course, some varieties had changed, and certainly none of the plants had lasted that long. The yews in the family cemetery, of course, were of that vintage, but yews were expected to age well. The oaks along the drive, too, they could get to a wonderful age.

Now he passed from flowering bushes to a few roses, to plants he couldn't name, looking for signs of movement. He saw a flicker in the distance, as if someone had stood up, spotted him, and fled like a hare. But he couldn't tell who it was, or even if he'd been right. That flicker had been in the back corner of the second walled garden. The greenhouses were beyond. The glass just peeked over the top of the stone walls that were lined with ivy and climbing roses and other plants threading their way along the stone and brick.

By the time he'd reached the corner, he found Gerald Waters coming through the archway from the greenhouses. "Sir." The older man tugged on his cap. It was one of the stereotypical signs of service, and Jeremy did not know what he felt about it. He had never expected to have this many people dependent on him and his good will.

It wasn't that he couldn't manage people. He had two people working under him in the Ministry, and he also had the work of two analysts, shared among the three senior staff in their department. But that was different. The Ministry had salary scales. It had lists of expected job duties. It had a process for applying for other positions if two people did not suit working in the same place. It could all be conducted without, necessarily, a great deal of disruption for anyone involved.

Here, all the staff knew he could turn them out with next to no notice, with no character, with only what they had saved and a few possessions. Their homes, their beds, were owned by the estate, by and large. It seemed a terribly precarious way to build a life, while simultaneously being the way people had lived here since the estate was built. The dissonance wore at him, and more with Waters than with Mrs Summers, for some reason.

"Master Waters." Jeremy nodded politely. "I was reviewing the estate accounts, and I had a few questions."

The man straightened, and it was an uncomfortable sort of straightening. Jeremy almost expected a pitchfork or something of the kind to appear in his hand, a physical ward against whatever came next.

"Sir." This time the other man's tone was flat.

"First, erm. I am still trying to understand the estate. The long-term options and all that. But may I ask, about your living space, and the young men?" He had not met them, not straight on.

"Ernie and Henry, sir. Henry's my nephew, also Waters." The elder Waters had to stop and consider, like he used the other young man's surname so rarely it was hard to bring to mind. "Ernie Harrow. There we are."

"Yes. I wanted to find out, first, if you..." Jeremy stuttered to a halt. 'Have everything you need' was presumptuous. 'Everything you want' left the door open for unfulfilled desire. "If your housing is sufficient, at the moment, if there are any repairs needed, that sort of thing." Now he sounded like a pompous idiot, but that was probably one of the better failure modes. Probably.

"Ah." There was another long pause, and Jeremy suspected he would normally chew on something physical. A pipestem, maybe. Jeremy knew he had a pipe. "I have one cottage, sir. The lads have t'other tucked in the woods. Used to be the gamekeeper and his wife. They keep an eye out for poaching and other trouble."

"Oh." It was one more aspect of a large estate that Jeremy hadn't considered, and that didn't seem to be documented. "Is there much of that?"

"Not at the moment." Those four words were rather weighty. After another lengthy silence, Waters added a few more. "Mostly boys scrumping apples and berries and all. A few people going after rabbits, sometimes deer. Not so many."

"Not too much trouble for the young men, then?"

Jeremy cleared his throat. "Do they need anything? More furniture, or linens, or some such? We're looking at the goods stored in the house. There might be some."

"Oh, a wool blanket never goes amiss. Or sheets, I suppose. The maids at the house, they do our wash, they'd know what's worn. Nice girls they are, quick."

Jeremy inclined his head. He would convey the compliment to Mrs Summers to pass on to the maids. He'd had nothing to do with their selection, their training, or the quality of the work. "I'll let them know. And the meals, I know they package some up for you."

"Aye. The lads, they're not comfortable with people. Not now." Here, then, was that protective streak, come out again.

Jeremy hesitated. "Bad War, then? One or both of them." He tried to keep his voice neutral, but it wasn't something he could be neutral about, and that probably showed.

"Aye." This time was curt, even for three vowels. "You didn't serve, sir, I understand." While that was polite enough on the surface, Jeremy heard the disapproval those words always conveyed.

"A poor heart. They wouldn't take me." He'd felt the shame of it, repeatedly. "Office work, for the Ministry. Doing what I could to get supplies to the right places. Materia and such, mostly, not directly to the War, but some of that too." Now he was justifying himself.

"Then you'd not understand." Just for a second, Waters glanced back toward the greenhouses. "They get on well together, the two. And I'd give Henry the shirt off my back, day or night. Ernie, too. But they don't get on with others now. Don't you be speaking to them, I'm warning you."

Then, suddenly, his teeth snapped together. "I should beg your pardon, sir, but I won't."

"You care about your nephew. And Ernie. I respect that." Jeremy did. He wished someone— anyone— had been like that about him. He'd never provoked that sort of loyalty in anyone except his mother. And Mother had been complicated in the end. She'd been poorly much of his adult life, and the tables had been turned. He'd had to do for her what she'd done for him, and far too soon. "Would you ask them if there's anything that needs tending? Leaks or whatever."

"I'll ask. I'll be telling Mrs Summers if there is."

"Thank you." Now Jeremy took a breath. If this part had been touchy, the next question would be worse. "I'd like to understand the expenses and, I gather, income from the gardens. I'm not asking you to talk me through it now, but could you prepare and do so next week when I'm out? Friday or Saturday, perhaps?"

"Ah." It was another measured pause. "What sort of records do you want, then? I'm not much of one for reading or writing, you see."

Jeremy knew that was the case for a fair number of people. But he still had not got his head around how other people managed who didn't read and write with ease. Or do maths. He took a breath, because demanding that Waters learn wouldn't do any good. Certainly not in a week. "Can you talk me through it? Perhaps have one of the young men help you with some reminder notes to make sure we discuss everything relevant?"

"I'll see." Waters rubbed his forehead with a dirt-smudged hand. "Would that be all, sir?"

"Yes. Yes. I suppose. You have work to get back to?"

"Always, sir." Water shrugged. "Let me see if it'll be

raining, come Friday or Saturday. Probably. The omens suggest it. I'll be letting the house know, and come by." In other words, Jeremy should not come looking for him.

"All right." Jeremy almost turned away. "Oh, the woman we had looking at the tapestries, she thinks some of the plants depicted might be local here. Of particular interest to the gardens, when they were made. Perhaps we might have you take a look, sometime, and see if you know more about them?"

It provoked another of those defensive, stiff reactions. "Sir."

Jeremy did not press. He was certain that every word he said would make it worse. "I'll leave you to it, then. If you have anything that needs tending in the cottages, let them know and we'll see about fixing whatever it is."

Waters just nodded, and then stood in the arch of the wall until Jeremy made his way back out of the walled garden. When Jeremy glanced over his shoulder before ducking back into the knot garden, Waters was still standing there, legs a little apart, arms folded over his chest.

CHAPTER 7

MAY 30TH AT EDA'S WORKSHOP

"How's your aunt, Ferry? And her people? Innis and Kay are still out." Henny promptly spoke up as soon as she saw Ferry come in through the hall into the kitchen. Eda went back to staring at her copy of the proposal, totalling up the different options.

"Aunt Annonia sends her regards, and Aunt Julia said if you need more of the weaving needles, she's glad to do a batch. Or make sure a batch is done." Ferry set the basket she'd been carrying on the bench by the door.

"Bless, she's always got the lightest touch. Never get a blacksmith to do a jeweller's work, that's how the saying goes." Henny was in fine form today, all laughter and teasing.

"There's no such saying." Eda didn't look up, but she tried not to sound cross. She wasn't at all sure it was working, though.

"Ought to be." Henny set a mug of tea down in front of Eda's hand. She put one at Ferry's place, and then went back to get her own, as well as a plate of biscuits. Those had come from Ytene's kitchens this morning. The cook there had a way with them. No one in the workshop turned them down when Ferry brought them. "Come on, Eda. You showed Ferry most of what you wanted to this morning. What are you fussing over?"

Ferry settled down next to where Eda had the papers out, the short end of the kitchen table, and Henny slid into the chair opposite. Eda leaned back a little, rubbing her eyes. Ferry looked well. She had her hair back in a tidy bun. She was wearing the sort of dress for visiting much-loved relatives, with a chance of running into less-loved ones who'd find something to criticise in the street. It was like dressing for a chance of rain, only much trickier to balance.

Ferry had come into an apprenticeship older than usual; she was in her late twenties now. It made her steadier, and she'd learned faster than most. She knew how to learn. That was the thing Eda had taken away from it. And Ferry, somehow, had got away from being caught up in what she ought to do. Instead she went and did the thing that needed doing or explained why she couldn't. That saved no end of time and fuss.

Eda sighed. She really was tangled. "I can't decide what to do if he wants someone."

"Antecedent, please?" Ferry offered. When she'd started with Eda, four and a half years ago now, she'd not have dared that. She'd become more confident, and that mostly wasn't Eda's doing. Ferry had settled into the New Forest cottage with her husband, children, and an increasing number of horses right out the door, like she'd been born to it. Lord Carillon had done a lot to convince her that her skills were worthwhile. And there, well, Eda had taught her plenty. But Ferry made it her own.

"We mentioned I did a consultation." Eda took a breath. She had to explain it to Ferry anyway, including why she wasn't considering Ferry for it. And maybe spelling it out would help her decide. "First, we put off talking about it this morning. How are you getting on with the tapestries at Ytene?"

Eda had talked Ferry into taking on the restoration of Ytene's tapestries, a sequence about a bit of local folklore, the Bisterne Dragon. They'd been tended well for a good long while, then more or less benignly neglected. As Ferry had worked, however, she'd discovered a whole range of minor oddities, from the dyes used to the enchantments woven in. It was turning out to be more of a challenge than either of them had originally expected, but in the best way. It would certainly establish Ferry as able to take on delicate enchantment work, as well as the weaving restoration. Lord Carillon had been entirely willing to fund the necessary training with a specialist in the right sort of enchantments, the ones beyond Eda's own ability to teach.

Ferry shrugged. "I'm into the tedious part. I need to dye another batch of thread and see if I can get a better match for the yellow. Fortunately, Mistress Drummond had time for a consultation on Monday. I'll be coming into town again for that. But she wanted me to have a go at it first, and see what I got. I'll set the dye baths tomorrow."

Henny looked bemused. "How'd you get time with her? She's always busy, a dozen places."

"Cassie's her good friend, and I see Cassie for supper most nights?" Ferry said. "I know, my life's— I don't even know. Besides good. Anyway, I was talking to Cassie about it, because she at least appreciates the challenges of colour matching properly. She said she'd ask Mistress Drummond, and here I am." Mistress Castalia, as Eda knew her, was one of the dressmakers in high demand. And, also, these days, she was living at Ytene when she wasn't in her shop. Eda made a mental note to see if they might draw on that to swap some skills sometimes, a bit of woven border for sewing up some of the fabric for wearing in an interesting way.

"But nothing you can't sort out, it's just the time and magic?" Eda pushed them back to the actual topic.

Ferry took a moment to think about that. Eda appreciated that, rather than getting a rushed answer that had to be changed later. "Not for a month or two, at least. I can't swear about beyond that. It's that third tapestry. There's something about the two mastiffs that feels different to me. But at least a month before I get to that. Probably longer."

"All right." Eda took a breath. "We mentioned that I'd had a consultation with someone who'd inherited Oakburgh Hall, out in Norfolk. It's miles from a portal, seven from the nearest. He has ten tapestries, four narrow, four wide, two above the doors, and they need rather a lot of attention. It'd be within your skill, but of course the travel. I wouldn't ask that with the children."

Ferry jerked her chin, more or less instinctively, then she let out a breath. "No. You're right. I know well how long it takes to ride seven miles, and I certainly wouldn't want to do that regularly, the way the weather's been."

"Ha." Eda agreed. "Much worse in the rain. Dreadful. So, I can take it on. Henny technically knows how." Everyone who made it through apprenticeship in this workshop did.

"But Henny finds restoration like that near enough hell on earth," Henny said, amused. Henny enjoyed seeing the inches of cloth forming, the waves of something new out of threads. She could mend and do the fiddly weaving by hand that restoration required, but only in tiny doses before she rebelled. It took all sorts to make a workshop.

Ferry nodded. "And it's not Innis's sort of thing either." Innis had an excellent line in twill weaves for magically protective cloaks and other clothing, and that was profitable as well as being to her taste. Besides being responsible for Kay's basic training, though that part they could solve some other way.

"I wouldn't ask her to give up the coin for that, no. I quoted Master Royston fair rates, but she'd be giving up too much." Eda agreed with that.

"She's got both grandparents and her aunt to keep, as well as her brothers and sister." Henny nodded solemnly. She'd been around for all of that and seen how Innis had fought so hard to keep everyone going. Innis's father hadn't come back from the War, and her mother had died in the middle of it. No wonder she'd gone straight into a line of work that was all about protection and that would be in demand as long as people had differences.

"So, if someone does it, it's me. If he can afford it. Or it's waiting for you to be done with Ytene, Ferry, and figuring out a space you could work on them somewhere with a portal."

Ferry spread her hands, then nodded. "So, do you think he'll be willing to pay your rates?"

"He's rather well informed about them. He works at the Ministry, I'm not sure where, but he's used the scales as a reference. And of course, there are additional considerations." Eda flicked her fingers. "That's why I can't decide."

"You'd live there. Maybe come home on the weekend? Or Friday to Sunday, if you wanted to keep an eye here," Ferry asked, more confirming than an actual question. "So the fee for being away from home, your own things, balanced by room and board. What's the estate like?"

Eda snorted. "You have a lot of thoughts, don't you?"

"Lizzie and Benton talk about managing the estate, and that sort of contract from time to time. There have been a couple of people out as consultants. Not for long, though, tapestries would take a long time."

"My thought was that I could at least do the one, and he could decide how to proceed from there. That could be hiring more people, bringing them somewhere more people could work on them, all that. And of course, they don't all need the same amount of work. Whatever else, they seem to have been spared most of the moth damage I'd have expected. It's more about wear, where they brushed up against furniture, or the threads having snapped with the weight in a few places."

"That's something," Ferry agreed. "How do you feel about being away for a long time, then? This has been home for ages."

"Since I was apprenticing myself." Eda had grown up in the Lake District, her family mostly keeping sheep and other livestock. She'd moved to Trellech for her apprenticeship, and to lend a hand with Grandmum as she was getting older, and she'd stayed. She hadn't even moved out to a husband's house. He'd come to hers. "I don't know, honestly."

"What's the house like?" Now Ferry was leaning forward on her elbows, her head tilted.

"Big moated manor, I don't know, attics for miles. Not that I saw them. Dozens of rooms. There are gardens, I didn't see those. And most of the rooms are closed up, I think. There's a great hall. That's where the tapestries are. Lights up above, but really it was designed for charmlight. I think Master Royston had an office somewhere on the ground floor. And the servant's quarters and kitchen and I don't know what else." Eda shrugged. "I've been in enough houses like that. The housekeeper seemed competent enough, I suppose."

"And the food?" Ferry pressed the point.

"They gave me a sandwich. Well, two sandwiches, decent bread." Eda hadn't really thought about it. Honestly, she'd been so focused on the work. "Freshly made tea, when I want it, not stewing in the pot. I suppose it wouldn't be horrid. Everything that was in use seemed clean. A bit neglected, I mean, I saw plenty of spots that could use more whitewash or repairs to the plaster or whatever, but nothing out of the ordinary."

"And every old house has a dozen places you see like that. And several dozen you don't." Ferry sounded like she was quoting someone. "You could do a trial period. One tapestry, like you said, one with a modest amount of work needed. If you hate it, you can present other options there. And you'd know what you needed to warn anyone else about."

"That's true." Eda let out a sigh. "Henny, I know you can manage here, but if you'd rather I didn't."

Henny shook her head, looking very thoughtful now. "I think you should. It might do you good to go do something else. You've been a little, I don't know. Not restless. But it's a good life you've got, but you've been having it just like this for a decade now. A change might show you what you want to do next. You still hadn't decided on the next weaving. We haven't warped the high loom. It's a good time for it, not much left in the middle."

"No, I'll finish that black silk by Friday." Eda let out a breath. "All right. I'll see if he wants anyone. Tell him what it'd take for me, and give it a trial." She glanced from one woman to the other. "Thanks for letting me talk it out."

Henny, of course, came right back with the answer. "Got to make sure everything slides smooth. No tangles."

"Here, let me pour more tea all round, and Henny, you wanted to hear about Anna getting into the yarn, didn't you?" Ferry's daughter was two and a half, and had an endless curiosity about anything with colour in it. Eda was fairly sure she'd follow her mother into the fibre arts. It was just a question of which ones and how many.

CHAPTER 8
JUNE 2ND AT EDA'S WORKSHOP

J eremy knocked on the door precisely on time, as arranged. It was five, the time Mistress Fellowes had requested. He could see a couple of people moving back and forth inside, and then someone came and opened the door. "Master Royston, Mistress Fellowes is in her study." This was a woman, not one he'd met yet, with pleasant dark hair and a smile, maybe in her mid-twenties, much younger than Jeremy.

"Of course." He waited to be shown the way, though it was certainly not a large house, and he remembered from last time. It was curious, having a home that was also a workshop. He wasn't entirely sure how that worked in practice. And certainly he wouldn't inquire about it. He could hear footsteps above. The woman guiding him knocked. "Master Royston, Mistress Eda."

"Thank you, Ferry. I'll be out to see your current work on Monday, whatever else. At ten, yes."

"Ten is excellent, thank you. I'll pass that along." The young woman ducked out of the way. "A pleasant evening, Master Royston." Then there was room for him to step into the study. The woman closed the door behind him, as Jeremy looked to find a chair, and spot the source of the delightful smell. There was a vase with fresh flowers on the windowsill, specifically with fresh lilacs, and he was struck by how simple a thing was so pleasant.

Now he bowed. "Mistress Fellowes. I hope this is still a convenient time."

Mistress Fellowes nodded. She settled in the chair she'd used in his last visit. "It is, we've just wrapped up for the day. I gathered from your note, and your presence, that you wish to proceed with the work, but we should talk about the specifics and the practicalities."

"Yes, please. Your notes have been clear in several respects, but confusing in others, I expect because of how little I know of the art form and the work required." Jeremy reached into his satchel for his notebook and a pencil. "And you mentioned in your note that you would have some requirements and specifications."

"Yes." She tapped her fingers on the desk for a moment. "You understand that this is a terribly time-consuming process, even for just one tapestry. The ten pieces you have all have different degrees of damage to them. The estimates I gave you are guesses. Educated guesses, informed by two decades of work, as well as what I learned from my own apprentice mistress, bless her, in her own time."

"She is, I beg pardon, no longer alive, then?" Jeremy coughed. "I could not get a sense of how many there are who do this kind of work."

"Mistress Hollingsworth died a few years before the War. I was one of her last apprentices." Mistress Fellowes considered. "There are few of us with this speciality. Ferry Pride, who met you at the door, is bidding fair to do well with it. Five or six others still regularly taking commissions. It is a problem, balancing supply and demand."

"Mistress Pride is the one you mentioned, with a current project and young children." Jeremy didn't quite make it a question. "But able to take on such projects in the future, perhaps?"

"Yes. She's blessed to live somewhere she could, in fact, set up tapestries for repair at home in due course. But I'd hesitate to transport yours, as it stands. Besides the fragility, I have been wondering if they may be tied into other enchantments in the house."

"There is some odd family lore. I don't know the truth of any of it. And I haven't found much in the way of documentation in the family records yet." Jeremy did not want to admit to the old stories about lost treasure. Here, in this sunny and bright study, they seemed ridiculous. And certainly such things did not fall into his view of how things worked in the world.

"I might be interested in hearing more about that, if there's anyone at the estate who would know those stories." Now Mistress Fellowes shifted, pulling her notes over. "As you have guessed, there are few people who could do this work, or who could begin it any time soon. I have a proposal for you, which I think you may find more agreeable in terms of both money and the level of commitment required."

That did sound promising. And again, Jeremy was struck by how soothing he found her approach. She obviously had a gift for the art form, but she was also as relentlessly practical as he could have hoped for. He didn't have enough information to know if this was something common to weavers, or specific to her. "Please, go ahead."

"What I would propose is beginning with one tapestry.

Gaudium, perhaps, it would provide an excellent test for matching colour and fibre, given both the design and the work it needs. It needs work, but is in the middle range in terms of overall needs. I would work on that until completion, and at that point, we could negotiate for the next steps. That might be arranging to have the other pieces brought somewhere I or Ferry could work on them. It might mean finding another restorer. It might mean stretching out the timeline of the work to suit your budget and resources."

"Ah, quite." He could see the benefit of that. "To be honest, I am uncertain of the long-term sustainability of the house. Having the pieces mended would allow them to be sold, and I gather they would likely fetch significantly more as a set than individually."

"They would." Mistress Fellowes tilted her head. "Though more likely with an American buyer. Too many of our families are scrambling for resources themselves, given death duties and the demands of the estates, and even simple matters like rebuilding stables for working horses."

"Yes." It came out curtly, but Jeremy knew about that. It had taken six months, apparently, to replace the cart horse who currently served the estate. Far too many horses had died in the War. There were many places automobiles couldn't manage, and horses took time to grow and be trained. "I see your point. And you seem, pardon, as if you disapprove of selling them abroad?"'

"I think they are a piece of art, made in Albion for an Albion home. A specific home. This is not even one of those times where the hangings went from place to place, trooping about the country as the family moved. It would be a shame to separate them if there were other opportunities. And that's beyond whether there's any attachment to the enchantments or protections of the house." She lifted a finger. "I know someone who might consult on that, but he's booked up for months. He did promise to write when he thought he might have time to have a look. His consultation fees are about the same as mine, for an initial review, but he'd want records in hand, as well."

"Which I do not have sorted yet." Again, Jeremy felt it came out too crisp and sharp. "I beg your pardon, this is all very new to me, and I am not entirely sure what to say or how to say it."

"Are you willing to meet my terms?" She passed a slip. "The same as I included."

He glanced down at the paper. "Yes, in principle, but I am confused by some of them? A bedroom and your own bathing room and water closet. We can arrange that well enough. Privacy, a door you can lock and ward, that is understandable in a house you don't know." As he said it, he saw her tense and then relax, oddly, and he didn't know what to make of that. "We have plenty of rooms. If you'd like to be nearer to other people or entirely on your own, you have your choice. Mrs Summers will need a few days to arrange them and tidy and make sure there are fresh linens."

"And meals, and the ability to come back to Trellech Friday evening and return either Sunday night or first thing Monday morning." She seemed a little nervous at this.

"Absolutely. I am still figuring out what my best options are. I normally work in Trellech during the week, and go out to the house on Friday evening, returning Sunday. But I could adjust to make trips you wanted sensible and spare Douglas and the horse."

"So you are not there during the week?" Something about this surprised her.

Jeremy shook his head. "I haven't been. I have been considering taking a leave from my work— this time of summer is busy but not our busiest, usually. A leave would give me more time to focus on the house, but I would want to make good use of that time." He was, in all honesty, not sure how he felt about living on the estate day in and day out. That was part of the problem. He felt like if he did, his life would change forever in even more ways, and he did not want that.

"You enjoy your work, then? You said you're a senior clerk, the Ministry of Materia, but I'm not sure what that entails." She leaned forward a little, but he was unsure if that meant she was interested or not.

"We make sure that the Materia used in Albion is up to standard. That if it says it was harvested on St John's Eve, it can be confirmed to be so. That it is not adulterated, that it is not one thing simulating another. That the provenance, when that matters, is correct. Sometimes it matters where something comes from."

"Ah, we get that with sheep and wool. Only in that case, skilled spinners and weavers and knitters can tell when there's something wrong, much of the time. We might not know what we have instead, but we can tell when something does not fit what we expected. Our fingers can."

Jeremy nodded. "Most of my work is with the paperwork, you understand? We bring in specialists when something falls outside that. But there is a great deal to do in the spring, with planting, especially for Materia that is heavily used by the Ministry itself, to ensure sufficient stores. And then again with tracking the harvest. June and July, it is usually busy growing, and I am less involved in that part."

"Except those things harvested on solstice or whatever, and I suppose you are not the only one in your office." She said it thoughtfully, and Jeremy nodded, agreeing with her. "My second will oversee things here. I have some preparations to make, as I mentioned. And ideally, I'd like several large tubs, some non-reactive surface. I don't care whether it's enamel or created magically."

Jeremy blinked. "May I ask why?"

"Dye baths. And somewhere safe to hang up the results - somewhere cats or animals can't tangle the yarn, ideally. A greenhouse where I could open up the glass would be ideal, but they are not exactly in the ordinary way of things. And then I'd need working frames. Do you have someone on your estate or in one of the towns that does carpentry for you?"

The question, what felt like out of the blue, startled him. "Um. Yes. If it's not terribly complex. He's good at mending things, but sturdy, not beautiful."

"I'll want frames for working on the tapestry. It's not terribly difficult to set up, other than the piece that they roll onto. I have plans, I can explain and supervise; that is one of many things I know about my work. But I'm not terribly good at the actual woodwork. And I'll need someone to help me lower the tapestry when we get it off the wall. Strong arms, steady on their feet, we'll need two stepladders."

Jeremy blinked several times. "You have a list, I hope?"

She nodded once at the papers in his hand. "Those have all the specifications. I am not a terribly picky eater, but I included a few of my preferences. If they're a bother, let me know and I'm glad to discuss with your Mrs Summers."

Frankly, Jeremy thought that Mistress Fellowes was more comfortable with him having a housekeeper than he was with having one. "If there's nothing much out of the ordinary, I'm sure she'll sort something agreeable, but I'll let her know you're glad to discuss." He took a breath. "I believe we've come to terms. When would you be ready to begin?"

"I put some things into play, since I could use them even if you didn't go forward. A week from Monday, if that's convenient? You needn't be present to get me started. Not so long as Mrs Summers knows where things are and there are people on hand for the carpentry and to get the tapestry down."

"I'll make arrangements. I admit I'm a little curious?" He offered it tentatively. "The thirteenth, then. Would you prefer to go out Sunday evening, to be there and settle in?"

"If that isn't a bother for the estate, certainly." Then she tilted her head. "Do you have further questions?"

"Not at the moment. I'll be out there tomorrow, and I'll confer about the staff matters. I will let you know, a note on Monday, if there's anything you should know. And then a week Sunday, at the portal."

"Just so." Mistress Fellowes stayed seated, but Jeremy stood.

"I won't take up more of your evening. Thank you, and I'm pleased you'll be giving your expertise to the work." It seemed a proper thing to say. A moment later, she stood as well, offering him a smile but no further commentary as she showed him to the door.

CHAPTER 9
JUNE 12TH AT OAKBURGH HALL

Eda was not sure what to make of the house. Or the people in it, not yet. She had taken the portal out to Swaffham at the time indicated on Sunday, arriving at half-five. Then it was another jostling ride in the cart. Master Royston had not come along this time, and she couldn't decide what to think about that. Part of her was glad she didn't have to make awkward conversation in the cart. Part of her wondered why he hadn't come himself. Douglas, the carter, had just grunted and said, "Master Royston had things to tend."

She had rather a lot more materials with her, and at least the cart had room for them. She had a carpetbag with her personal items, a travelling trunk, also inherited from her grandmum, and then two chests of materials, mostly wool. At least those weren't heavy. She'd also brought one of the table looms, in its own case, because she would want to do something with her hands in the evening. Not weaving at all sounded like torture. She'd warp it and do some lovely patterned strips that could be used for a bell pull or the charmed equivalent somewhere.

Once they arrived at the estate, she was starving. The housekeeper had come out to meet her. "Master Royston suggested we hold supper for you, perhaps half an hour? I can show you to your rooms. This way." She left little space for Eda to say yes or no. But Eda wanted to see the rooms, put down her bag, and have some reassurance she wasn't making a dreadful mistake.

Eda managed to say, "The two chests are going where I'm working, please. The trunk and the rectangular case should come to where I'm sleeping."

She didn't actually think people here would hurt her, not like that. Henny and her guild knew where she was. Master Royston had not hesitated at any of the usual contractual precautions. And there was, in fact, a town quite nearby. It just didn't have a portal or a train. Now, she just followed Mrs Summers through the courtyard, up a flight of stairs, and then toward one corner of the building.

"Master Royston said he'll give you a proper tour in the morning, of course." Mrs Summers turned over her shoulder, then opened the door. "Three rooms here, a sitting room, bathing room and water closet through that door, bedroom there. The maids cleaned everything out properly, but let me know if there is anything they missed, or anything you need. And the rectangular table you asked for, there, by the window for better light, I hope?"

The furnishings were more expansive than Eda had expected. The sitting room had a good-sized table up against the window and a couple of easy chairs. There was a fireplace on the wall shared with the bedroom. Not that she expected to need that terribly much in June or July. Or August, if she were here that long. And it all looked quite clean. "If I could have a couple of minutes to set my things out? How do I find my way down for supper?"

"I'll have one of the maids come up in twenty minutes." With that, the housekeeper near enough vanished out the door, leaving Eda alone. She unpacked the carpet bag, laying her hair brush and such out in the bathing room. It had a startlingly well-maintained copper tub. She wondered if the hot water was up to filling it properly. The bedroom was just as tidy as the other two rooms, with a carpet in good repair and a pleasant floral pattern. She unpacked the changes of clothes she'd brought by hand. As she was finishing, Douglas and someone else who was not introduced brought up her trunk and the loom case.

As soon as they were done, they were replaced by a maid, perhaps in her early twenties. "I'm Alice, Mistress. Mrs Summers said I should show you down to supper when you're ready."

Eda was not at all used to the sort of house where maids appeared out of nowhere. She had a cleaning woman come in at home. Running the workshop left little time for the housecleaning. But that was usually two hours in the morning, while they were upstairs, and they tended the workroom themselves. But she knew how to be polite. "Thank you. I'm sure I'd get terribly turned around."

"Yes'm. It took me a while to learn, even with it being square. This way." Alice led her down a corner stair, gesturing. "The great hall where the tapestries are is that side. The dining room is this way." That meant she was above where the tapestries were, at a right angle to them and a few doors down the corridor. That should make it easier to go back and forth. They went through a larger dining room. It had a long table covered in a dust sheet that would likely seat twelve. Next, they entered a smaller room, with a more modest oval table that might seat six with not much crowding. About the same size as the table in her kitchen, actually, though it was rare everyone was down there at the same time.

Jeremy stood politely as she entered. "I'm sorry for not meeting you at the portal. There was a problem with one of the drains." He ducked his chin. "Not on this side of the house, thankfully. I hope the rooms are sufficient, Mistress Fellowes?"

Eda inclined her head, and he came around to push in her chair for her. That was not the sort of manners she'd been used to from Bert, not unless they had been out somewhere with people to see them, fancier than a pub. "I haven't had a great deal of chance to explore yet, but Mrs Summers showed me where things are." Then, some imp of the perverse, or at least the difficult, brought her to ask, "May I ask about the general state of the hot water?"

"Oh, vastly better than the drains. My great-uncle had a whole new system put in a few years before he died. He was very specific about his baths, I gather. Let us know if that isn't true. I don't think anyone's slept in those rooms in a few years."

"It seems a large place, for just a few people," Eda offered, cautiously.

"It was used as a convalescent home for officers for a few years during the War. Few at any one time, because it's so awkward to get to, but for men who had to be somewhere quiet and undemanding. But since the War, it's been quiet."

Eda nodded and turned her attention to the food as it was served. Adding a list of her preferred foods and such when they settled the contract formally was just as ordinary as the contractual protections of her spaces and person. Now, she was presented with chicken, fresh vegetables lightly cooked, and a quite presentable dinner roll.

"It looks lovely." She settled in to take a bite, then another. "My compliments to your Cook, please. It also tastes lovely."

Master Royston looked pleased at that, though he immediately said, "Cook also came with the house. I think she's pleased to have someone else to cook for. She knows all our tastes by now." He added, after a brief consideration, "Besides the two of us, there are a number of staff. You've met Mrs Summers. Mr Haldane is the estate steward and acts as butler when that's needed. He's away this evening, to make some materials purchases tomorrow. There are two housemaids and a kitchen maid, Alice, Margaret, and Ruth. And then a man of all work, three gardeners, and you met Douglas. They all live on the estate, but Cook sees to their meals separately."

Eda nodded slowly. "I appreciate having a sense of the people. I don't wish to disrupt anything. And I know it takes a lot to keep a place like this in good repair. Though I've only been a visitor, and often at houses that are mostly closed up for whatever season. It's considered untidy to have restoration efforts going on during a house party."

Master Royston considered. "And from your point of view, Mistress Fellowes, I'm sure everyone wants to wander around and rub their grubby hands on what you're working on?"

It was more humour than she'd expected from him based on her limited experience so far, and it surprised her into an actual laugh. "Exactly." Then she considered. "I appreciate your consideration for the etiquette, but if you would prefer, I am agreeable to moving to a first name basis or something of the kind. It seems awkward to keep saying Master Royston and Mistress Fellowes all the time when we're the only two people in the room."

"I had not wanted to presume." He ducked his chin. "Also, the contract made it clear that appropriate forms of address should be suggested by you."

"I'm surprised you read that part. People usually don't." It was in the fourth appendix. That one didn't actually have anything that needed to be countersigned in it, unlike the second, which had all the food and housing arrangements.

He blinked at her, owlishly. "I beg pardon. People don't read everything they sign?"

"No." Eda considered his expression. He looked as if someone had told him that grass was, in fact, the vibrant red produced by cochineal and alum and cream of tartar. "Most people just look at the places they actually sign. Silly of them, but true far too often."

"Is that why there were so many specific statements to initial?" Eda nodded. "I suppose the matter of names and forms of address could be discussed later."

"Exactly." Eda took another few bites of her food. It really was excellent, and it wasn't the sort of thing she got from one of the places near her, for takeaway, the many nights she didn't want to cook for herself. "But it's in the contract so that if there is a problem, someone insisting on informality, or the wrong sort of nickname, we have something to point to."

"Ah." He set his fork down, leaning on his plate, as if he couldn't use it neatly and talk at the same time. "I am Jeremy then, if you like. The staff insist on their various appropriate names. Mrs Summers gave me a lecture about it a few weeks ago. It matters if they're in the village, picking up small things, apparently."

Eda nodded. "Eda, then." People often weren't entirely sure how to pronounce it, but she'd always said ed-ah, a bit like better, but with much less in the way of consonants.

Now she had to cast around for a new topic. "Mrs Summers said she thought you might give me a tour of the house tomorrow. Or are you going back to Trellech first thing?" No, Mrs Summers would have known about that. That was foolish.

"I'm hoping to arrange some leave, but I'll need to go in on Wednesday and see about that. Of course, I won't get in your way or be a bother. I've a number of matters of estate paperwork to figure out, and I might as well do it when I can be handy if you have questions." He said it as if he'd been rehearsing that, perhaps to say to someone in his office. "I thought it might help to see a bit more of the house, in good light, but I am glad to do that at a convenient time for you."

"Perhaps tomorrow afternoon, last thing, three or half-three?" Eda made an estimate of how big the house was, and what a reasonably thorough tour might involve. "That will let me get things set up with no need to pause too much. I might just want a sandwich for lunch, so I can eat quickly, if that's not a bother."

Master Royston - Jeremy - shook his head. "Just let Mrs Summers know at breakfast. She's entirely used to that from me. Though of course if you do want company for a meal, and I'm available, I would not be so rude as to make you eat alone."

The way he put that was also not the ordinary sort of thing, but Eda wasn't sure how to ask about it. She would likely want company somewhere in there. She was used to people chatting away in their breaks in the workshop. She just wasn't sure how that would go with this man, whose conversational tastes she didn't know, but which likely didn't include wool staple lengths, the various dye formulae, or particular techniques. And she certainly wasn't much good at talking about most other things. Bert had always complained about it.

Now she took a breath. "Perhaps we might talk a little now about the surrounding area? I know little about Norfolk." That seemed a neutral enough topic to begin with, and it might end up being useful.

CHAPTER 10
THE NEXT MORNING

J eremy gestured. "The building has changed quite a lot over the years."

"A Tudor property." Eda tilted her head. "So they weren't thinking about sieges."

"Not at the time. Though I gather during Cromwell's Protectorate, there was a battle nearby. By then, of course, the non-magical community had forgotten entirely that we were here, and the protections were quite good. Still are." Though he should double check on when they were supposed to be renewed and make sure that money was set aside for that. He only had any idea about both schedule and cost because his great-uncle had kept good notes.

Though he'd also have to check the current costs. Post-War inflation and the rather vastly reduced number of specialists who could do that kind of work had likely sent the prices up. On the other hand, he certainly knew people in equivalent positions in the Ministry who could point him at suitable people to consult.

On a number of levels, dealing with the tapestries was a

lot less essential, but also felt a great deal more manageable. From what Eda had explained in her proposals, most of what she intended to do could be undone if it turned out to be a bad idea. He'd be out her fees and expenses and such, but it was not remotely the same category as the non-magical wandering in.

Then he realised he'd been quiet too long again. Eda was staring, rather deliberately, at one bit of leading in the window. It made a pleasant arch, encouraging the eye toward the gardens visible from this angle, but the leading itself did not merit that kind of interest. "I beg pardon. Let's see."

"Is it properly a castle?" Eda's question came out a bit abruptly. "I suddenly realised I don't know what the defining features are."

This was yet another question Jeremy had not expected. "I admit I don't know either. I ought. Or at least how the estate fits into that." He considered. "There is a gatehouse, of course, and the moat. But I don't feel like we have proper fortifications. It's not a defensible bit of landscape, or positioned to overlook something important. Rather, the middle of nowhere."

"It makes you wonder who made their home here, and put so much effort into it." Eda considered. "I gather Baddock Hall, down near Ipswich, is the same design, a moated square hall. Though I don't think they have the same sort of gatehouse anymore, if they did."

"A little earlier, I believe, maybe a decade? But I admit I've not made much of a study of the demesne estates." Jeremy hesitated. "Have you seen many?"

"Quite a few, there aren't that many who do tapestry restoration, and of course it's places like the demesne estates that are most likely to have a tapestry. You've seen the lists of the others, obviously." Jeremy had. There were maybe a dozen names, but connected into various webs of people, by apprenticeship ties. "I've been out at Ytene a number of times recently. That's where Ferry lives and is working. But that's a very different sort of building, much older. It dates back to not long after the Conquest."

"But also not a castle." Now Jeremy would be stuck on what the actual definition of one was until he could get to the Encyclopaedia Britannica in the library. For this, he'd likely need to consult both the non-magical volumes and the additional ten volume supplement that the magical publishers put out. It was the 1910 edition, of course, and Great-Uncle Dennis had not kept up with the supplements. On the other hand, Jeremy was fairly certain the definition of a castle had actually been untouched by the Great War and all the other events of the last seventeen years.

"No. A hunting lodge, I think, originally, or something of the kind. It's not like this, all the deliberately designed squares, or that courtyard." Eda tilted her head. "Do you know much more about who made the tapestries?"

"Only the sort of formal biographies." Jeremy walked down one hall, trying to remember if there was anything in this direction Eda might want to see. "Pardon, may I ask a personal question? It applies to the tapestries."

Eda stiffened. Jeremy could see that, but he didn't know why. She took a few more steps herself, then nodded. "You may ask." That was cautious, and it made him sure he'd mis-stepped, but he wasn't sure how.

"I beg your pardon. I wondered if you're religious at all. There's a history of the family being Catholic recusants." Jeremy offered the additional information in the hopes it would ease things, and something in the last bit seemed to help.

"Not the bits of history I know best." Eda's voice was quiet, measured, like she was tending to weaving, a rhythm to it that made sense to her. She went on a step or two, then paused. "Pardon, where are we going?"

Jeremy coughed. "I admit I was trying to figure that out. There's not much of interest in the parlours this way. Did you want to see the gatehouse?"

"As you wish." It was not a rousing statement of delight, but she nodded, letting Jeremy open the door to the courtyard for her to go ahead of him.

The gatehouse stood at the front of the house, two great towers standing up on either side. "How many storeys is it?" Eda shaded her eyes with her hand, looking up and up.

"Oddly, only three floors, but the ceilings are rather taller than the rest of the house. It looks more like four or even six, doesn't it?" This was a question he had an answer to. "Quite a lovely view if the weather is clear." It was not raining at the moment, but the clouds and mist obscured a lot. "There was a porter's lodge, down here at the east. And then the rooms above, they're known as the Lady's Room. It's unclear if that's because they were used by visiting Council Members several times, or the local Lady."

"Not a place that would get a regnal procession after the Pact," Eda agreed. Then, before Jeremy could say anything further. "I'm not particularly religious, no. I keep the customs, May Day and Solstice and such, but whatever religious feeling I had got impossibly tangled by the War. Like many people, I suppose. Now I'm wondering about people who felt so strongly about it, to keep going on with it, when the world made it difficult."

"An interesting question." Jeremy nodded. "Would you

like to go up? The stairs are rather steep, but solid. All stone, no worries about how well the wood has held up."

"Oh, I suppose. Do you want to go first? I don't know where we're going." Eda stepped back to let him lead, and Jeremy opened the door to the stairway, then went up the stairs. There was plenty of light from the small windows. He didn't need to worry about a charmlight or a lantern. They came out in the first floor room, with its large windows, and Eda inhaled in delight.

"This is lovely. Unexpectedly lovely! And that bed." There was a great four-poster bed. "They must have brought it up through the window. Or built it in place. Now I'm going to wonder about that. Not the sort of thing you have notes about, I suppose."

It certainly wasn't what Jeremy had wondered on seeing it. "Not that I've seen. There are some hangings there, but not particularly well known. There's a sitting room, above, or something like it." He felt entirely baffled, and he must have looked the same, because she immediately added something of an explanation.

"Oh, I think about moving looms about a fair bit. It makes you think about the turns in staircases. In the workshop, the upstairs windows are more than big enough to bring in something, at least partly assembled. I think you could do it here, if you removed the glass. Or were exceedingly careful with it." She took several steps to look out. "The view is fine."

"There are stories about this part of the house. Well, slightly more stories on average than the other parts, it's honestly a little hard to tell what's noteworthy right now. But it's not been much used in a century. Awkward to get to. My Great-Uncle's mother didn't care much for stairs, and certainly you'd not want small children up and down them all the time." He suddenly realised there'd been no indication if she had children, or had had children, or whatever applied. If she had been that wary of the question about religion, he certainly couldn't inquire about that.

What she said didn't give him any clue, either. "No, and it must have been a challenge in any long gown, or anything with much padding. Your Great-Uncle's mother, when did she live here?"

"Great-Uncle Dennis was born in 1825, and his mother, that would have been around 1800, but I might be a year or two off. That was Great-Great-Uncle Cornelius. His wife came from a cadet line of the Howards. She was very proud of the connection. There's some embroidery and such somewhere, and some framed images, the heraldry, and family trees and genealogies." Jeremy wasn't sure what he thought about that. "But Great-Uncle Dennis never married, so there hasn't been a woman as mistress of the estate since Caroline, his mother, died around 1870."

"And your great-uncle does not sound like someone much interested in the hangings or embroidery." Eda said it fairly lightly, as if she weren't entirely sure how he'd take it. "I'm far better on weaving, obviously, but I could have a look if there are pieces you're curious about. At least suggest some approaches for preservation or who to talk to."

"I'd like that." Jeremy coughed. "Perhaps I might show you the library, and then let you get to work? It's an eclectic collection, and the household papers are stored separately, but you're welcome to borrow what you like from it."

"Thank you. I suspect I'll be wanting more reading material of some kind in due course. And it's probably the sort of library that has interesting local history tales, isn't it?" Eda let Jeremy go first again out the door, and he went downstairs. Once they were back in the courtyard, he went to the other side of the house and the library. Here, at least, he felt slightly more on solid footing.

The library was the place he'd spent the most time in the house, besides his sleeping room and the muniments room. It was pleasantly arranged, panelled in wood, with shelves of books stretching around three sides. The windows weren't particularly large, but they had small diamonds of coloured glass inset along the top, casting a rather enchanting light on the floor as the sun moved.

There were two chairs by the fireplace, and Jeremy gestured. "I use that table most often, when I need a desk, but please claim the other if you'd like. We shouldn't need the fire this far into the summer, but that fireplace draws well, at least."

Eda tilted her head, then smiled suddenly. "And that's not true of all of them, I gather? Well, old house."

"Exactly. We're getting them cleaned out one by one, but it's taking rather a long time. The kitchen chimney, the great hall, here, my rooms, and we just did the one on the corner with your rooms last month." Jeremy nodded. "I should let you get to work. Luncheon at half-twelve?"

She nodded once, distractedly. "I will come back." That sounded more firm. "To get to the Great Hall, it's out into the courtyard, ninety degrees right, the room on the left?"

Jeremy had to make a brief gesture at each step to make sure that was correct. "Yes." Then he felt himself blushing. "Pardon. I still get turned around as well. If you need, stick your head out a window and shout for Mrs Summers?"

Eda seemed to take that in good humour. "I suppose that will serve. I'd rather not sacrifice my thread to the labyrinth. Thank you for the tour. It is a help to get more of a sense. I'll see you at luncheon." Without waiting for him to reply, she went out, following the directions from what he could see. The comment about the thread made him go and pull out one of the volumes of Greek myth off the shelves. That would do for pleasure reading. Then he turned to go look for the many volumes of the encyclopaedia along the far wall.

CHAPTER 11
JUNE 14TH AT OAKBURGH HALL

By Tuesday afternoon, Eda had made a good beginning. But as it got on for three in the afternoon, her shoulders were aching, she had done something to her neck, and she needed to be somewhere else. It was not currently raining, and it had not been since just before luncheon, so going outside seemed a reasonable choice.

She tidied up her supplies, that was habit trained into her long ago. On her way out through the courtyard, she spotted Alice. "Just going for a walk to clear my head, I'll be back in a few." Eda knew she didn't need anyone's permission, but it felt odd to wander off and not tell someone where she was. On the other hand, Eda still wasn't entirely sure what to do with a home that had a staff, and more staff than the people being served, to boot.

It wasn't even as if Jeremy were here; he had gone back to Trellech for the workweek, first thing Tuesday morning. As soon as she'd been remotely settled in. That was understandable, but it meant Eda didn't really know how to handle things today.

Alice just nodded, and Eda walked on. She crossed the bridge over the moat, then followed the paths around to what she had been told was the kitchen garden, then through to the walled garden. The climbing roses were in full bloom, and the scent of them filled the air thoroughly. She was inhaling, trying to decide whether to sit on a bench or keep walking, when she caught the motion of someone in the far corner.

It was a young man, maybe in his middle twenties, and he looked like a startled hare or deer, so frightened he couldn't move. Eda put her hands down beside her, before she called out, carefully. "I'm staying at the estate, working on the tapestries. I didn't mean to bother you."

The young man ducked his chin, tugging the peak of his cap down over dark hair. Then he dashed for the opening in the far end of the wall, disappearing almost without any sound. That was not what she'd expected. Eda certainly hadn't wanted to startle anyone. The man hadn't seemed to be doing anything wrong or suspicious, he'd abandoned some pruning shears by the wall where he'd been working.

She considered retreating. But Jeremy had been clear she could walk in the gardens. Eda wanted to enjoy the smell of the roses a bit more, and the light here was pleasant. And she also hadn't done anything wrong. She was fairly certain, anyway. In the end, she sat on a bench, only to realise it was rapidly soaking the back of her skirt.

Before she could decide to retreat with what shreds of dignity she might still have, there was a sound, shoes on gravel, across the garden. "Beg pardon, mistress?" A different man was standing there, same peaked cap on his head, and he ducked his chin.

"Yes?" Eda wasn't sure what else to say.

"Might I have a word, mistress?" The man gestured,

then came closer, rather than shouting across the garden, though he didn't rush. She nodded, tilting herself to show her focus on the conversation.

Once he was closer, a few feet away, in comfortable conversational range, he cleared his throat. "Beg pardon, mistress. You're staying here, I heard from Mrs Summers." He spoke clearly and precisely. "I'd be Waters. Gerald Waters, head gardener. Learned here, didn't do no proper apprenticeship."

Eda nodded. "I am, yes. I'm Eda Fellowes, I'm a weaver working on the tapestries." She glanced back toward the opening in the wall. "Did the young man— is he all right?"

The man in front of her blinked, as if she'd gone entirely off the script he'd expected. "Erm, mistress." Then he coughed. "I wasn't sure what happened, see."

"I came into the garden— the roses are stunning, the scent's so lovely— and the other gardens, of course." Eda was babbling now, but she was trying to ease things and complimenting someone's efforts in a garden rarely went badly. "I'm sorry if I startled him."

"Aye, you did, mistress." Waters ducked his chin. "He's my nephew, you see. He had a bad War, he's not good with people. Him or his friend, they both work here."

"Oh, I'm terribly sorry. And here I was, showing up out of season. A snag in the weaving." The second example obviously baffled Waters. She added, "I'm here to repair the tapestries. I think about snags all the time. The damage we do living, and how to make it smooth out so it won't keep catching."

She'd startled him again, she could see that. He took half a step back, his hands folded in front of him, as if he weren't sure where to put them, before he shoved them into his pockets. "Aye, mistress. Something like that."

"Well, I'm sorry I startled him. I'd love to be able to enjoy the gardens, now and again. It's hard on the back and the neck, weaving and mending!" Eda did her best to keep her voice cheerful and relaxed. "Is there something I could do so as not to startle your nephew again? Not get in your way."

"Ah. Well." Waters shifted his feet, bracing a little, settling in for a good think. "Did you know people, came back from the War? To live with?"

Eda hesitated, then shook her head. "Not like that. I know a few, but not living with." She hesitated, then added. "My late husband died in the trenches. Not the same thing." She kept her voice as neutral as she could.

"Ah, my condolences, mistress. That's a hard thing too. Buried over there?" There was an odd note in his voice now.

She nodded, once. One of the countless stones in the great cemeteries somewhere in France. They'd sent her a letter. She could go and look if she really wanted to, but she hadn't. There wasn't anything in that trip that would do her any good. At least she knew where he'd been buried, which was more than many people did.

"Henry's my nephew. My brother's son, he died in 1919." Of the flu or the Naples Scourge, whatever one called it, Eda suspected. "And Ernie's his friend. They came back together. It was Henry you startled."

"Dark haired?" Eda asked, carefully clarifying.

"Aye, Ernie's tow-headed." That much information seemed easier for him. Now she would know who she'd upset, at least, which didn't seem a terribly useful piece of information, but it might come in handy sometime.

"I certainly don't want to startle them again. Would it be a help to whistle, if I'm out here on a walk? I'm not a great whistler, but I can manage a tune or two." Eda was trying to think of reasonable solutions.

"Oh, I suppose. Something that doesn't sound like a bird, if you can?" Waters shoved his hands a little more in his pockets. "I wasn't sure what to expect, mistress."

"I'm not posh. I work on some very posh things—tapestries take a lot of time, they're expensive to make. And tricky to mend. But I'm from a crafting family, in Trellech. I don't know this bit of countryside well. Maybe you could suggest some places to walk, not in the garden, too?"

Something in that seemed to reassure him. "And Master Royston, he had you come here?"

"Yes. It's tricky to move tapestries, especially if they're not in good shape. I'm working on one of them to see how things go, and from there we can decide what to do with the rest. I'll be here, oh, much of the summer, probably, but it's a little hard to tell yet. And glad to appreciate the gardens, when it won't cause you or the young men trouble."

"Ah, well, you're right that a garden ought to be seen. I can't right now, we've things to tend to, but perhaps sometime I might show you the place? And if you'll have a care about the boys." There was definitely fondness there to go with the protectiveness.

"Definitely glad to. I know a few men who don't like to be surprised. Whistling's easy. I'm not likely to come out before eleven in the morning, or if not then, mid-afternoon. When I want a break and to stretch and be out in the sunlight, really."

"And from that, I'm thinking you're not a morning sort of woman?" The way he put it caught her ear. Eda certainly hadn't turned out to be a mourning sort of woman. She'd got the telegram about Bert, followed by the letter from the

Ministry a day or two later, and she'd just kept on with her life. It had been the sensible thing to do, and honestly, she hadn't been entirely sure how she felt. She'd trod through the necessary social steps, glad to let them buffer her, to follow the expected pattern. But she hadn't wept for days, like she had when Grandmum died. But she could answer the actual question Waters had asked.

"Not really, no. I take a bit to get going. A good cuppa, maybe reading for a few minutes, some exercise to get my hands nimble. So you needn't worry I'll be out here at dawn."

"Can't deny that's somewhat of a help." Waters considered. "May I ask, mistress, what you think of Master Royston? He's still new to the place. I'd understand if you'd not want to say much."

"But you're curious how someone else sees him." She considered. "He's very attentive to details. I expect because of the work he does at the Ministry. When he first talked with me, it was clear he knew how that kind of consultation works, but he'd not done it on his own behalf often." When Waters looked confused, she added, "There are set rates for such things. Most people don't know much about them, but they're meant to keep things fair. We can charge a wide range for the actual work."

Waters nodded, but he said nothing.

That got Eda wanting to see if she could provoke him just a little. "We charge based on the work required, whether there are annoying parts about it. And of course, it lets us tack on a fee if the person is difficult to deal with. I didn't do that for him, of course. He's been very considerate. But there was a fee for me being out here, not able to be at home, or with my own big looms, for however long I'm here."

85

"Convenience, then. Or inconvenience, then." Waters nodded. "I was wondering, mistress. Some people come in and they want to change everything, just for the sake of change. Master Royston's cousin, Hieronymus Royston, he was bidding fair to be like that. Wanted his hands in everything. Now, hands in the dirt's good for a man, and I dare say a woman. But only when it's making the garden better, aye? Not fiddling for the sake of the fuss."

"Oh, I think that's a fair way to put it, yes. Tangling everything up, putting your stores out of order. Just because they took the notion they got a better idea. I've had an apprentice or two like that. Either they learned or they didn't last long." And Kay, for the other concerns she had about his ability to do the work to the standard she required, at least had avoided that one. He listened and took instruction well enough and didn't get ahead of himself.

"Like that." Waters nodded. "Right then, I should get on. But a tour, mayhap. And Master Royston, too, if he'd like to come along. I'll let the boys know you'll whistle and who you are."

"Give them best, if that would be any help. Or—" Eda hesitated. "I have a small loom with me, big enough to make a strap or a bit of ribbon. For fun, I think that sort of thing's fun. If there's anything like that that they'd like, find useful or a bit of pretty, I'm glad to work something up. I was planning on bell pulls, but they work for a strap for a bag or to hold curtains back, anything like that."

"A bit of a pattern, then?" Waters asked.

"Like that. I was thinking something geometric, not flowers, but I can do leaves easily enough."

"A bit of leaves never go wrong. Or maybe a rose or two, if you can do a rose? I think they'd like that. They share a cottage. Curtain ties would be a thing. Have a bit of the garden with them, besides whatever's been clipped the last day or three."

"Excellent." She'd only warped the loom last night. She could easily set up the weaving for that. "Thank you for coming to explain to me, and having an eye out for them. I'm sure it makes a world of difference to them."

Waters hesitated at something in that, then he just nodded, pulling his hands out of his pockets and tugging on his cap with the right. "Do my best, mistress. Have a good afternoon, walk in any of the gardens here. Just not beyond the wall. That's back where they are much of the day, the greenhouses and such."

"I'll have plenty to keep me busy here." Eda smiled up at him, and waited until he'd disappeared before standing and casting a drying charm awkwardly at her backside. Then she made a slow circle through the gardens, taking time to admire the different plantings.

CHAPTER 12

JUNE 16TH IN THE MINISTRY QUARTER, TRELLECH

"Good morning, sir." The door cracked open, and Jeremy was already standing.

Arranging this meeting had taken a dozen specific skills, the sort that were only honed by years in the Ministry. It had meant knowing how best to ask Mistress Norris, who ran the administrative offices with an iron hand. Other men tried to get around her by flirting with her, and that never worked.

Jeremy treated her with absolute respect and the occasional round of bringing biscuits for the entire office. That worked rather better. It meant she'd managed to get him fifteen minutes with Master Fulbrook on three days' notice. Master Fulbrook was two steps up from Jeremy's actual supervisor and the senior administrator for the entire Ministry of Materia, and Jeremy needed his permission for what he wanted to do.

"Master Royston for your ten o'clock, sir. Shall I take notes?" Mistress Norris did not stand yet, but she was perched on her chair as if sure it would be required in a moment, anticipating.

Master Fulbrook nodded. "Please, Mistress Norris. Come in, Royston. What's all this about? I hope it's not a problem with the St John's Wort harvest again this year. Greaves assured me it was handled." Jeremy was not entirely sure he'd trust Greaves on such points, but it was not his place to say so, at least not so directly.

"Nothing about that, sir. A personal matter. I appreciate having a few minutes of your time." Jeremy followed Master Fulbrook into his office, a large corner office on the third floor. Minister Iyer's was directly above it, suitably distant from the lift to avoid all the noise. Though, of course, in practice, most of the lower level staff took the stairs. It was the first time Jeremy had been in here since he'd inherited the estate. Now he looked at the room with eyes newly educated about what went into a building.

Of course, it showed off the materia, as much as anything. The oak panelling was burnished to a warm glow, but it was all the other little touches that caught Jeremy's eye now. The brass for the fittings, the way the handles were set with contrasting ebony wood, or the delicate mosaic work on the side tables. He was almost certain the colours of the glass in it were chosen for particular reasons, and not just to be aesthetically pleasing.

Master Fulbrook took his chair behind an imposingly large desk, and Mistress Norris took a seat by a side table. That was set up for this sort of work, with a small chair that pulled out, angled so she could see Master Fulbrook comfortably, her notebook at the ready. Jeremy took the indicated chair on the other side, keeping the portfolio with the necessary forms he was carrying right at hand in his lap.

"Now, what is this about, Royston?" Master Fulbrook leaned back slightly, looking relaxed.

"With your permission, sir, I'd like to put in for personal leave, six weeks if possible." It was an option, the Ministry recognised that sometimes situations came up. It could be an unexpected magical obligation, an injury, all sorts of things. Whatever leave he got in this case would be without pay, of course. But that wasn't an urgent worry. There was enough in his accounts to cover his personal costs for far longer.

"Personal leave? Your forms, then. Tell me about why you need the leave." Master Fulbrook held out his hand. Jeremy took out the forms, hearing the little scratch of the pencil and paper as Mistress Norris took shorthand notes.

"Through a range of circumstances, I inherited a country estate. I would like some time to attend to what it needs and get it on a solid footing going forward. It's rather far from the nearest portal, seven miles, which means travel back and forth to Trellech takes a long time. I've been going out Friday night and coming back late on Sunday, but matters would benefit from more attention for a period."

"Not a landed estate, of course." Master Fulbrook peered up over the papers, thumbing through them first to make sure they were all there and in triplicate. "Six weeks, you said? How does that suit with your responsibilities in the office?"

"As of yesterday, I've confirmed all the plans for materia to be harvested on solstice itself. I have a complete set of notes. Master Wedgeworth has really been coming along, and I'm confident he can oversee the details. I'll be available by post, and I had considered whether a journal would permit easier contact."

Master Fulbrook considered, tapping the paper. "I suppose it would be good to see what Wedgeworth can do on his own." Elias Wedgeworth was two years out of his apprenticeship. He finally had enough experience to take on more of the work of Jeremy's particular sub-department. The trouble with a cycle that ran a full year, of course, was that it took several years to get a grip on what was needed. But Elias was a quick learner, he took excellent notes. Jeremy had spent the last couple of weeks pulling his own notes together while he thought about making this request. "Why six weeks?"

"That would give me a good chance to get things in better order at the estate, sir. But beginning the first of August, there is, of course, an increasing list of harvests coming in, and the proper records and documentation. I'd not want to leave the department short-handed in the busy season."

"But possibly ask for some additional time in December or January?" Master Fulbrook raised an eyebrow, looking steadily at Jeremy in a way Jeremy found uncomfortable.

But he knew what he needed to do, so he looked back, then nodded. "Exactly, sir. Though I'm hoping six weeks will make it easier to figure out the further steps. The current staff are excellent, but I am still learning many details. My great-uncle kept excellent records, but the two cousins since then have not, I'm afraid." Jeremy hadn't been entirely sure about saying that, but he had actually checked.

As far as he could tell, there was no particular overlap between Master Fulbrook and either cousin Gervase or cousin Hieronymus. They hadn't been at school in the same years. And he didn't think they'd have shared a secret society, though that was hard to tell. But Master Fulbrook was also a Dunwich man, like Jeremy himself, and Dunwich men prided themselves on practicality. It wasn't a terribly big risk to complain here and now that paperwork wasn't up to snuff.

"Ah, it's itching at you." Master Fulbrook chuckled. "That, I entirely understand. If you were considering a journal already, having one would ease my mind here. But I won't require it. Just make sure Mistress Norris has the fastest means to contact you, and the delay on messages."

"Of course, sir. I appreciate the trust in the department's work. And of course, if something comes up and I'm needed back here, I'm glad to oblige." Jeremy did not stand just yet. He knew there were the formalities for the papers to be properly signed.

"I think it does a department good to have someone out for a few weeks every so often, honestly. Something I preach more than practise, mind. But it shows where there are gaps in knowledge and cross-training. I'd much rather find that out when you're handy by post than because of some calamity. And as you say, Wedgeworth is doing well." Master Fulbrook pulled over a pen in a penholder, then his sealing wax and seal stamp. He promptly signed the forms after glancing through them once again. Then he applied the seal to the last one with a touch of a charm to firm up the wax and imprint his own magic. "There we go. And of course all the forms are properly done. I wouldn't expect anything less."

Jeremy ducked his chin, pleased at the compliment. "Thank you, sir. I'll plan to be out from Monday?"

"Certainly. Though if you have things wrapped up here, no reason you couldn't start tomorrow." Master Fulbrook offered it easily, and Jeremy was startled, now searching for the trap.

"I'll get the paperwork filed right away, sir." Mistress

Norris stood. "You won't need me for your half-ten, you said?"

"Not until after luncheon, no. I've some files to go through on my own once I'm done with Craft and Hancock." Jeremy recognised those names as two of the other senior Ministry staff, though in other departments. He thought the three of them got together to coordinate regularly. And perhaps it was the sort of discussion where formal meeting minutes wouldn't be much help later.

He'd reconciled himself, long ago, to the idea that while most of the Ministry ran on order and structure, well-documented, some of it didn't. It was why he was unlikely to rise much further in the department. He didn't have the gifts to build connections with people in other departments, to have a casual drink that solved three problems in an informal conversation, or prevented something from becoming a problem in the first place. He could keep the details in his head. That was easy. But he couldn't figure out how to make them come out and sound natural in the moment. Now he stood, reclaimed the papers from Master Fulbrook. "Thank you, sir."

Then a thought occurred to Jeremy. "Do you have a particular preference for flowers, sir? The gardens are doing quite well. I could get the gardener to put together a bunch or two next time someone is coming to Trellech for the day."

Master Fulbrook blinked at him, as if he'd overstepped. Then he was smiling. "Oh, whatever looks good. Surprise me. We could use a bit of delight around the place here, I'm sure."

"We certainly could!" Mistress Norris sounded cheerful. "Here, this way, Master Royston." She ushered him out, efficient as always, then took the papers from him.

Jeremy stood, waiting; she had to stamp the copies, and then they went into files. She filled out a quarto-sized piece of cardstock, then another, stamping it with a stamp from an ink pad. "There you are." She glanced up at him. "Master Royston, may I ask a personal question?"

He blinked. That was not something that had happened before. He hesitated, then nodded, partly because he wasn't entirely sure how to say no. He didn't think she'd be improper, certainly not right here and now. "Yes?" Then he added, stammering a hair. "About the leave?"

"About the estate. Do you like it?" Mistress Norris peered at him over her glasses.

It didn't make the question easier to answer. He knew all the proper answers. Yes, he loved this massive new challenge that had been dropped in his lap with near no warning, by a death and a solicitor. Yes, he loved having more land than he could walk in a day, not that he was a fast walker. Yes, he loved a building he had no idea how to heat in winter or care for in summer. And one filled with furniture and historic magical items that weren't at all well-tended or documented with what they needed.

Then he thought about walking across the moat, the ducks in the water, and the way the light came into the library, and he swallowed. "I'm still finding that out. I'm hoping more time there, not constantly rushing back and forth, that will help."

Mistress Norris nodded at that as he spoke. "Well, I hope the leave does you good. If you get a journal, let me know. Here's the card with how to reach the department. Otherwise, what's the best portal for post and the delay?" He noted down the details, his own handwriting nearly as neat as hers, where she'd labelled it. When he straightened up, she handed him the paperwork. "And if you have a few flowers from the garden to spare, I'd love to see them, if you get a chance."

He blinked several times. "We'll see, I— yes. I should get back downstairs, see if I can wrap up today. Do have a good afternoon, Mistress Norris, and thank you for your help with the scheduling."

She smiled at him. She didn't seem offended or put off. But as he turned at the staircase to go down, he could see her watching him, before she bent her head over her desk and her work again.

CHAPTER 13
THAT AFTERNOON

Eda had settled into the work now. With the help of the staff, she'd got the Gaudium tapestry off the wall safely, and settled onto the work stand, charms cushioning it from damage. She'd taken the measurements for the backing fabric they'd want, and she'd either bring them back to Henny on Friday night or send a letter in the post. This was one of the wide tapestries, so it took quite a lot of effort to set it up properly on the stand.

Part of her wanted to retreat to Trellech, but the rest of her wanted to stay put. She could work on the tapestry for a few hours on Saturday and Sunday, less than a full day's work, and perhaps arrange for a picnic basket and a ramble. Part of it, she knew, because she'd done this often enough, was just the itchiness of being in a new place, that ran by customs she didn't know yet.

It was worse here, though. As far as she'd been able to tell the last three days with Jeremy gone, the staff were fine with him. They didn't show any of the signs that staff did when they feared or disliked someone. They weren't sure what to do with him, that was clear. And he certainly wasn't used to having staff like this. Eda didn't think he was high enough up in the Ministry to have his own valet or cook, as he'd mentioned something about rooms. But that meant likely someone who saw to the cleaning and the cooking for several sets of bachelors or professional women.

That was how Henny lived, in a rooming house with three others. Each of them had a sitting room, a bedroom, a shared bath for each floor. The woman who ran the place provided breakfast and supper, luncheon on Saturday and Sunday, and did the general cleaning. Now, Ferry was more used to having servants. She'd grown up in that sort of family. And of course, she was working all day, and so was her husband. They had a nursemaid and got a fair number of their meals from the main kitchen at Ytene. But Ferry could make up a perfectly good hearty tea. She'd done it when they'd been working late.

And all of that differed from half a dozen people who ate somewhere else in the building, who bobbed and nodded and deferred when Eda talked to them. Even Mrs Summers, who certainly needn't.

The thoughts along those lines certainly kept Eda busy all afternoon. She took a few breaks to stretch, but other than that, she didn't pause. She'd just begun to lay out the foundation for mending a bit of the tapestry near the bottom. It didn't look like mouse damage, that was distinctive, but perhaps a piece of furniture shoved up against it, rubbing when people stood or sat.

She was still working at half-six, when Mrs Summers came to see about supper, and only finished up around quarter past seven. First, she set out what she'd want the next day, lining up the skeins of the shades she'd want for the repair work. Next she'd covered it all with a clean cloth to keep any dust off. Eda retreated to the rooms upstairs, taking a few minutes to wash up, rebraid her hair, and pin it back up into a crown around her head.

Mrs Summers had said, or at least implied, that Eda would be eating on her own again. But when she got to the small dining room, she found Jeremy. He'd just sat down, but he bobbed right up again. "Eda, good evening."

She blinked several times, surprised. "Good evening. I hadn't— erm." It seemed rude to say she hadn't expected him to be here, in his own home, even if that was true.

"I'm sorry for startling you. Please, sit. Mrs Summers said you were working hard all day, you must be starving." He at least didn't come around to push in her chair. That would have been entirely too much nonsense. Instead, Eda sat down, this time choosing a seat on the side of the table, rather than putting herself at the end, the length of the table away from him.

He blinked at her, but he didn't comment. A moment later, Alice was right there, with their first course, a creamed vegetable soup. Eda had a few bites before he spoke again. "I hope I won't be a bother. I did request leave, and have permission to be gone from my usual work until the beginning of August. Oh, and before I forget, I stopped by your workshop before taking the portal to see if there were any messages. I promised to see a package of supplies into your care."

"Oh, bless Henny. I assume that was Henny?"

"She indicated a name along those lines. She was firm that I shouldn't open it. I felt like something a little out of a fairy tale, honestly." Jeremy sounded a little more relaxed now, as if being released from his usual work had changed something in him.

"Oh, that's more thread for the mending. Henny has an immensely useful knack for packing yarn and thread so it won't tangle. But heavens help someone who opens the package and tries to seal it again." Eda considered what she could say here. "You've seen cartoons in the papers, people trying to shove some large item in a closet and hide it? It's like that, only less of a rigid closet to help."

The sound she heard didn't make any sense for a moment, then she realised the man was chuckling. It had a sort of rusty sound to it, like he hadn't much, but he was smiling. "That is quite an image. Does your thread usually like to escape confinement? It sounds like one of those exaggerated adventure stories, a creature from the depths or some mysterious chasm."

"Not nearly that mobile, thankfully. Unless you add a cat. Or a dog, perhaps." Eda shrugged. "I like a cat, but with the workshop upstairs, and people coming and going all the time, not in a few years."

"Was your workshop elsewhere, then? At some point previously?" Jeremy asked it, then focused immediately on his food, as if he weren't sure it was too personal.

"Before the War, my husband and I lived in the cottage. My late husband." Clarifying that point seemed relevant. Certainly if she'd been married and Bert had been alive, she wouldn't be here for weeks on end. "He was killed in the War, and since, well, we turned the upstairs into a workroom. I enjoy having people around. Before, I leased a space in the Crafting quarter. Looms can be a little loud, but a solid building does well, and there are charms for the noise."

"But it would complicate a cat, yes." Jeremy looked curious. "Loud?"

"If you get us going at the same time, the shift of the

wood, the thunk of it, it makes it harder to talk. And the height of the ceiling, too, there's often more of an echo."

"Pardon, how tall is a loom? I thought they were mostly not that big?" The man actually seemed interested. Eda thought looms were one of the most interesting topics imaginable, but most people didn't agree. She knew that. Bert certainly hadn't wanted her to talk much about her work, nor had any of his friends. Grandmum had tolerated quite a lot, but she had been a glorious sort of knitter, and she appreciated other fibre arts properly. But even Eda's Mum and Dad had limits on how much weaving talk they'd put up with, never mind her brothers and sisters.

She took a few more bites of her food, mostly to give her time to think. "You're honestly interested?"

"Yes?" He sounded puzzled. "Should I not be? I don't know much about it, but that's how to learn, isn't it, finding someone who knows and listening to them?"

"It is not how most people go about things." Eda couldn't keep an odd note out of her voice, but then she swallowed. She could in fact talk about looms for days, even weeks, and she'd done the beginning explanation often enough. "Looms come in all sorts of sizes and shapes. I brought a small one with me just to have something to do in the evenings. It fits on a table. You can't make anything very wide on it, of course, but sometimes you want something narrow."

"So the tapestries here, they were made on two different sized looms? One for the wider tapestries, one for the narrower? No, wait, three, possibly?" He was sharp to put that together.

"It might be two, I'd have to check the measurements on the tapestries over the doors. It might be more than that. I'd need to look at the pieces in detail. They're all warped at the same distance." She had obviously confused him. "The warp are the threads that run the long way, up and down while you're weaving. The weft goes back and forth horizontally. Only tapestries are more complicated. You can take a larger loom, a wider one, and just warp part of it, but it can be trickier to balance. And like most things made of wood, a loom can have a mind of her own."

"Her? Like ships?" Jeremy took another bite of his food, like he'd remembered he was eating.

"I think of them like that? I suppose it's sentimental. But a loom is making something, bit by bit. Not all in one..." No, that was decidedly not the sort of insinuation one made to one's employer. What on earth was she thinking? "Though there are as many male weavers as female, both now and historically. Though that varies by time and place."

"Is that true? You always hear about women as spinsters." He seemed not to have noticed that she'd been on the edge of indelicacy, items going into orifices and such. Eda took a breath and went on, more evenly.

"Ah, that's because weaving, and also knitting and such, goes through a tremendous amount of yarn and thread. And spinning is something you can do as piecework, while you're doing other things at home. On a wheel goes faster, but you can carry a spindle with you while you're keeping an eye on children or livestock or sitting with your friends."

"Do you spin, then? No, wait, didn't I see some spindles?" Jeremy set down his fork. "And please tell me if I'm being impertinent."

"I enjoy talking about it honestly. Please tell me if you'd rather I stop. I spin. Not very much, not for production, but I like a bit of knitting as a change, and I'll spin yarn for that.

But it's a part of our training, because we need to know what we're asking for. How to evaluate a thread or yarn for balance and quality, and whether it's made from the materials it claims to be."

"Ah. I go at that problem a great deal differently. We do it with records and charms, mostly." Jeremy tilted his head, as if considering that.

"I could show you a bit of the thread once I've unpacked it and sorted out. Oh. I wanted to ask if someone's going near the portal soon. I have a letter for Henny. The details for the backing fabric. She'll be working on that. And I didn't explain the looms, did I?" Eda felt she was being a bit scattered here.

Jeremy shook his head, but he answered the actual question promptly. "Someone will go to the market on Saturday, and they can drop a note in the portal post without any bother. The looms?"

"Well, there are table looms. You make the patterns of the cloth by moving the warp up and down, in different sequences. On a table loom, you set those with your hands, and it can be a bit of a strain on them. A floor loom is wider, and you change the patterns with your feet, with pedals. Rather like a pipe organ. And tapestry looms, you need a lot of height to work the complicated patterns properly. That one goes almost up to the ceiling, the way ours works. But it's slow work, and it takes two people to run. May we ever be rich in apprentices."

"But for mending you can do yourself? Or at least with some help for your— however you have it set up to work?" Jeremy asked, more cautiously.

"Yes. And it's delicate, you don't want anyone jarring the frame. Or breathing near it, while you're working, honestly. I use charms to help, but even then, you're working with threads, reforming the fabric. I can show you at some point, maybe in a day or three, when I've got more of the current patch sorted."

"I'd like that." Then he looked up. "Oh, Mrs Summers. You wanted a word tonight, I beg pardon." He stood. "There will be some berries in a minute, but I promised I'd see to something, a repair needed. Do excuse me, Eda. I'll see you tomorrow, I suspect."

"Tomorrow." He excused himself from the room, and Eda paused to look after him, more than a little perplexed by several pieces of that conversation. It hadn't been unpleasant. The opposite, in fact, having a conversation with someone who appeared to find her preferred topic interesting. But she was not at all sure what to do with it now.

CHAPTER 14
THE NEXT DAY AT OAKBURGH

J eremy frowned again at the accounts book in front of him. Then he peered at Mr Haldane over his glasses. "These accounts make no sense. You know that."

To his credit, Mr Haldane did not prevaricate. "No, sir, I suppose they don't."

"Do you have any explanation? You are the steward of the estate. You managed these accounts for Great-Uncle Dennis, and then for my cousins." Jeremy leaned back. The thing of it was, he knew there was something wrong, but he couldn't figure out what it was. Some people had an eye for actual Materia, for plants and leaves and sprigs and dried leaf or cut up root. Some people, like Eda, downstairs, on the opposite end of the house, had an eye for colour.

Jeremy had an eye for the patterns of accounts. Something in him knew when a column was off. It was the wrong shape, the wrong shade, whatever metaphor he could stick to. There was something wrong on the lists in front of him.

"Explain to me again where this bit of income comes from. What is it? What has it brought in over the last two decades? Has there been variation due to the weather? How was it affected by inflation since the War?" Not whether, but how, he was sure it must have been. "Will it continue?"

Mr Haldane cleared his throat. "I have every reason to expect it will continue, sir. Your great-uncle cared it was steady. He did not ask questions."

"And my cousins?" Jeremy leaned back to tap his fingers together.

"Your cousins, sir, were not in the position for long enough to look at these details." That was accurate enough. Cousin Gervase had had the place for about eighteen months, but he'd also had his own work in London, and it was hard to get away. And Cousin Hieronymous had inherited for less than that, under a year. From everything he'd gathered, neither of them had been particularly inclined to look at the accounts, letting Mr Haldane handle all of that.

Jeremy considered. "Look. You know I can't let this go forever. I can give you a month to get records in order, so I can understand the estate income and expenses and make informed choices going forward."

"By Michaelmas accounting?" Mr Haldane leaned forward. That was the twenty-ninth of September, three months from now.

Jeremy was not a man designed to be imposing or intimidating, either by whatever forces determined such things or by his parents. He managed to raise an eyebrow. "Three times the length?"

"It would take us through this growing season and most of the harvest." Mr Haldane had the good grace to look unsettled, at least. "I believe I might arrange a more satisfactory answer to your question at that time, sir."

"Or you hope I'll be back in Trellech and not breathing down your neck." Jeremy sighed. He should not have said that part out loud, but something about this situation confused and frustrated him in ways he did not know how to handle better. He let out a breath, counted to five, and then said, "I beg pardon."

"You've made your interest in the estate clear, sir, and we appreciate that. We take care of each other here, and we take care of the estate. But there are, pardon, things you don't know. And where it's not a matter of my simply being able to tell you."

"That sounds entirely mysterious." Jeremy looked up at the ceiling. It was a decoratively patterned ceiling, with one darker spot visible among the interlaced geometric framing. "Is that another leak?"

Mr Haldane looked up, peered. "To be precise, sir, that is the same spot as in the winter of 1917. I will go see about getting someone out to look at the roof, shall I? It's Friday, but if I go now, we can have someone out here first thing on Monday. It might not actually rain until then."

Jeremy knew when he was defeated. "Please. And Mr Haldane?"

The older man pulled his notes together, but paused when Jeremy spoke. "Yes, sir?"

"Michaelmas. Not a day longer."

"As you say, sir. If you'd tell Mrs Summers I'll get my supper in town, please?" Jeremy nodded, letting the other man get on with it. He supposed it might be a chance for the man to talk with friends in Swaffham. Or perhaps his steward had a secret life as a ringer for the local darts tournament. Jeremy certainly had no idea. The staff kept their personal lives strictly private.

Of course, by the standing rules for country houses, servants weren't properly permitted much in the way of a personal life. They were supposed to be up and down at his whim whenever called for, with a scarce afternoon off once a week. Jeremy had insisted each of them get a full day, though obviously not all on the same day. And an additional afternoon, and it wasn't as if the ordinary daily duties were all that onerous. But the bare upkeep of the place took a surprising amount of ongoing effort, even with magic. The ceiling here was just one example.

And beyond that, someone had to walk through the house every day and make sure there was no flood or leak or sign of mice. There were the household charms to renew, dusting to be done, all of that, even if no one was really using the spaces. Others had to tend to the kitchen garden, or get the eggs from the chickens, or do whatever other food preparation was required.

Jeremy pulled the notes over again. He'd go through them one more time, in hopes he might spot the problem. And then, yes, it would be about four, he could go down to see how Eda was getting on and tell Mrs Summers about Mr Haldane being away for supper.

He did, in fact, wrap up right around four, and ran into Mrs Summers on the way downstairs. That dealt with, he made his way to the Great Hall, pausing by the doorway so as not to be startling. Eda was bent over the frame, a charmlight lantern hung on a stand that cast clear light over the area she was working on. When she looked up, he cleared his throat. "I came to see how you were getting on, if you needed anything?"

"Oh!" She didn't sound unhappy, at least. "I was trying to decide how much more to do today. Would you like to see? I need to stop for a couple of minutes, at least, and let my fingers relax."

"If it's not a bother." He came over carefully, not crowding her. She stepped to the side and indicated the area under the light. "I am just about done with the first part of this. I'm reweaving the warp threads by hand, anchoring them into the stable, undamaged portions on the top and bottom."

"And the next step is what, exactly?" Jeremy peered down at the threads, trying to make sense of them. "And don't your eyes ache?" He took his glasses off, peered again, and put them right back on. Without the glasses was absolutely worse.

Eda tilted her head. "Are you far-sighted, then? My close vision is quite good, thankfully. I have glasses I wear sometimes, but it depends on the day. Other than that, it's practice, really. Being able to distinguish the threads. It's close work, but I've built up a sense for it over time. And charms." She sounded cheerfully exasperated. "I don't know how people do it without charms."

"What do the charms do, then? Not move the needle, surely?" Jeremy thought that was a particularly delicate sort of work, and easy to have an error.

"The weaving motion, once I get to the weft, the charms can help with that. With magnification, though I don't like to use that for too long at a time, it can make you a little dizzy if you look at anything else after. And today, I was using charms to hold the thread in place until I anchored it properly. Here, you want the physical anchoring. Charms can wear off. If they did that unexpectedly, there would be more damage to the tapestry. Can't have that."

She sounded briskly firm about how things ought to go, which Jeremy was finding rather reassuring. Mr Haldane, earlier, had also been clear about what ought to happen. But the way Eda did it felt like it included Jeremy, rather than shut him out. He coughed, not sure what to say, or rather how to say it in a way that didn't sound awkward.

"Please, ask. I like it when clients take an interest in the work." Eda took a step back, beginning to stretch her hands out a bit. It was a series of exercises opening and closing her hand, then stretching each finger against the palm of her other hand.

"People don't?" That confused Jeremy even more. "They just, um. Pay you and let you do your work? You could do it badly, or hide a problem."

She cocked her head, and now she definitely looked amused. "You hired me for my skill and the quality of my work. Even if clients don't notice, others in the Weaver's Guild notice. And we see each other's work. We'll get called out for a small issue when the person who did the larger work isn't available, or sometimes we're invited to look when we're working on another piece." She shrugged. "Anyway. I prefer people understanding what I'm doing."

"Does it mean people value your work more? I do. I couldn't do that, not even with training and a lot of practice." Jeremy gestured at it again.

"Ah, do you do any crafting at all? Beyond whatever your record keeping is with pen and paper?" Eda went back to stretching her hands, and he couldn't help watching the motions. They had an elegance to them, a dance of sorts, something she knew intimately.

It also meant he almost forgot to answer. "Not much of one. I'm a reader, more than anything, but that doesn't take much dexterity. Enough to avoid paper cuts..." He offered the last tentatively. People rarely found his attempts at humour actually funny.

Eda snorted, amused, so apparently she did. Or at least didn't find it abhorrent. "Plenty of people find themselves with paper cuts. If you don't, that suggests something to work with. But nothing else?"

He shrugged. "I have had little space for a hobby, not anything like crafting." He hesitated, then confided something he had told no one else. "I wondered about what it would take to refinish some of the furniture. Clear up some of the cracking varnish, stain it again, polish everything up."

"You could do that. I'm sure there are some very boring dressers or desks or something like that. It's a skill people learn. And simpler than making them." Eda added, "I enjoy making something better. I like making something new with a loom, but I also like this. Restoring it. And you know about materia, you said, you could experiment with stains or polishes if you wanted to do some of that."

The thought hadn't occurred to him, but it was a good one. "Oh. I suppose I could. Do you think, are there books about that sort of thing?"

"Possibly in your library. If not, I'm sure booksellers in Trellech do. I know the shops that cater to crafters." Eda considered. "Look, I might as well stop for the day. I want a walk, but you could look in the library."

"Just like that?" It was still early, not that he was going to argue too much. He didn't want to argue with her.

"You're used to someone else telling you when you ought to be working and not working, aren't you? You had to arrange leave, you said. Get permission? You couldn't if they said no?"

"Of course not. It's a matter of, of proper procedure. Didn't you have to plan to be here?"

"Yes, but only in the sense Henny has to take over some things in the workshop, paying the bills and keeping up on supplies and all that. I didn't need her permission. She wouldn't need my permission, except that if she was rude about it, I might not want her back. But it's not..." Eda shrugged. "It's not permission. It's providing relevant information. I don't have a right to say yes or no to when she works, only if she's doing that work in my space with my looms. And our guild custom is that I'd have to be rather awful not to have her back when there was good reason for her to be gone for a bit. Point of fact, she took six months after her Mum died, to get her Da settled properly. We didn't know how long it'd be, just left it open."

"And that didn't affect other things you were doing?"

"Not really? We shuffled some of the apprentice duties around, but that's not a bother. We do that anyway. Sometimes people want a break from it. Or they want to work on a different kind of weaving. Anyway. You're not paying me by the hour, even if I used that for a rough count of how long it'd take to set the fee. You're paying me for the project. If I don't hit the benchmarks for the contract, I don't get paid until I do, which is my incentive to do enough work. But I'm actually a little ahead of that right now. A couple of hours?"

"In one week?" Jeremy blinked. "Is a couple two, three, five? People have different ideas of what it means as a number. Very imprecise."

"Four, in this case, I think. And I got bored on Wednesday evening. I put a bit of extra time in. So. Shall we go look at the library until supper, and if not, I can write down the bookshops you can send a letter to? Or probably there are some options somewhere around here, stain and polish and rags and such." Then she stopped. "Tell me if I'm too much? Too bossy. I'm used to deciding for myself."

"Not too bossy." Jeremy got that out immediately. "Confusing, sometimes, but not too bossy. It's a good idea. Do you need to wash up? Can I do anything to help you tidy up for the night?"

She shook her head and sent him along to look in the library while she put things to rights. He went, his hands in his pockets and his mind whirling about the whole conversation. But he liked the idea of doing something with his hands, not just his head. And doing something that would be hard to mess up, or at least that could be fixed if he did.

CHAPTER 15
JUNE 18TH

Eda spent Saturday working. She'd considered going back to Trellech, but she trusted Henny to keep an eye on the workshop, and she didn't much fancy the long trip back to Swaffham again so soon. Instead, she'd sent a note along to go in the post, to let Henny know she'd plan to come back next Thursday evening. That would give her time to check in, and then spend Friday at the Midsummer Faire before taking the portal back to Swaffham. Jeremy had said that would be fine, and everyone should go to the Faire, though he had said nothing about his own plans in that regard.

At any rate, getting ahead on the work now would make all of that easier. Especially if she was going to lose a chunk of Thursday and all of Friday next week. And of course, Eda liked the work she did, rather a lot. She liked the delicate parts. She liked the puzzle parts. She liked figuring out how to make a repair that wouldn't show. And she especially liked the intimacy of being up close with threads that told a story. All told, Eda had put in about six hours between lunch and the time she should wash up for supper.

That meal found her back in the small dining room. Jeremy seemed distracted by something, or at least more distracted. The man seemed to often be thinking along several other lines. Eda was fairly sure she was not boring him. He asked thoughtful questions, for one thing, right on point for what she'd just said. It wasn't just pleasantries, the sort that eased social connections but popped without a trace like a soap bubble. And it certainly wasn't like Bert, who'd pretended to listen to her, and hadn't wanted to be bothered.

Some of her mood must have come through, because when they had finished up the fruit for the pudding course, Jeremy cleared his throat. "Perhaps a walk, a postprandial walk?"

"Is that a word people actually use?" Eda knew what it meant, but she'd never heard anyone actually use it in a sentence who wasn't being a pompous twit. And whatever Jeremy was, he wasn't that.

"Postprandial?" Now she'd made him self-conscious. "I use it? Sometimes. Mostly with my landlady, honestly, to escape the decorous conversation after supper. By which I mean her continuing to gossip about the neighbours, often for a block in every direction."

"Every night? That seems exhausting!" Eda then swallowed. "A walk would be lovely. It's not raining. And we shouldn't startle any of the gardeners."

"Oh, have you been worried about that?" Jeremy stood, waiting for Eda to do the same and join him. Then he walked out into the courtyard and across the little moat, and Eda took a second to think about how to reply. That took her until they were on the bridge.

"I startled one of them - Henry, I gather - just after I got here. Master Waters came out to talk to me about it. I was in the walled garden." Jeremy looked a little baffled. "The gardener. Is that the wrong title for him?"

"Everyone just calls him Waters, but I honestly don't know. Mrs Summers keeps having to educate me about what's done. And not done. She's very kind about it, but I keep running into something that ought to be simple and isn't. Have you been out in the gardens since?"

That was a delicately put question, and Eda appreciated how he didn't either get upset at Waters or at herself. But he had a right to know if anything was interfering in the work, of course. She nodded. "Waters - there, all right - suggested I whistle or make a bit of noise when I came along, so they'd know where I was. I haven't seen either of the two young men since, and I saw Henry for just a moment."

"That's more than I have, honestly. Waters does a grand job— I mean, you can see it in the gardens. He knows what he's doing. But I've not met the young men. Mrs Summers has one of the maids leave meals for them, I gather."

"At least with charms, they can have a hot meal when they want. If you get a glimpse, well, Henry's got dark hair and Ernie is blond." Eda offered it because that had been helpful to her.

"That will be a help if I have to apologise." By now, they had turned along the path toward the gardens. "May I ask what you whistle?"

"Oh, a folk song of some kind." She considered and began whistling "English Country Garden". She got through one verse, heard the shift of branches near the far end of the walled garden, but when they got there, the space was empty.

"Do you have a garden? No, wait, you said something about a dye garden?" Jeremy offered to let her go first on the walkway, but Eda stopped to smell the roses and the mix of the other flowers. "And that's a most suitable tune."

"Mostly dye plants. Not a significant amount of anything, and of course some have to be imported, or grown elsewhere. A few flowers - including roses, I love them, and some foxglove and hollyhock. And some kitchen plants, of course. Chives and dill and some garlic. Practical plants. Of course, it's Trellech, so a lot of things come through the market, or the shops."

"But then you have the question of provenance, and—does it matter, for dye, precisely when something was harvested?" Jeremy was not pressing her to walk on, to be anywhere in a particular hurry, and Eda liked that. It turned out. She gestured at a bench and he nodded, so she settled herself on one end. After a tiny hesitation, he took the other end, leaving plenty of space between them. He was tidy about that, as well as his other manners. He didn't let a hand wander out of his control. It would make him a good weaver, possibly, if he ever wanted to try it. She suspected he'd be the sort who'd have no trouble with the tension of a piece, either. He measured out his movement the same way each time.

Eda considered. "The batch of dye makes more difference for us. Each one is a little different. We know some reasons— the temperature, the humidity, the material. But often, you just get what you get. For what we're doing here, it's not too much of a problem. It's small runs of colour, and as long as we can match to what's near it, everything looks like it fits. But if you're knitting something, or weaving large portions of cloth, you want to dye all of it together." She made an exasperated face. "All of us get very good at the relevant maths if we make it through our apprenticeship. Yardage and all that."

Something in that surprised him. "And you run your own business, you do your own inventory and such? Accounting?"

"I do. Oh, there's a firm who checks over my records, every quarter. Some of our dyes are also poisons. There's paperwork around that, and then taxes and tithes and such. But I do most of it, and they just double-check it."

"Ah." He stared off into the distance, across the garden, for a long moment, then he muttered a charm she didn't know. "Pardon. That's to check no one could overhear. I've — there are irregularities in the household accounts, and I can't figure them out."

"That must be driving you around the bend!" Eda said it before she thought better of it. But she knew how she felt when her accounts didn't line up properly, and he was used to doing that professionally.

Thankfully, he didn't take offence. He let out a sigh. "You understand. Mr Haldane asked me to give him until Michaelmas for an explanation. But the more I think about it, the more that worries me."

"May I ask more about what the puzzle is?" Eda turned a little more toward him, keeping her hands in her lap. He looked a little like a hare who might startle at anything. "Unspecified expenses?"

"No. That's the odd thing. Income. It's been fairly steady the last few years, but it's not annotated at all, anywhere I can find. Just a lump sum coming in. It's not an investment or something like that. I checked with the Grindlays. And then with the Bardi and the Scali, because I might as well be thorough. Great-Uncle Dennis banked with the Grindlays, I haven't changed that."

Eda frowned. "Did he do much trade with the empire, then? Rather than domestic?" When Jeremy blinked at her, she said, "There's a long history of cotton imports from India, and some places in Africa. It's complicated, and I don't work in cotton. It's not as useful for magical weaving."

"Oh?" He seemed distracted, and more importantly, to welcome the distraction.

"Wool and silk. Both take dye well. A lot of our standard work, the sort of thing where we make four or five yards and it's used for ritual robes or something of the kind. It's a blend of the two. We almost always use British wool, there's a long tradition of that, as well."

"Oh, that one I know about. Or at least, some of. I suspect you know different aspects than I do." Jeremy sighed again. "It's confusing. And I don't know if I can count on the income this year. Technically, it doesn't entirely matter, because it's not needed to keep the house running. But I can't decide about larger repairs or— erm."

"Or the rest of the tapestries?" Eda offered it gently.

"Just so." He ducked his chin. "I can't plan anything. It keeps wobbling about in my head."

"I know that feeling. When I was starting out, year to year— well, month to month— could vary a lot. It's one set of costs and income if someone wants, oh, ordinary wool-silk cloth, and another if they want highly skilled tapestry work. The one will keep me fed. The other will let me expand or take on fewer projects, not be weaving until all hours or making sure everyone in the workshop can." She shrugged. "My late husband found it frustrating. He was a carter, he worked a certain number of hours, he had a steady amount of income. Occasionally a bonus, for something difficult or done faster than expected, but it was predictable."

She remembered when that had changed, when his

frustration had turned to something more complicated that hadn't made sense. Eda didn't realise how long she'd been quiet until Jeremy coughed. "Pardon. I didn't intend to bring up a, a sad memory."

"Confusing." There was something about being out here, in the increasing twilight that made her feel a little confessional. "I was thinking about how he was about the income. He got, well, irritated is probably a better word than frustrated. Eventually. I still don't know why. Not that it matters much now."

Now it was Jeremy's turn to go quiet. He stared off at the far wall before he cleared his throat. "Beg pardon, but may I ask something a hair more personal? Speaking in terms of something I've seen professionally a few times, with some of the Ministry suppliers?"

"I suppose?" If it was something he'd seen at work, it couldn't be that personal, surely.

"May I inquire if your late husband's difficulties began, perhaps, at the point at which you reliably out-earned him?" Jeremy's voice held steady until the last few words, and then he looked away from her, as if that had been entirely too much.

"Oh." Eda felt the sound come out of her in a puff of breath, like getting hit in the stomach with a pillow. Not hard enough to actually hurt, but the sort of blow one felt, anyway. She couldn't move for a minute. She was stuck in the memory, trying to trace it back to when he'd changed. Jeremy said nothing else. He didn't move. Finally, she nodded. "I think so."

She stood suddenly. "I'm sorry. I need to go think about that. I'm not, it's not your fault I'm upset, please don't think that? You were very careful. But I need to go now."

He stood, automatically, but he didn't try to walk with

her. She hurried back along the path, pausing to glance over her shoulder just once as she turned into the kitchen garden. Jeremy was standing there watching her, but he didn't move or say anything.

Eda fled back to her room, closing the door and turning the lock, before flinging herself at her bed. Was it true? It felt like it was true, and she couldn't, right now, think of a reason it wasn't. But why hadn't she noticed, then? It was the sort of thing she ought to have noticed. It was even the sort of thing that her classes at Alethorpe had talked about back in the day.

When she was in Trellech, she'd have to look at her old account books. And her private journals. Eda absolutely didn't trust her memory entirely, not enough to upend what she'd been telling herself for what, nearly two decades now.

CHAPTER 16

THE MIDDLE OF THE NIGHT

J eremy woke up, suddenly fully awake. He couldn't figure out why, not at all. He didn't think it had been a dream, or at least he didn't remember dreaming. He was asleep, then he was not, and his heart was racing.

It was racing more than enough that trying to go back to sleep, simply rolling over and willing it, would not work. If he'd been in his rooms in Trellech, he would have gone to the sitting room, though he might not have dared much of a light. His landlady didn't like that sort of thing, even when it didn't shine anywhere that might bother someone else.

It was not a preference without some reason. Apparently there had been a commotion some time ago, before Jeremy had moved in there. A flickering charmlight had made someone in the next house over sure there was a fire. Commotion had been entirely the proper word, with the Guard summoned, and the fire equipment. There had been water coming in at several windows before the man with the lantern had noticed the problem.

Here, though, Jeremy could go down to the library. Or a sitting room. Or somewhere else. It might startle the staff, possibly, but he could keep well away from their spaces. And he didn't intend to go out of the warding, that would be too much bother. He found his slippers and dressing gown, along with his current book, and he padded off to find the staircase.

Jeremy was crossing the courtyard from the stair down from his rooms toward the library on the other side when he caught a shift of something by the gatehouse. The moon was visible, just a little away from the full moon earlier in the week, but what caught his eye wasn't the moon at all. It had something of the pale grey of the lunar light, but this was distinctly shaped like a person. Or enough like a person. It had visible arms, head, and robes, but no feet.

He staggered back a step, realising suddenly that this might be the ghost he'd heard about. He took several steps closer to the gatehouse, enough to see it disappear through the door to the left. Certainly, it wasn't anyone human. He'd never heard of a magical ability to move through solid wood. There were no windows, well, none sufficiently large, to tell if it moved inside the staircase or even in one of the upper rooms.

Good sense suggested retreating, or at least not advancing. Jeremy apparently lacked good sense, at least in this particular. Instead, he padded forward, first to the arch of the gatehouse above him, then through, across the bridge over the moat. It wasn't as if they locked the place down with a portcullis at night. This was not that sort of fortress.

At first, he thought he saw nothing at all. But then there was a shiver of movement, off toward the hedges to the right. It made him think again of a frightened hare or deer, something quivering in terror and unable to move. Something, someone, huddling down, hoping that danger would not come swooping in.

Jeremy was no owl, no hunter, and certainly neither brave enough nor competent enough to go charging after some danger. If it was out there, it was on the other side of the moat. That would do. Instead, he stood there, waiting, scanning the moonlit grounds in every direction he could see. There was no other movement he could spot.

He didn't even know if that was unusual, actually. He had heard birds outside his windows, often at exceedingly unfortunate times of night, at least for his falling asleep. Jeremy sometimes heard the servants going by, in the hallway, or more rarely someone talking or whistling in the garden. Some of that might have been Eda, he realised now, especially if she used the same song. But those sounds, unlike the birds, had been muffled. He knew they were happening, but they were not bothersome.

Nothing moved. Nothing made a sound. It was as quiet as the proverbial church mouse. Jeremy stood there, hearing only the thump of his own heart, and the slight inhale and exhale of his own breath. He counted to two hundred in his head for good measure. Then he turned, and went to brush his hand against the warding in the gatehouse, the way the ghost had gone.

The door was solid and closed. He felt the wards open to his touch, and then the door latch gave and he opened the door. He went up, stair by stair, the light through the windows enough that he didn't feel he risked slipping and falling.

On the first floor, the room was as he expected. He crossed over to the other side of the gatehouse, through the arch and small door between the two rooms. At first, nothing seemed out of place, but then he caught something fluttering. A thread, multiple threads, on the curtain. It didn't look like a tear, or like they'd been pulled from someone's clothing.

In the middle of the night by moonlight was certainly no time to do a proper examination. Jeremy peered around, craning his neck, but he couldn't see anything else. He could come back in the morning, a proper morning that had daylight.

He turned to go back across to the stairs he'd come up, then down, latching the door as closing the wards as he did. Three minutes later, he was in the library. Jeremy rather wanted a pot of tea, but of course, he had no idea how to make that happen without waking one of the staff. Not that he didn't know how. He did. But he didn't know where a kettle he could use was, or whether it was a stove that needed to be turned on, or one of the magical kettles.

Mrs Summers had been insistent about calling one of the staff, letting them do their duties, not getting in their way. Jeremy appreciated that as a philosophical model. Certainly, he didn't want to make them feel they were about to get turned out for lack of need. And also, all of them had skills, decidedly practical skills, that he didn't. As well as a much deeper understanding of the property.

But that didn't help right now. Perhaps he could ask Mrs Summers if there could be a small magical kettle added somewhere convenient, in case he woke again in the night. But how likely was that? This was the first time he'd had in months. Though, the accountant in him had to note that the percentage of nights he had slept here was rather different than the number he'd been its inherited steward or whatever the proper term was. Landholder, not that he found that at all comfortable.

It made him grimace, then consider. He was in the library, perhaps there might be something here that would serve instead of tea. There were books, and books could certainly distract him from his thoughts. Jeremy had had a thought about some of the garden plants, what grew here that was different than in Trellech, and probably there was something in the library that would be a start. He could ask Waters, of course, but that was delicate. Perhaps he'd ask Mrs Summers to arrange a conversation with Waters, so that no one was startled by the prospect. Including Jeremy.

Jeremy made a slow circuit of the shelves to see if anything caught his eye. There were a couple of books he made a note of. Then he came to the sideboard and realised, for the first time, that it contained a decanter and glasses. He had never drunk from it, and yet, here it was, filled. It was one more thing to ask Mrs Summers about. Had that been here the entire time?

CHAPTER 17
JUNE 19TH

On Sunday morning, Eda woke up unexpectedly early. She'd had a hard time getting to sleep after the previous night's conversation. She'd done a bit of weaving on the table loom, working her way through a repetition of leaves and vines, and the occasional thorn. It was a pattern she hadn't done in a while, but she knew it well.

Weaving hadn't helped. Not much. She kept hearing Bert's comments in her ears. How, when the workshop had been in a rented space, three blocks down, she'd been too far away. How he'd had to get his own tea if something kept her late. The brief comments he'd made about colour.

The thing of it was, he hadn't been an awful husband. And even if he had been, in some ways, no one was perfect, surely. She had plenty of her own faults. Eda was finicky about how things were placed. She'd rather weave more than do a bit more spit and polish to make everything in the kitchen shine. She wanted to make do, and save money for boring but necessary things like roof repairs. Bert had preferred a good time, out to the pub, or maybe a fishing day with his friends.

And Bert had had his sweet moments, absolutely. When she'd been a journeyman, working hard on the tapestry that had been her masterwork, he'd been thoughtful. He'd been the one to pick up food at the market and bring it home. He'd helped her fix her loom, twice, and found a carpenter for what she couldn't do herself. She didn't have the tools. For a while, he'd talked her up. He'd sounded so proud of her.

Then it had changed. And that was the awful thing. Jeremy was right. He had to be right. She could go home and check her journals and notes, but she was sure it was right around then. When she'd been bringing home more coin than Bert, and it wasn't just once, in a particularly fortunate month. It was when it was an average month, then even a poor one.

It taken her a couple of years to get to that point. But even at the beginning, when it had been luck and blessing, Bert hadn't really seen it like that. Oh, he'd been glad enough they didn't have to scrimp about groceries, that she didn't keep close tabs on his money for the pub. That they'd both been able to buy new shoes, not have old pairs with cracked leather resoled one more time.

All right, if that was the truth, and she had admitted it was, once she'd stared at the ceiling for ages, she still didn't know what to do with it. The fact Jeremy had said it made her uncomfortable. That was unfair to him. He'd gone out of his way to be gentle and thoughtful in bringing it up. He'd asked first, for goodness sake. And he'd known it might upset her. Jeremy hadn't even tried to stop her when she needed to be alone.

Everything he'd done was the opposite of Bert, really.

And that felt disloyal. Bert had died fighting in an awful war, overseas. He'd done his duty when it counted. And if he'd griped about things, he'd also been a steady sort as a husband. Bert had worked hard, been dependable and predictable. He hadn't turned harsh when he was drunk. He'd never hurt her, not with anything more than a bit of a word. And Bert had kept up with his chores, mending and fixing things in the house, making some clever changes that eased this task or that. Plenty of women had it far worse.

He'd never have thought about her feelings like that. Bert would certainly never have given her that information, and not just because it put him in a bad light. He wouldn't have thought she needed it or wanted it or should have it. It wasn't practical to know, and he was a practical man, about the concrete objects he was taking here and there, as efficiently and safely as possible. He'd been a good carter.

None of that helped her sleep. She had got some, Eda knew that, but not much. Now it was morning, and she had more or less finished the book she'd borrowed from the library while she wasn't sleeping. She didn't have plans to work on the tapestries today, her hands wouldn't be steady enough, but she could find another book, read, take a walk. Something like that.

Eda got dressed, then padded down the stairs, through the courtyard, and across to the library. She'd closed the door behind her before she realised she wasn't alone. Jeremy was there, at one table, folded over with his head in his arms. He was asleep; he seemed to be staying asleep, and she didn't want to wake him.

Both because someone ought to get some sleep. And because if he woke up, she was going to have to talk to him, and she did not know what to say. Instead, Eda eased the door open again and backed out of it. Once the door was closed again, she found herself in the hallway holding a book she no longer needed, and unsure what to do next.

Mrs Summers would probably want to know Jeremy was in the library. Someone ought to know. Probably? Eda wasn't sure how that worked here. Obviously, servants and staff were supposed to cater to the whims of the people they worked for. But Jeremy had seemed a person unbothered by whims so far. He was someone who had an orderly life that did not involve falling asleep at a table in the library.

The problem was that Eda had only the faintest idea where the staff spent their time when they weren't visible. There was a kitchen, obviously. Houses like this had servants' halls, a room for the housekeeper or a butler's pantry, various other rooms depending on the needs. A cold room, for example, maybe a dairy. Probably not a dairy right here. Eda would have noticed cows by now.

She had at least been through most of the house now, and it wasn't as if the servants' hall would be upstairs. That didn't make sense. Eda angled herself toward the most likely corner, keeping an eye out to see if she saw anyone about. The halls were empty, but she came up to a green baize door, the classic sign of the below stairs space, whatever number of stairs were actually involved.

Eda pushed it open cautiously, finding a hallway with doors opening off of it. She could hear voices, a little further down, then Alice came out of a doorway. She saw Eda, squeaked, and then stammered. "Mistress?"

"I beg your pardon, I didn't mean to scare you. Is Mrs Summers around, possibly?"

"Yes'm. Mrs Summers? It's Mistress Fellowes." Eda could only assume that Mrs Summers had made some gesture, because Alice took a step or two back, gesturing at the door.

The room inside was quite pleasant, a sitting room rather than a sleeping room. It had a small table, suitable for two, four at a pinch. It held a desk and chair, a pair of easy chairs, and a couple of shelves and potted plants along the windowsill. As she came in, Mrs Summer stood up from where she'd been sitting. "Mistress Fellowes?"

"I'm sorry, I didn't mean to, erm. Upset the usual order? I went to the library to bring a book back, and Jeremy was asleep at one of the tables. I thought you might want to know, so no one was startled. Scared?"

There was a flicker in the other woman's eyes, to something further down the hall, through the wall, but she nodded. "That is considerate of you. I'd be glad to bring the book back, in due course, and we'll make sure Master Royston's needs are tended to."

That didn't actually answer any of Eda's concerns, including about the book. She took a breath. "Oh. May I ask — if there's something like this in the future, how best could I let you know?"

"Any of the bell pulls, Mistress, in any of the rooms. Or there's one in each hallway, as well. There's no need for you to come down here. Now, would you like your breakfast in the dining room, or up in your rooms? It's near as easy for us to do the one as the other. And will you be wanting luncheon at half-past twelve?"

Eda sighed. She could tell she would not get very far with this. "My rooms, please. And— does it look like rain? Do we expect rain? Would it be a bother to put a picnic lunch together and I could have a long walk?"

There was another flicker of Mrs Summers glancing further toward the corner of the building. "I'll put together a basket, it has a shoulder strap, easier to carry, and a map of the grounds with some of the more likely walks. A few are waterlogged right now, Waters was saying. Is there anything else?"

Eda swallowed hard. "If, perhaps. I mean. I was hoping to change out my book. If you could let me know if Jeremy's no longer in the library, or perhaps bring me back a novel of some sort, something for pleasure reading?"

"I'll see about that, Mistress. We'll have your breakfast in, oh, fifteen minutes."

It was as clear a dismissal as any Eda had heard, precise and unyielding. Certainly, she could take the hint. "Thank you." She tried to think what else to say, but all of it sounded awful in her head, and would be worse out loud. Instead, she turned and retreated with as much dignity as she could muster. It wasn't much, but at least she didn't get lost on her way back to her rooms.

Somewhat to her surprise, it was Mrs Summers who brought the tray, not one of the maids. She closed the door, set the tray down, then cleared her throat. "If I might have a word, Mistress?"

Eda turned, stiffening. "Yes? If there's something else."

"I know you're not terribly familiar with how things are done in the great houses, or in this house. But you have some knowledge, yes?"

"Some. I've visited a number of homes, stayed overnight in a few. This is the first I've been at for a length of time since before the War." Eda remembered those days. She'd certainly read enough pieces in the paper about how those times were gone.

Mrs Summers nodded once, precisely. "Master Royston is not as familiar with how things are done on this sort of estate. He might, perhaps, understand some pieces of it better coming from you than from one of us. I have talked to him about the customs. Mr Haldane has done so."

"Without much success?" Eda frowned. "I don't know why you think I'd do any better." She took a deep breath. "On the other hand, I know how problems can happen if one person in a workshop doesn't understand the rhythm of it. Would you tell me what you wish he understood better? I can't promise anything." Certainly not today, when all her own complicated feelings about Jeremy were churning away. "But perhaps I might get an opportunity."

"He respects your knowledge and skill, Mistress. That has been clear from when he first considered the repairs." Mrs Summers cleared her throat. "We enjoy our work, Mistress. We each know our part, and we find pleasure in tending the house and the people in the house. Master Royston is very little bother. He is much easier to tend than his cousins were. Much more like his great-uncle. His requests are reasonable, made with appropriate warning. We, the staff, we understand that our jobs exist because there is a house and people of the house to serve. And we do not wish to risk that."

There was a great deal unsaid there, but Eda felt she saw the bulk of it. "So you want him to— let's see. It's not that change would be unwelcome if it made sense for the estate. But you would want changes made with the good of the estate in mind. Not just now, but in the future. And Jeremy does not understand, perhaps, the scope of his requests, or what sustaining the number of staff here means for the estate?"

"Just so, Mistress. We would not ask you to persuade him to do anything in particular. Just to understand the system of the house." Mrs Summers coughed. "I have perhaps overstepped in saying this much. But it will be awkward when he wakes up and thinks we should not have tolerated him being out of place among the shelves."

It was a clever little play on words. Eda nodded. "I can't make any promises. But he appreciates a system rolling smoothly along. I'll see what I can suggest along those lines. Thank you for breakfast. I'm afraid I didn't sleep well last night. Is there perhaps a potion in the house's stocks I might take tonight, something mild?" Something inexpensive and easily replaced. She was fairly sure Mrs Summers would translate that appropriately.

"Of course, Mistress. Please let us know if any change here would be a help. I'll check our apothecary cabinet and leave something for you while you're out." She went on to check that Eda had no particular ingredients or such she needed to avoid. It gave her the excuse to leave before Eda had to figure out how to dismiss her. Mrs Summers departed, promising to have the picnic basket for her when someone came to collect the tray, and with any luck, a book as well.

The food was perfect, the toast crisp and warm, the egg jammy in the middle, the butter, whatever cows it came from, perfectly smooth to spread. The jam smelled wonderful, early strawberries, and tasted better, like sunlight and sweetness condensed. Whatever else the staff were, they were good at what they did. Superb. At least the parts she had any ability to measure.

A walk, perhaps, wouldn't solve anything. But it would get her out of the house. And right now, that certainly seemed less confusing than being in it.

CHAPTER 18
JUNE 21ST

J eremy had not seen Eda, not more than fleetingly, since Saturday evening. It was Tuesday now, and he'd only paused briefly to say good morning or good afternoon while she was working. She'd taken her meals in her room on Sunday, worked through at least lunch on Monday, and he wasn't sure what she'd done for supper. Eaten it, obviously. He was fairly certain Mrs Summers would mention it if there was something to worry about.

He hadn't wanted to press her. Jeremy was certain he'd overstepped somehow. He'd certainly done this type of thing before. He'd offer information, information that people might want to have, and then they'd go away. And be stiff and awkward, as stiff and awkward as Jeremy usually felt, after. They'd let the awkward show, and most people didn't do that.

Eda had not been dismissive when he'd stopped by to be civil. She hadn't told him to go away. But of course, he was employing her. She was doing specific and skilled work for him. But he had fractured the offer to come see what she'd done. He realised that somehow, without noticing it, he'd looked forward to seeing what happened as she did more of the repairs. Now, of course, he'd see the finished thing, but not how it got there.

Tuesday evening, he had just sat down at the dining room table, a book to one side, and Mrs Summers was about to bring in the meal. He looked up at the sound of the door, then blinked, pushing back in his chair to stand politely. "Eda. Good evening. Happy Solstice eve."

Eda looked flushed, as if she were shy or nervous, possibly. It was that sort of blush, the right amount of red on her cheeks for that. "Happy Solstice eve to you. Mrs Summers mentioned Cook had something special in mind? May I join you?"

"Please." Jeremy stayed standing until Eda had taken the other chair. Going around to help push it in would be too much. That sort of thing required physical proximity. And if she were feeling nervous, that was the last thing he wanted. Once she was settled, he sat, clearing his throat. "I owe you an apology for Saturday. I didn't wish to upset you."

Now her eyes widened. "Oh, no. You were very careful. I've been thinking, since, how you were thoughtful. You asked me if I wanted to know. I said yes. If I didn't like what I heard, that's not your fault." She looked away, to the corner of the room. "You put my marriage in a different light. Different shades of colour. I've had to do a lot of trying to figure out what that means, that the foundation was different than I thought."

Jeremy nodded, uncertain. Then he ventured, "As if you'd been weaving with a different thread than you thought?"

There was a long silence, and Jeremy waited. Then Eda

nodded. "Like that. Linen instead of wool maybe. I don't know." She looked up again. "It's not your fault for telling me. I had to think, and then that took longer, and I didn't know what to say. But Mrs Summers said, the meal tonight. I didn't think it was fair for you to be on your own, and...." Her voice trailed off as there was a gentle knock on the door.

Jeremy tried to decide whether Eda needed another moment. But she looked composed enough to manage the first course being brought out. He called out, "Come in, please."

The first course was a summer salad with early vegetables, fresh herbs, with a little jar of salad cream to go with it. "Chicken for the entrée, sir, and Cook has made a splendid trifle for pudding." She put out the main course plates next, leaving them both, an informal service as Jeremy understood it.

"Ah, thank you. And my thanks to Cook, as well. I hope you're all getting to enjoy something lovely?" Jeremy offered it cautiously. He wasn't sure if this was overstepping, but Mrs Summers beamed. "Thank you, sir. And the staff are very grateful to have the day on Thursday, for the Faire."

With that, she went out, and Eda glanced after her. "I see why she was hoping I'd join you. Trifle is a lot of fuss for one person. Even two."

"I know I enjoy eating it, though it's been rare, not the sort of thing at a table in lodgings." Jeremy said. "Do you know about the making, then?"

Eda hesitated, but then she nodded. "You have a layer of sponge cake, spread with jam, then doused with sherry. Well, usually sherry?" She sounded a little less certain.

"Then fresh fruit, a layer of custard, a layer of whipped cream. If you're being very fancy, you can do multiple layers of each, but that takes a special sort of bowl, and we were never that fancy. My grandmum liked it a lot. She'd make it for special occasions. Birthdays, holidays." Eda glanced up, as if not sure how he'd take this. "Maybe strawberries, today? It's the right season."

Then she took a bite of her salad, leaving Jeremy to pick up the conversation. He didn't want to spoil the meal by asking about something personal again. He was trying to find a topic when a rather unsuitable one popped out of his mouth. "I think I saw a ghost." He hurried to add, "Not just now. The middle of the night, Saturday to Sunday."

"You what?" Eda looked up wide-eyed. "Where?"

"Going up to the gatehouse. I saw her— I think her?— go right through the door, and it was latched and warded when I checked. Nothing upstairs." Jeremy coughed. "I, well. I fell asleep in the library, after. I wasn't scared. I don't think it's a terrifying sort of ghost? But I had trouble settling down."

"I— oh, I went to return a book, Sunday morning, and you were asleep at one of the tables. I didn't want to disturb you." Eda offered it tentatively.

"And I'm sure you didn't want me to make things more awkward for you. I am..." He let out a slightly bemused sigh. "I am particularly awkward when I'm not really awake. Either end of the day. I learned to get up a good ninety minutes before I need to be in the office, and have a good strong cup of tea to start the morning."

Eda blinked, and then there was an honest smile, the kind that crinkled both her eyes and lips. "I can understand that." She ate a few more bites of her salad, making a pleased sound. The salad was rather excellent, the blend of ingredients and the salad cream seemed perfect. "Do you think the ghost means anything in particular?"

"I know there's a great deal of lore about them, but I don't know what's true. Or what you do with that, even if you can figure out what it might mean."

"Not at all my sort of speciality, I'm afraid." Eda said. "I — I probably know someone I can ask? A couple of some-ones. But it's solstice, and they have obligations. I mentioned Ferry. There's Lord Carillon. There's a ghost at Ytene, Ferry's seen a glimpse once or twice, but she seems a different category? She mostly is seen in the music room when she approves of the music."

"But Lord Carillon will be very busy, yes. And perhaps the Faire, as well?" Jeremy coughed. "I was planning to go out. The staff have the day on Thursday. You said you were going to go back to Trellech for the day, yes? If you'd not mind taking the cart with them, that would sort things out nicely."

"You could go to Trellech too. Though I suppose there's a limit on what the cart can hold?" Eda frowned. "Mrs Summers, Mr Haldane, the maids, surely?"

"Not Waters and Henry and Ernie, no." Jeremy said. "And there's a larger cart, a pair of draught horses, coming." He hesitated. "I suppose there'd at least be someone at the library, even if many people take holidays. And I could check in quickly at the office, there are some harvest we oversee that will happen tomorrow morning at dawn."

"The library seems a reasonable sort of thing. And you might— I don't think it's the sort of thing people have stalls and shout about at the Faire. Though I admit I haven't paid the most attention to that? But there are lectures, and maybe that would suggest someone to talk to, even if you can't make the actual lecture?"

It was an approach to tackling the problem that Jeremy hadn't considered. "That is clever." He could say that, and with truth and earnestness that he hoped she heard properly. "I wouldn't have thought of that. And I didn't think of it. I was just spinning around wondering how you even found someone."

"Ah, that's— you don't have a guild, for the Ministry, do you? It's just sort of people in different departments, and you know which departments handle which aspect?" Eda had finished her main course and set down her fork.

"Is a guild so different, then?" Jeremy took another bite or two of his chicken; Cook really was a wonder. It was tender and moist.

"It means we know that everyone at a given rank has certain skills, and we also know who has what specialities. It makes me wonder if there's a guild of people who know about ghosts. I suppose some of the architectural magic people must know, but I don't know how you find out who and where they are, who might consult."

"And I don't have a great deal to spare for consulting fees. Not with..." He cut himself off. "Well." Not without understanding where that mysterious income came from. "But the history of the house might be informative. That seems the sort of thing a librarian could help with. Maybe not immediately, but I could get started. Though probably there's a book in this library that has as much as there is."

"You'd hope." Eda shrugged. "Sometimes there isn't, though. Or the copy here had an accident with a fireplace or a mouse or a minor flood or something? If some accident befell it in the last few years, would your cousins have noticed?"

"No." Jeremy was certain of that. "Not unless the book was worth a fair bit as an object, I expect. Those, they inventoried well enough." He'd thought about that on Sunday, actually. It had struck him that the mysterious income might come from the sale of items from the house. But he'd looked at the lists of furniture and art and books and such. While he hadn't gone through the attics in detail — that was a project that would take at least a year of determined visits— he had seen most of the more valuable items and recently. And the lists had been compared to Great-Uncle Dennis's inventories, several versions, and all with the charms that confirmed the documents hadn't been tampered with. "Thank you. I think that gives me somewhere to start, rather than flail around."

"I'm glad. And I'll ask Ferry once we're through the Faire." She added, after a moment, conversationally. "Lord Carillon breeds pavo mounts, good-sized ponies. I don't know anything about the game, really, I don't even watch the bohort much. Too hard on the hands for a crafter who relies on unbroken fingers, the way some people play. But Ferry's husband is the head of the stables, so of course she knows a lot about it now."

Jeremy nodded, hesitated, and then before he could think better of it, he asked, "A happy marriage, then, your apprentice?"

Eda looked up, like a deer caught out in the open. Then she swallowed. "She's happy. And lucky. And she knows how much of both. I'm glad someone has that." Before she could say anything more, Mrs Summers knocked on the door. The trifle was a triumph indeed. Three layers rose up in a straight-sided glass dish, unsmeared and perfect, dotted with deep red strawberries.

Neither of them risked spoiling the evening with

further potentially difficult conversation. When they finished, Jeremy asked if Eda might show him what she'd been working on, if it was convenient, and she did that comfortably enough. As Jeremy took his leave, he felt that had gone better than he deserved.

CHAPTER 19
JUNE 23RD AT EDA'S WORKSHOP

I t felt grand to be back in her own home. The ground felt different, the sunlight was different. Well, there was some, today. And everything smelled different. Smaller. Manageable.

She had been chewing on that feeling all day. The cart had got the lot of them, Jeremy included, to Swaffham by nine in the morning, but it had meant leaving at half seven. Jeremy had come through to Trellech with her, but he'd immediately said his goodbyes, rather than offering to walk her to her home. She wasn't entirely sure what to make of it. Eda hadn't wanted him to. She was still figuring out what she felt and thought about their recent conversations.

But he hadn't even offered. Of course, he had several places of his own to be: his office, his own rooms, the library, in some sort of order. He hadn't talked much about it this morning. Neither of them had been quite awake yet. Then there was the awkwardness of talking with the staff right there, the maids bubbling over with delight about the Faire. She'd not known how to start a conversation or continue it.

Now, she'd spent the day catching up with the workshop. It had been a mix of checking over the work of the apprentices and doing some of the administrative tasks. Kay had learned a few things, Aliane had sorted out a problem she'd been having keeping patterns straight. And Eda had gone over the bookkeeping and paid the bills. While she did that, Henny had been tidying up, and when Eda emerged, Henny handed her a mug of tea and gestured with her chin at the sitting room.

"Not the kitchen?" Eda was bemused.

"In the kitchen, you'll be twitching to do the dishes. I'll do them when we're done talking. You've been working your fingers off. Are you actually taking tomorrow as a holiday?"

"Well." Eda curled her fingers around the mug. "I plan to go to the Faire, eat a number of sweets and baked goods, chat up the people with interesting wool, and, I don't know. Depends on what looks interesting. I need to be at the Swaffham portal by seven, but it's not like I was going to stay for the dancing. I never do."

"You sometimes like the music, though. Sure you don't want company? I was planning on going Saturday with my sister and her boys." Eda shook her head at that. She would rather go on her own. Henny leaned forward. "Right. Tell me what it's like. You've been there ten days. It's long enough to have an informed opinion."

The problem was that Eda did not know where to start. She sipped from her tea, trying to figure out what to say, and that still didn't help at all. When she looked up, Henny was waiting, watching her as deliberately as she watched patterns forming in the weaving. "It's fine?" That sounded weak, and Eda knew it. "The food is excellent. The house is..." Her voice trailed off.

"That's no help at all. Master Royston? Is he treating you properly?" Henny looked intent now, like she was a hound who would go baying after someone who didn't.

"Jeremy?" Then Eda caught herself. She closed her eyes, resigning herself to a conversation she'd known she was going to have to have. Well, probably. "Look. Let me get my knitting. You get yours or whatever?"

"I'm working on that jumper for my niece, that's no good. No mind, I'll start some socks." They both set their mugs aside, the same gesture at the same moment, in sync like they were weaving, stood, and went their separate directions for their supplies. Three minutes later, Eda had the knitting out of her bag, a simple shawl. It was getting too big to be easily carried around, but she'd manage. And at least right now, it wasn't even complicated.

Henny came back a minute after that, rapidly casting on stitches for a sock, counting them off. Eda didn't interrupt her, just waiting until Henny had done a row or four, and Eda was halfway done with her tea. "Jeremy's been very thoughtful. The tapestry's interesting. It was well-tended in the past, and I think with a number of protective charms, there isn't nearly as much damage as there ought to be."

"That's about the tapestry." Henny said. "Master Royston? The house? There are other people?" Her needles kept up a pleasant even clicking, stitch by stitch, an echo of the rhythm of a loom in some ways, a soothing sound to both of them. The shawl Eda was working on wasn't a hard pattern. Right now she was still on the body of it, but the border wasn't much harder when it came to lace. Mum had taught her this one when she was tiny. Now it was easy, anyway. Certainly, it was a lot simpler than tapestry work.

It was also a deeply satisfying vibrant red. She'd hovered between choices for this. It was meant to be a shawl for her bedroom, to replace one that was getting a bit worn. No one else would see it. Eda had bought it, rather than dyeing it herself. It was good to keep up cheerful relationships with the dyer's guild. And Greer, who'd done it, had a deft hand with colour. She was almost Eda's first choice for whatever she bought. Now, she just delighted in the red as it moved across her fingers.

Eda sighed and laid out the basics, mostly so that Henny would stop fussing about the unknown so much. She talked about what she'd seen of the staff, the size of the house, how much of it was under dust sheets. At the end, she said, "I don't know what his plans are. It's a vast place. It's ridiculous for a couple of people."

"And it's in the middle of nowhere." Henny pointed out. "Not even like he could, oh, have boarders. He could set up a tutoring school or something like that. Somewhere where people didn't need to come and go too often."

"Maybe. But he went to Dunwich, and they don't do tutoring schools the same way. Some fostering, I think." Eda tried to remember. It wasn't something that came up in her circles often. "And he's been pleasant with me, but I don't think he knows how to deal with, I don't know. People?" That came out wrong. "Different kinds of people. I think he might be fine with people at the Ministry. He knows what's done there."

"But now he's not there. Or at least not for another month or so." Henny tilted her head. "What do you think about the house?"

"I like it. More than I thought I would. The gardens are lovely, though it seems a shame almost no one gets to enjoy them. The gardeners do, I think, though I've only met Waters. And the staff seem happy. It's silly to have so many, for just one or two people living in the house who aren't staff?" She shrugged. "And I'm unusual that way. Neither fish nor fowl, isn't that the phrase?"

"Hired for a task, but not eating or whatever with the staff. I suppose it's good they're happy."

"Better than the alternative. And no, they were all cheerfully chattering along this morning in the cart. Not afraid of speaking up or anything like that." Eda hadn't really put it together until now. "Jeremy is, he's considerate. I like that about him. He doesn't elbow in to bother me while I'm working. But he's interested in it, asks me to show him the new bits. He doesn't forget something once I've told him. It's rather novel."

"He hasn't been inappropriate?" Henny had never married; she'd seen far too much from her extended family, she said, to want that unless it was absolutely the right person.

Eda opened her mouth, hesitated, and then knew Henny had seen it. Henny had that look in her eyes, insistent. Eda swallowed. "He made a comment, a very insightful one, that I'm still thinking about."

"Which was?" Henny's knitting needles hesitated in their quiet clicking.

"It was about Bert." The thing was, Henny had known Bert. None of the other current folks around had, really, though Innis had met him several times. Eda stopped trying to do her own knitting, letting it rest in her lap. "He saw something I hadn't realised. I hadn't even said much."

"You don't, about Bert." Henny looked up from her hands. "Just saying."

Eda couldn't argue with that. She twitched one shoulder. "We'd been talking about erratic income. He'd been trying to figure out the estate finances. There's enough to pay me, before you ask. He's been clear about that, but sorting it out makes a difference in how much more I do. Or someone does."

"I was going to ask," Henny agreed. "You trained me to be as attentive to the business as the thread. What got you on to Bert?"

Eda swallowed. "I said that Bert hadn't liked the erratic income. Not being able to plan on it. He liked his work, which was steady, so long as he did his hours. Predictable. And then Jeremy asked if he could ask something more personal, about something he'd seen professionally, some of the Ministry suppliers."

"Well." Henny tutted slightly. "He asked. That's considerate. And you said yes."

"I did. And he asked— didn't tell me that was what happened— asked if the difficulties, when Bert got difficult, started when I began making more than he did, reliably."

"Was that— no, that was right around when I apprenticed. A year or two in?"

"1905, 1906." Eda agreed. "I'd got well-established by then. I'd earned my mastery the year before, 1904. And the workshop, I had you. There was Cedric, bless him, and Linley." Cedric had had a Bad War, and while he'd come home, his hands weren't steady enough for most weaving now. Just simple things, though Eda made sure he got enough business to keep himself together. His wife did a lot of spinning, fine quality stuff that got top prices, such as it was. And Linley had married, and she still did weaving, but mostly for local use, nothing complex.

"Do you— do you think Master Royston was right, then?" Henny sounded uncertain, and that wasn't like her.

Eda looked at her more steadily. "I think he was. That's the complicated part. I excused myself that night, and he let me go. He didn't try to, I don't know, make it less? And we've talked since. It's not awkward anymore."

"Anymore?" Henny began knitting again.

After listening to the sound of the needles, Eda picked up her own, letting the stitches slide from needle to needle in a soothing repetition. Knitting made the world orderly, as did weaving. It put all right with the world. "He left me alone for a day or two. But we had supper together on solstice eve. Cook had gone to some extra bother. Trifle, even."

"My. That is a fuss." Henny let out a huff of breath. "I don't like you being on your own out there. I suppose he's being respectful." Then, before Eda could ask her, she said, "You know I've no patience for romance. And I don't comment on other people's marriages. But I guess it'd be honest if I said that when I thought about it, I didn't want one like yours with Bert. You're so much happier now, you're not shoving yourself into a corner to avoid bothering him. He didn't do the same to you. If it were both of you, avoiding jogging each other's elbows, that would have been fair. The dance of the weaving, you're the one that taught me that. Instead, it was you working around him, and him not getting out of the way. It wasn't right. And you weren't happy."

Eda's needles stopped now, but there was truth in that. "I was happy some ways, I suppose. But you're right. I'm happier now. Have been. I wish we could have done better while he was here. I think that's the part that hurts."

Henny let out a sigh. "Want me to stay for supper? Or I can run out and grab something. There's only the ordinary things in case someone needs a meal. Eggs, bread, jam, cheese."

"Would you? As good as the cook is, I've been really wanting one of Rhian's meat pies."

"Just the thing. Let me finish this round and I'll go get a pair. Sorted for breakfast, or should I grab a pastry or two?"

"I'll get it at the fair. And I'll put the kettle on. And do the dishes." Eda grinned at her friend. "You can do supper. But I sort of miss doing my own."

"I won't argue." They both finished their respective rows and rounds of knitting at about the same point. Henny went off with a basket for the errand while Eda ran the water, charmed it hot, and then scrubbed at the dishes and set them to dry. That was satisfying, a chore that was begun and done in just a couple of minutes.

CHAPTER 20
JUNE 24TH AT THE MIDSUMMER FAIRE

J eremy had made it out to the Faire in good time. He'd got up early, more than early enough to avoid the crowds. It was one of the more pleasant parts about being a naturally early riser. He enjoyed the quiet at the start of the day, before anyone expected anything in particular from him.

Matters at the office were in good form, though there had only been a junior or two in the Thursday. Jeremy had checked over the records and the details of the harvest. Wedgeworth had been working through a tidily ordered list. The harvesters had reported in that the solstice morn harvests had gone without a hitch.

It would be a fortnight at least before any of the final weights and measures became relevant. Every year, the plants dried down differently, or rather the amounts came out differently. Jeremy had confirmed that there would be more than enough for the Ministry needs, and plenty for the open market. Having both was excellent.

He'd spent the rest of Thursday afternoon checking in about correspondence and routine notes that hadn't followed him to the estate. Mistress Norris was in the office, upstairs, and she'd come by briefly to see how he was doing. Some mysterious chain of information, a spider in a web of connections. But she'd been pleasant and not confusing. Or not too confusing. Anyway, she had to work on Friday. So he didn't have to navigate whether she'd be at the Faire or get free to be at the Faire, or anything like that.

His landlady had been pleased enough to see him. Though she'd wanted to bend his ear for half an hour after supper after one of the newer lodgers who wanted to come and go later than she approved of. Jeremy had listened patiently enough, but then said that the man was past his apprentice years, and his work took him among musicians on a regular basis. Not theatre— Mistress Brown wasn't entirely sure she approved of theatrical types, and she certainly didn't care for the number of trunks and parcels involved in their lives.

Kerran White was a musician, instead, a chamber musician. He played the viol, or perhaps the viola. Jeremy wasn't entirely clear. He gave music lessons; he accompanied singers on the piano or sometimes on the harpsichord. And a couple of evenings a week, he would be at one gathering or another, either performing himself or being a pleasant artistic addition to the conversation. He did not make any of his music in the lodgings. He didn't even apparently have a radio or a gramophone in his rooms. The only bother, as far as Jeremy could tell, was that he opened the door, quietly, and went up and down the stairs - quietly - at times Mistress Brown did not care for.

"You might add some sound charms on the stairs? Or something that would let you know when all of us are in, if it's the locking up you worry about. Or perhaps he'd be glad to do the last stage for you, to avoid being a bother? He seems to have a fairly regular schedule, from what you've said." She'd harrumphed. All Jeremy could think was that she'd wanted to complain. "You've had far less pleasant lodgers, I know that. Weren't you telling me about the man before me?" That had got him a good half hour of the man's every failing before Jeremy made his excuses and went up to his bedroom.

Which had been both reassuringly familiar, and unsatisfying. There was no denying that the bed at Oakburgh was vastly more comfortable. Larger, that was part of it, but Mrs Summers had mentioned they'd replaced the mattress recently, rather than this one, which was in its last year or two. Maybe three, the way Mistress Brown tended her finances. That was admirable in many ways. Jeremy appreciated sensible use of funds. But perhaps his back did not appreciate it as much as his intellect did. He'd spent a good hour Thursday night alternating between thinking about reading and staring at the ceiling before he actually fell asleep.

Friday morning had been taken up with getting to the Faire, leaving his overnight bag in storage for the day. That part was easy. There were people who did good business doing that, both for people coming for the day and for people's purchases that they didn't want to carry around. They also ran a series of hostels for people who wanted to stay over. They weren't anything fancy; people with money paid for the portal and the extra fee for a reserved and convenient time. But they were pleasant, well-kept, and close to the Faire. It was also where the people who had to be handy for livestock and such stayed.

Once he'd left his bag, he made a round of the Faire. This time was different from his previous visits. In earlier years, he'd have stopped by the Dunwich or the Ministry tent, to see if there were people he knew. There usually were, of course. Then he'd find something for lunch and spend his day at whatever caught his attention.

Today, though, he was interested in a number of the agricultural and domestic presentations. There were all sorts of people with new, or at least newish, devices that promised to save labour, costs, magic, or all three. Jeremy noticed that most of those danced around the topic of employment for people who'd done those jobs in the past decades. He couldn't figure out in most cases whether that was avoiding the deaths in the War, or the fact many people still were looking for good steady work.

At any rate, Jeremy wasn't interested in putting people out of work at Oakburgh, but he was interested in some of the agricultural items. He wasn't sure what Waters would think of any of them. But Jeremy could at least attempt a slightly informed conversation about them, and collect pamphlets and cards for later discussion if they turned out to be potentially useful. The range was rather astonishing. There was someone who had a vast automated irrigation system that looked like it might break down in fascinatingly complicated ways if anyone looked at it wrong. And getting it to Oakburgh to install it in the first place would probably be on the order of one of the labours of Hercules, given the size of the storage tank on display.

Another display had a tractor run on a combination of steam and magic, apparently. Jeremy listened, but he didn't have the expertise to understand what the risks and benefits were. And he might be old-fashioned— well, he certainly was— but he liked the softness of a horse, the way they had personalities. It seemed like the tractor might be tricky to repair, given where they were, too. It was easier to find a blacksmith in the village or a veterinarian than a mechanic.

One speaker talked about people in an area going in on a piece of equipment together. That might make more sense, only Jeremy wasn't exactly on close terms with any of the other magical estates remotely nearby. He'd have to make an attempt at that, at least. If nothing else, they might have advice or specialists with a little spare time, or something like that. He'd learned that plenty of people hated accounting or dealing with ledger books, and he could reasonably offer that as a fair trade.

Once he'd finished with those, he continued circulating, pausing to watch one of the equine competitions. This wasn't the pavo, the main matches for that would begin tomorrow. But it was people on horses with both jumps in the arena, and then doing other things, displaying their speed or dexterity. Or whatever it was called when it was a horse. He was so absorbed in it he didn't notice someone calling his name until the second or third time. Whoever it was sounded decidedly irritated.

"Jeremy Royston, are you ignoring me deliberately?" Now the voice had got shrill. It was attached to— oh. Aunt Mabella. Not a person he was excited to see.

Jeremy turned, making a slight instinctive bow. Aunt Mabella was a distant sort of aunt. Technically, an aunt. Jeremy's father had had an aunt by marriage, who had three sisters. Aunt Mabella had been the second wife to someone, Jeremy forgot the name now, who'd died relatively young. Or rather, when she was relatively young. And she'd been migrating from household to household ever since. "Aunt Mabella, I beg pardon, I was enthralled by the Faire. Good— good afternoon." It was edging into evening, but only in the sense it was coming up on six o'clock. The daylight and the Faire would be going on for hours yet.

"You were ignoring me. Well, I suppose I shouldn't have expected any better, if you had proper manners you'd have conceded to young Algernon. He has proper plans for the estate, not trying to preserve any of that old rubbish. Algernon's certain that turning the whole thing over to industry would be the way, and well, some housing, nice tidy little houses for workers. He says there's a lot of money to be had in airfields and aerodromes these days, and you could do well off the timber." Her voice got a bit more shrill as the sentences went on. Jeremy took a couple of steps away from the fence, no reason to startle the horses or riders, but that brought him closer to Aunt Mabella.

"I beg pardon?" He was not, it was true, fond of cousin Algernon. Cousin Algernon was careless with money and even more careless with record keeping. He kept hoping other people would bail him out of both. As an added insult he'd tormented Jeremy on and off when they were both children.

Jeremy might reasonably expect the last point would no longer be an issue decades later, but he was fairly sure the first three were still relevant. They had been as late as last year. No, October 1925, Jeremy had not had a holiday card for two years running now and didn't miss that at all. At any rate, the ideas Aunt Mabella was listing off were horrid. They careened between the destruction of the property and the fact that it would be hard work to make a go of an aerodrome in the middle of the county.

"You know perfectly well that estate should have come down to Algernon. He needs it, he has a family to support, children to set up in the world. You've no need of anything, and certainly you oughtn't to have the pleasure of it." Now her voice was pitched to carry the plummy too-much gossip voice that made Jeremy want to flinch.

Jeremy blinked several times. Algernon was absolutely not in that line of succession in any way, shape, form, or legal standing. "Did Cousin Algernon think he was? It's not even his side of the family." It was not a solid response, and he knew, as he said it, that he was giving her an excuse to be more awful in about six directions. He couldn't predict what. This was exactly the kind of social situation he always fumbled. But he knew it was about to get worse for him.

"Well, I never, you don't have a bit of familial loyalty in you. You ought to have just come right to us, rather than whatever you're doing. Nothing good, I'm sure of it, from a boy you never amounted to much."

Jeremy retreated half a step. He wanted to turn and flee, but she'd just follow him, and his thoughts were whirling. He certainly didn't want to bring her near any people he respected. Before he could get too much more tangled, he heard a bright sound, a friendly one, cutting across Aunt Mabella's commentary. "Jeremy! Good evening, I hadn't expected to run into you."

There were few people who called him Jeremy. And not in that tone, which was confident and sure of herself. Jeremy twisted to see Eda coming across. She was wearing an entirely lovely dress, one that flattered her, in a summer-vibrant green and gold, her hair pinned up. It wasn't like her working clothes. He thought she'd got a fair bit of today's sun. It was in her cheeks and her nose was a little red, but in the sort of way that made her look like she had loved what she'd been doing. Most of all, she looked like an angel, not that he really believed in them, sent to at least change the conversation. She stopped a few feet away. "I beg pardon? I don't believe we've met?"

"Mabella Pound-Hepplethraite. From Surrey. Do you know —" Now Aunt Mabella stumbled. "Jeremy is a relative."

"By marriage, on my father's side." Having someone else there had broken Aunt Mabella's spell, somehow, and Jeremy felt relieved.

"Ah, yes." Eda's glance moved from Aunt Mabella to Jeremy and back to his aunt, before she clearly made a dozen rapid calculations. "I'm a specialist in tapestry restoration. Only the most unusual and high-quality tapestries, on the whole." She launched into a discussion, without letting Aunt Mabella get a word in edgewise. There were comments about the estates she'd had the pleasure of seeing, the states of their gardens, the ornamentation of their households. And, of course, Eda mentioned plenty about the tapestries. She didn't let on she was doing work for Jeremy, and she certainly didn't let Aunt Mabella round into him again.

Jeremy found, much to his bafflement, that Eda was even leading his aunt away, guiding her with one hand. She seemed to be saying there was someone Aunt Mabella must see, if she was at all interested in embroidery. Jeremy felt like a coward doing it, but he began taking small steps in the other direction until he could melt into the crowds around the tents.

CHAPTER 21
JUNE 27TH AT OAKBURGH HALL

Eda had done a good day's work already before she took a break in mid-afternoon for the gardens. Mostly, that was because she'd woken absurdly early, and got up rather than lie in bed staring at the window. It wasn't the light that had woken her, or the birds, it was something else.

Her day at the Faire on Friday had been lovely. Even the end. She'd come across that woman, and she'd known, even before hearing the commentary, that whatever she was saying wasn't kind. Jeremy had looked trapped, some poor animal with a foot in a poacher's snare, trying to decide whether to do the desperate thing.

And the thing was, Eda knew how to handle that. For one thing, it was something Alethorpe taught, as rigorously and repeatedly as they taught the crafting skills or how to manage a business. Especially to people like Eda, who'd be working for clients who had status, money, both, or aspirations above their actual holdings of either.

For the other, it was a great deal easier to deal with someone like that when you didn't know them and didn't owe them anything. Mrs Pound-Hepplethraite - and Eda did not use 'Mistress' quite deliberately - would be an amusing story at the pub in Trellech at some point. But she wasn't the sort to either have tapestries or commission bespoke fabric. Eda had, of course, been entirely polite and appropriate; one never knew who might overhear. But she hadn't much worried about whether the woman liked her at the end of it.

When she'd gone back, though, Jeremy had disappeared. She'd expected to meet him at the portal, either on the Faire end or back in Swaffham. Instead, the portal attendant had handed through mail. Mrs Summers had opened it, mentioning that Master Royston would be spending the next few days in Trellech. He expected to be home Monday evening.

If Eda had known that earlier, she might have stayed at the Faire longer. But she hadn't. She didn't want to put the staff out further. So she'd retreated to the house and spent the next three days weaving, while it poured outside. She hoped the weather at the Faire was better. While she worked, she made good progress, and she could set aside wondering about Jeremy for a bit.

But of course, she couldn't work all her waking hours. And her current knitting was not absorbing. Reading only got her so far, somehow. Eda felt like her wheels were stuck in mud, like she wasn't putting something together. When the rain finally broke, it seemed well past time to at least try something different, and so she went out into the gardens.

Everything was still damp, but Eda first made a circuit of some of the walking paths, keeping clear of the bits that looked particularly boggy, more or less successfully. Her boots would be all right when they dried out, probably. From there, she finished up with a pass through the gardens. She'd brought her book with her, and the bench wasn't too soaked; a charm solved that. It felt good to be outside for a bit.

Maybe it was the Faire that had put her in mind of it, but she found herself thinking of the network of people needed for an estate. She hadn't heard everything that woman had said, but something about selling up the estate. That would be a shame for the land; there were ancient trees, for one thing. And years, decades of work had gone into the gardens. Abundant rose bushes didn't happen overnight, never mind the climbing plants or many of the magical ones that took years to come to bloom or harvest.

The house might be draughty and creaky and entirely too big for a handful of people to be living in. But it had a lot of beauty. Not just walls designed for these specific tapestries, but the rest of it. There were plenty of options other than tearing it down, if the income was a problem. A school of some kind, or someone who needed space for apprentices to lease it out. It was remote, admittedly, but some people saw that as a benefit.

It would likely make a fantastic artist's or crafter's lodging, if Jeremy could be sure of finding artists and crafters able to pay their bills reliably. Each could have a bedroom and a studio or something. There was plenty of space for meals and sitting rooms and what have you, for people who wanted company, and she'd seen a few outbuildings for larger projects. Thinking about that kept her occupied, and then her book actually held her attention, so it wasn't until she heard someone nearby that she looked up.

Jeremy cleared his throat. "Pardon. Mrs Summers said she thought you'd come this way?"

Eda was suddenly aware of what she must look like. The wind had tugged her hair out of place, she could feel the wisps. Her shoes were muddy, and she wasn't exactly wearing her oldest clothes, but definitely on the grubbier and more worn side, a blouse and skirt. Jeremy, for his part, looked uncertain but much better dressed, like he'd been doing something that day that involved more formality than usual.

"Oh." Eda ducked her chin. "I didn't know you'd made it back. Yes. I was working all day, and the rain finally broke, and..." Now she just sounded flustered. She'd put in plenty of hours of work. For one thing, she didn't have to justify herself to him.

"I'm glad you took time to enjoy the gardens. Oh, the white roses here have bloomed! Just a few days away, and it's entirely different. See?" There was an honest delight in his voice. "And are those sweet peas? There's someone near my rooms in Trellech who has an arch of them. I find the smell delightful." Then, without turning away from the flowers, as if it were easier to talk to her without looking at her, he said, "I appreciate what you did on Friday."

"My pleasure." Eda said it, then realised she meant it. It had been a pleasure to help him there, to see something she knew she could do. "I hope you didn't mind my stepping in? It seemed, she seemed, unpleasantly pointed?"

He snorted. "That's a reasonable term for it. I hope she wasn't awful to you, though? I should have. I mean, she's my aunt. Distantly. Not at all your problem."

"She was making you unhappy." Eda hesitated. "You are my client, and while it is not in our contractual agreements for me to deflect difficult aunts, it certainly isn't contrary to them. Covered under additional professional services as relevant, which is one of the line items."

That made him relax visibly, and turn back. "I admit, I

didn't know what to do. And you did. May I ask how you know, do you have— oh, I shouldn't ask that, surely."

"Do I have difficult aunts of my own? Actually, no, they're all rather pleasant. Some of them have very wrong-headed ideas about the best kind of wool for different projects. But as long as they don't make me knit with their choices, we manage just fine." Eda shrugged. "Alethorpe teaches us how to deal with people like that. Depending on what kind of crafting you do, it can come up rather a lot."

"Enough that there's a class in it? A formal class?" Jeremy cleared his throat. "May I sit?"

"Please. Also, it's your bench, isn't it? That's part of the point. I dried it off, but you might check I got all the rain?" Eda shifted slightly, to give him a bit more space.

He glanced at it, then sat, turning a bit toward her, his feet tucked under the hollow beneath them. "It is lovely out here. I don't really want to go inside yet." That sounded a little confiding. "Do go on. I don't know much about the actual classes at Alethorpe. I've picked up more about Schola, since of course so many of the Materia specialists went there, or other people who work with materia."

"Well, we have the ordinary classes, about materia and materials in general, and how they get made. Some of those are practical, depending on our focus, some of them are more theory? Or at least a desk and pen and paper sort of active, not our hands making things. But there's also a lot of time set aside for us to actually do whatever it is we do. I learned a bit of weaving there, enough to have the basics. But we also had to learn all the parts of making thread and yarn before you get to weaving. So I had a lot of time carding wool, and then spinning it different ways, sewing, all of that."

"Much more about the hands than we were," Jeremy

said, thoughtfully. "And that made a difference for, I don't know, other things?"

"Absolutely, yes We'd have our teachers, all sorts of different crafts, talk while we did that, usually smaller groups so we could discuss and ask questions. About how to deal with clients, how to set limits, what limits were fair and what weren't. There isn't just one answer, of course. And it's reasonable, say, to give one person better terms because you know they'll be easy to deal with. But it's awkward if they talk about it, and everyone expects that."

"Oh." Jeremy looked away from her, and down at his hands. "I suppose that makes sense. Rather than having set rates."

"Well, we have set rates, too. You came with those in your notes. Most people don't. But that's the, oh, that's the base fee for the work, so we don't undercut each other. We then decide things like how long the work will take. The surcharge for being away from home, expenses for materials. We can explain those, obviously, like I did, but there's a certain amount of space."

"I see." He sounded forlorn, suddenly.

Eda softened her voice. "If Lord Carillon wanted my time, I'd charge him the lower end of our rates, for whatever it was. I know he's good to his staff. I wouldn't be dealing with anyone being difficult, interfering. And I know the space I'd be working in would be clean and comfortable. Of course, what's funny is that he'd insist on paying more, or paying a bonus for good work, or something like that, precisely because he takes care of his people. You, I didn't know that about."

"No. I had no real idea what I was asking, now, did I?" Jeremy glanced at her, then went back to looking at his fingers.

"When I wrote out the proposal for you, there's the charge for being away from home. Because as pleasant as my rooms are, and as good as the food is, it's still not my home, and that's sometimes a little tedious. Though mostly, I'm very much enjoying being here, actually." That made him look directly at her with a rather pleasant shy smile. "But the rest of it, well, I was fairly sure you'd be reasonable once I explained what was needed. Your aunt, now, I'd have been tacking on charges right and left. All within my rights, but she's the sort who'd be jogging my elbow every minute unless I charged her for time spent talking. I don't with you, this is just, I don't know. Us talking. Like people."

"Oh." This was a more thoughtful sound, at least, so Eda felt like he might be taking in her explanation properly. "Thank you for explaining. That's actually rather a help." He took a breath and then let it out. "Do you mind if I talk through what I was doing today? It occurs to me you might have some ideas. It's about Aunt Mabella, and some other family, and some legal, I don't know, implications? Nothing that affects your work at the moment, I should say. But it's asking you as a..." His voice trailed off.

"As a friend?" Eda offered. "You don't seem like you have very many. I have a lot of acquaintances, anyway. And some friends. I'm glad to lend an ear. My shoulders were getting sore. I need a break from the weaving for a bit. We're not using up working time. And besides, you get some say in that."

It made him snort. "But not to chatter your ear off while you're doing terribly complicated dances between threads with sharp objects."

CHAPTER 22
THAT AFTERNOON

J eremy took a breath. In truth, he was still unsettled by what he'd learned earlier that day. And he'd been nervous about talking to Eda. He'd been sure she'd look down on him for, well, being a coward. It would be entirely justified.

Instead, she'd been kind. And she'd been interesting, far beyond being kind. She'd explained things in a way he wanted to follow. She knew far different things than he did, but she knew them in a way he could make sense of once she'd talked about it. That combination wasn't something he'd found often, even with other people in the Ministry or at the Dunwich club in Trellech.

Now he cleared his throat. "I was worried, enough to inquire about it, whether Aunt Mabella might have any, might have been right about any of it."

"Even though she's on the wrong side of the family? No, wait, you said your father's side, but not in the right line."

"A sister of my father's aunt by marriage. So not in the direct family line at all. Though more active than some about keeping up with the extended family." Jeremy wrinkled his nose. "She was a bit awful with my mother, actually, when Mama was declining. Until we arranged things so Aunt Mabella couldn't get into where she was staying without a direct invitation. You know the sort, probably, someone who turns up and spends three hours talking exhaustively about their own minor infirmities, when that person is dealing with more complex matters."

"Oh, yes," Eda said. "Not often. But that is decidedly a type. That Mabella is one does not surprise at all, no." She hesitated, then said, "You needn't answer if you'd rather not. But I gather it's just you now. Or it would have been your father, here, sorting things out."

"I was an only child. Mama doted on me. Papa died a little before the War, Mama five years ago. And he didn't have brothers, so there are some more distant cousins, but - well, that brings us back to today." He hesitated. "You? If I may ask the same. You're here. I suppose that's a partial answer."

"My husband died in the War. I said that. We never had children. I've sisters and brothers, but they're up in Yorkshire. Good solid farm and fishing folk, I love them, but we have little in common. They'd understand me better if I were weaving cloth for cloaks or hard wear, and that's not what I do. Not what I want to do. I go up for a week once a year, usually, in the middle of winter when it's quieter for them." Eda shrugged, and Jeremy wasn't sure what to say about any of it. Especially since he had not got the most flattering impression of her late husband. But of course, it was absolutely rude to say that sort of thing out loud. Mama had taught him far better.

After a moment, he cleared his throat. "I'm glad you get to see them. A manageable amount."

Eda's expression cracked into a smile. "It's taken some

experimentation to figure out when we will absolutely get on each other's nerves and leave the day before that happens, yes." She folded her hands a little different in her lap, like she was twitching to have something to do. "You were going to explain what you were doing today? I don't know if I can help, but I'm glad to listen."

"I was in Trellech, talking to the solicitor that handled the inheritance case. It had to be proved by the Courts, because of course it's rather a tangle of entailments. They're not terribly common outside the Great Families these days. I admit I still don't entirely understand how they work. At any rate, the courts are in recess over the holiday, but my solicitor was willing to meet with me. Aunt Mabella doesn't precisely have any rights, nor does her son. But I need to give some thought to the long-term. Or ought, anyway. Beyond the other reasons, like the finances."

"Because?" Eda asked it, cleared her throat. "Tell me if I'm prying."

"I'm the one who brought it up." Jeremy replied. "The entailment means that I not only need to sort things out now, I need to figure out who could inherit. And—" He looked away. "Doing either is overwhelming. Both at the same time is even more so. And come August, I'll need to be back in the office, even less chance to sort things out here."

Eda was quiet for a long time, what felt like forever. It was probably less than a minute. Jeremy used to be much better at patience, and then his life had changed, and he wasn't. Certainly, he felt like he wasn't. Everything crumbled away like old brick when he touched it. "What would you want to do if you could?"

"Make it a comfortable space. A warm space. With people. But that's not likely, is it? The staff, but that will go away. It already is a lot of places, I know that much. At least without other work to keep people busy."

"I was— may I offer a thought I had?" She was curiously deferential about it now, as if she were afraid he'd be upset. Jeremy didn't want her to think that, whatever else. Surely they were adults who could talk about topics without worrying about that.

"You have had well-considered opinions so far." Then Jeremy turned toward her, more directly. "Are you worried you'll offend me? It sounded a bit like that. Please don't be. I'm certain that's not your intention. You've been so careful with how you put things, how you explain the underlying parts."

She ducked her chin. "I'm glad you think so. And I am a little worried, I guess. It's not my place to suggest things. Only this isn't the ordinary sort of setting, really. And you haven't had many other people to talk to about any of it, have you?"

Jeremy shook his head. "People at work, the people a few steps above me. They might have a house, enough like this to understand? But they've had it for a while, if they do. They grew up knowing they'd have something like that. And the people my rank, they might own a townhome in Trellech or something like it, but that's a different sort of architectural implication."

"Landscape implication, too. Much smaller garden." Eda nodded, making a decision visible. "I was thinking that it might make quite a pleasant space for, I don't know, artists or maybe a tutoring school. The sort of place where people wouldn't need to come and go terribly often, and where the solitude might be a little of an advantage, even. The countryside's lovely. You have some outbuildings for larger projects, and you've certainly got plenty of rooms. You could have ten, maybe fifteen people, either sharing a bath or with their own, comfortably."

Jeremy blinked. "I hadn't really thought about it like that. I don't remotely know how to set up something like that. Especially a tutoring school. It's not as if I went to Schola."

"I didn't either, but I know people who did. You'd want someone who was looking to set something up, of course, and then arrange for them to use the space. Keep some spaces just for you, some for the staff, of course. But it would be steady employment." She turned her hand palm up. "Maybe tricky to manage the gardens, but thoughtfully applied warding might solve that."

"Which is more money for specialists." Jeremy ran his hand through his hair. "I'm not saying no. I'm flailing because it's very different from anything I'd thought about."

Eda was quiet again, then she asked, her voice suddenly gentle in a way that Jeremy found confusing. "What were you thinking about?"

"I wish I understood more about the gardens." Jeremy craned his neck around, but it was late enough all three of the gardeners should be in their own cottages having their tea. "I understand materia. Or at least, I understand it on paper, a great deal more than I understand most things. The patterns of it, the shapes of it. I suppose I'm not making sense."

"Oh, no. That is entirely sensible to me. I look at clothing, and I see the fabric, the thread and such, used to make it. I can't not. But put me in front of other materials and I'll stare blankly." She gestured. "Brick and stone, for example. I know there were deliberate choices made there, and they seem to be mostly good ones, since the place is still in reasonable repair for its age. But beyond that? No idea."

The way she put it, the way she made it sound reasonable, that cracked something open in Jeremy. "That." He suddenly felt overwhelmed, turning away and bringing his hands up, so she wouldn't see whatever expressions he was making, covering his face with his palms.

There was silence and stillness, and then, so lightly he thought he imagined it at first, a touch on his hand, not pulling or tugging, just there. "Are you— do you need me to fetch someone? To go away?"

His hand twitched, and her hand shifted, but didn't fall away. Slowly, he lowered the other hand, then the one she was touching. "It's been a long day. I'm, I'm."

"A tad overwhelmed. Shows you're sensible." He let his hand fall in his lap, and her fingers followed him, as if she were tracing some essential thread back to the source. "What do you want to do?"

"I want to make this place live and breathe. Keep it living and breathing and beautiful. And that's a ridiculous desire, far beyond the funds or the people, or anything. But there's something here, a heart, and no matter how impractical it is..." Jeremy's voice trailed off, and then he dared look at her.

She'd scooted a little closer on the bench, and she was looking down at their hands. "I think it's good to have dreams. I didn't for a while. Not beyond being a good businesswoman, steady, reliable. The world's better with dreams. Colours. An explosion of glorious flowers." She gestured with her free hand to indicate the garden. "Could you maybe spend the month you have figuring out if any of the dreams are possible?"

Jeremy sucked in a breath, then he nodded. "Will you,

will you let me talk it out with you? Please? I don't think I can sort any of it out by myself."

"If you like. You ask, though. I don't want to overstep." Eda hesitated, then she pulled her hand back. "I hope I didn't just now."

Jeremy looked down at his hand, at where her hand had been. "It's been a long time since anyone touched me in kindness, rather than practicality. Or courtesy." He glanced over at her, then back at his hand. "You didn't overstep. Thank you for having a care. For thinking it's worth having dreams about this place." He took a deep breath. "I'll do a proper inventory of what we have, rooms and furniture and what's in the gardens, and we can go from there."

"Glad to be an ear." Eda cleared her throat. "Perhaps we ought to go in, so Mrs Summers isn't worried about supper? I should probably wash up."

"Of course." He stood, waiting for her to stand and join him. "Perhaps I can rummage around and remember some of the historical tidbits, then? Or write them up tidily for you?"

"If you'd enjoy that, certainly." They walked back together along the path, across the little moat, before she split off to her own rooms and he went to his for a few minutes. Jeremy turned, just as he was about to open the door to his staircase, to watch her. There was something in her manner he found deeply soothing. She would put things in a flattering manner for a client, but he was certain, somehow, that she wouldn't lie. She wouldn't stretch what was true into something that wasn't or couldn't be.

CHAPTER 23
TWO DAYS LATER

Eda kept staring at the tapestries. Something wasn't matching up, something far bigger than the individual worn threads on the Gaudium tapestry stretched out on the working frame. She kept looking up from it, like a ray of light was nagging at her attention.

The previous day had, honestly, been entirely lovely. Jeremy had been up in his office all day, buried in looking at books and notes and a dozen other things. They'd had a pleasant break for luncheon and a lingering supper, not talking about the house in either case, but more about general types of people. It was intriguing how the types did and didn't overlap between her business and the Ministry. And it was more pleasant, honestly, having someone to talk over the variations.

For one thing, Eda could, and did, turn people down. Jeremy wasn't able to do that. He worked in a Ministry office. Short of active violence or some sort of criminal offence, he couldn't turn someone away from his work. On the other hand, he mostly dealt with the same sets of people over and over. Either they also worked at the

Ministry, or it was a stream of representatives from the Guilds or sometimes workshops, depending on the question at hand.

Today, she'd put in a truly excellent day's work. Everything had gone smoothly, no catches or tangles either in the thread or in the magic she was using to make everything sound again. But she'd wrapped up the section she'd been toiling over around four, too late in the day to make it sensible to start the next one. Of course, she set up everything to be ready for tomorrow. That meant adjusting the tapestry on the frame, rolling it carefully to bring the new area into comfortable reach, and making sure the tension was just right. Doing it today would help, too. It would let everything settle overnight and be easier to fine tune.

The thing was, the patterns of wear didn't make sense. She started out by staring at them, circling the room slowly, and considering where the marks would be on Gaudium, if it were hanging up. Tapestries, at least in rooms that got any use at all, showed signs of where they'd been hanging. Some of that was fading from the light, of course. Here, there wasn't as much of that. The windows were high up, above the tapestries, and whoever had glazed them had used sensible charms to filter the light and reduce the damage from it.

But people did reliably want furniture in their rooms. With tapestries this big, long enough to hang nearly to the floor, one expected to see marks of a table or chair, set nearby, and rubbing now and again. Even the best protective enchantments didn't entirely solve that problem. She was still staring at it when Jeremy knocked on the door, where it was propped open. "Eda, are— oh. Was I interrupting?"

"I'm puzzling something over. No sharp objects in my

hands, though, come in." She glanced over, and she thought he looked a little more settled than he had yesterday. Or even at lunch today. That was good. He got a pinched look around the eyes when he was anxious, and it didn't suit him, she'd decided. Not that she would share any opinions of that sort. It wasn't appropriate while she was working for him.

He came in, standing where she was, facing the same way, before he cleared his throat. "What am I supposed to be looking at?"

"I don't know if this is going to make sense to you. I don't know, honestly, if it makes sense to me. But I was looking at the worn patches."

"Worn patches." Jeremy gestured at several. "Along the middle there." They were looking at Obedientia and Alacritas, by the labels, both wide tapestries. Obedientia was a crowd scene, the glamour and crush of the Tudor court. Eda hadn't actually seen the portraits of that genera-tion, but she suspected the Roystons of the time had been woven into the image somewhere.

Alacritas, promptness, had someone on horseback, riding at speed into battle or carrying a message. It wasn't entirely clear, though the figure was armoured with a shield hanging against one leg and covering the knee. Quite possible to avoid having to make the knee come out right in thread. Knees and elbows were tremendously tricky, in Eda's experience. She'd far rather do plants and foliage. And that one had four legs of the horse to contend with. That didn't help at all. Horses had legs that were all joints.

"Here." She took a couple of steps forward, then added, "I think it's easier to see from there. And along here, on this one." She gestured at the two spots.

"All right." Jeremy frowned. "And?"

"Now, turn around, and look at, um." She gestured. "Abertas. Abundance." She didn't want to point it out to him in too much detail.

He twisted, coming to face the one that hung on the right of the other long wall, a hundred and eighty degree turn. Then he turned again, as if trying to trace things, before going and walking up to first Obedientia and then Abertas. "There's a mark here. On the right of Obedientia, and on the left of Abertas. As if there were the same object there. A table, something of the kind."

Eda nodded. "I think so. It's harder to tell, without them hanging on the same wall, and I don't want to move them. Well, and I can't, just by myself."

"Could we do, erm? Is there a method for doing sketches? You were doing something when you were figuring out the repairs, weren't you?" Jeremy tilted his head.

"I was. It will take a bit to set up, though. And some materia I don't have on hand."

"What sort?" Jeremy cleared his throat. "I don't know what we have handy, but I suspect something."

"Quartz, for a stone. You probably have that somewhere?" It was abundant, after all, and had several dozen magical uses. "Foxglove. Though that has to be handled properly." It was poisonous and could be dangerous when touched.

"Well, we've got that in the gardens, unless it needs to be dried."

"No. Well." Eda grimaced, then took several steps back to her working notebook. "Saffron. But Cook might have some, and I only need a thread or so."

"Let me go ask. Anything else?" Jeremy hesitated. "You don't mind me helping?"

"Good grief, no." Eda found a scrap bit of paper in the back of her notebook, and wrote out the list. Quartz, saffron, foxglove, vervain if it was handy, sage ditto. And a quantity of clean water, the best available, and a few drops of local honey.

"Right. I'll be back in a couple of minutes." It left Eda to stand there and stare at the walls, and then make another slow circuit of the space. She'd need paper, as well, but she had larger sheets in her working kit. She'd needed them for the planning for the repairs. Eda had cast the enchantment for Gaudium, of course, but she hadn't bothered to do the other tapestries yet. Normally there was no point in doing it until it was time to start the work, just in case something shifted in them.

She got the paper out, and the paintbrush that she'd need for it. It was part enchantment, partly sympathetic magic. She was not particularly talented at either, but she'd been drilled in this specific form over and over, because it was tremendously useful for her work.

By the time she had everything out and ready, Jeremy was back. "We'll need to trim the foxglove ourselves, I've a basket and tongs and the proper shears. Cook had some saffron, as you thought, and the sage is blooming now. Apparently, that's in the kitchen garden." He held up a hand. "And a flask, never used for food and drink, safe enough to use for the foxglove. Mrs Summers promised me it had been properly cleaned, but can you check?" It was a smooth glass, not purely translucent, but more clear than opaque. That would be easy enough to charm clean, unlike ceramic.

"I can. Let's get the plants first, though." Eda nodded, glancing around to see if she'd forgotten anything. No, the list was the list. This was exactly why she kept notes with the best items and the possible substitutions. "The garden, then."

Getting the sage was easy enough. The shears worked for that. But when they came out to the walled garden, Waters was there, a broad brimmed straw hat on his head. Jeremy cleared his throat. "We needed a bloom or two from the foxglove, if you don't mind."

The wheelbarrow was parked right in front of that. Waters lifted his head, something like an ox looking up, untroubled by whatever was about to happen because he was bigger and stronger and stubborner than anything nearby. "Say what, sir?"

"Eda— Mistress Fellowes— is investigating something with the tapestry, and it needs a spot of materia work. Can we trim one of the foxgloves?"

"Not safe to be doing that." It was not clear from his comments whether he meant the foxgloves, the magic, or, well, anything with the tapestries.

"I'm quite familiar with the precautions, thank you," Eda said. "We have the container for it. And we don't need much."

Waters blinked at her, slowly. "What does it do, then?"

It was, perhaps, more in the way of stubborn questioning than Jeremy knew what to do with. Eda considered it one more point in the conclusions she'd been drawing. The staff here were excellent at their work, but demanded it be done the way they thought best. Most of the time, that wasn't remotely a problem. Sometimes, however, it caused problems. Or could. As it was doing now. "We add the materia to clear water, let it sit for a little, there's a chant. Then I snip a tiny thread from the tapestry, add that to a smaller amount of the water, and brush it onto a piece of prepared paper. It will create a sketch of sorts of the design, and then I can do another layer of where the damaged spots are. Onionskin paper, for that."

"And you won't be touching the water?"

"No, I was trained in all the precautions. It goes in the flask. We make very sure that whatever we pour out goes into a suitable container. Everything gets cleaned by charm and water and another charm. Just to be safe."

"Right. I'll do the harvesting, then. Shears?" Waters stuck his hand out.

Jeremy looked rather startled, but then he held out the basket with the shears. "Thank you, Waters."

They were rewarded with a grunt, and then with Waters peering at the stalks of the foxgloves for a good minute and a half, trying to decide which to select. Finally, he chose one near the back, closest to the wall, a little more protected, and trimmed off two beautiful glowing purple blooms. "That enough?"

"Yes, thank you." To do seven tapestries, arguably nine if they did the long panels over the doors, it would take a fair bit of the water. "Much appreciated."

"I'll be taking the shears, I'll clean them, bring them back to Mrs Summers." Eda glanced at Jeremy, but this was apparently at least easier to manage.

He nodded. "Thank you. We'll be in the great hall for a bit, if she has questions." That said, he turned back toward the path back to the bridge and the house, just waiting long enough to be sure Eda was joining him.

CHAPTER 24
LATER THAT EVENING

J eremy gestured for Eda to go first into the great hall. "How may I help, or would it be easier if I stayed out of your way?"

She'd gone immediately to the worktable where she kept the cases of her supplies, but now she turned around, one hand on her hip. "You know how to deal with paper, though perhaps not at this size. I could use a hand making sure it doesn't roll up on itself. We'll want a long table to lay each piece out, while I paint."

"How does this work, precisely?" Jeremy stayed back as she bustled around, pulling a tray out of the trunk that had some of the supplies, then a long roll of paper. It wasn't the same broad size as the tapestries, perhaps a reduction by half. But it was far larger than ordinary paper. And of course, it was a roll so it could be trimmed to whatever size was needed. "Can you cut this into seven larger pieces, then two into halves, lengthwise, and one of them into four strips, widthwise? You want the proportions to match. Moment."

She whirled around, almost like a dance, to consult the

notes on her worktable. "Two-foot lengths should do for your starting point. Here's a measuring tape." Eda took three steps toward him, putting a measuring tape and pencil in one of his hands, scissors in the other. "Don't use these on cloth, these are the paper scissors, see the purple ribbon?" He went to work without asking why there was a difference. It wasn't like he was going to go anywhere near the thread with any scissors, not in this room. And certainly not when Eda was available to do it instead.

Instead, he focused on measuring out each piece, marking it in pencil, then making a line precisely and accurately, then doing the next. When he was done, there were seven curls of paper wrapping back around each other. Eda danced by him again, on a path between her worktable and one tapestry, different scissors in her hand. She dropped four weights onto the table, where they landed with a thunk. They were curiously beautiful things, with a flat base and dome topped by a peak and a rounded tip. Maybe to make them easier to get a grip on. He wasn't sure. He used two of them to weight down one of the rolled sheets, so he could measure and cut, then he did the other.

By the time he was done with the last sheet, cut into fours, Eda had a series of items out on the other table. They included the flask of water and seven small dishes that looked like they nestled together. They were maybe the size of saucers for a porcelain tea set, but deeper, enough to hold a bit of water. When she finally turned back to him, she nodded. "Come see? It's rather beautiful, actually."

Jeremy glanced down to make sure the paper wasn't rolling up on itself, but it was staying where it should. He came over, careful not to jog her arm. Besides the metal dishes, there was a paintbrush set out, and then clear water in a jug. "Do we bring the paper here?"

"Yes, one at a time, please. And then you can hold it down with the weights here. It will help if you can move the weight while I paint that section. See, so?" She gestured at what she meant, her hand sweeping like a brush across the empty table.

"So long as I am doing the simple part and you are doing the part that requires dexterity, I believe I can manage." He made it into a bit of a joke, and Eda smiled at him.

"All right. Don't touch any of the liquid. It's safe enough when it's diluted, when we wash it down the drain, but until then, no. If any gets on you, go wash that immediately." Eda considered. "I will add the thread, repeat the charm, and we will see what we get." There was a slightly odd note at the end of that.

"Wait." Jeremy cleared his throat. "What aren't you telling me?"

He caught the hint of the shrug, and he could see she was considering not telling him. "It's tiring. That's why I didn't do it at the beginning. It makes sense to do it now, and I'm curious."

"What sort of tiring are we talking about here? You'll want a chair? To retire to your rooms for a day or two?" Jeremy hesitated. "I am fairly certain we could find a fainting couch."

That last one made her smile, which was better than she'd hoped. "A chair, perhaps your help to clean up and make things safe."

Jeremy noticed she hadn't said she'd be fine. On the other hand, she was a grown woman. She certainly knew the charm she had in mind far better than he did. And while they were his tapestries as much as they were anyone's, her magic wasn't his to command or control. "Whatever help I can be, I am yours to direct, then." He offered a slight bow, hoping it'd take the awkwardness out of it.

"Thank you." Eda said it, focused on it, and then she turned away. She dropped one of the threads she'd clipped carefully into a bowl of water, picked up the brush. "If you could be ready to get the weights on that side."

The process was, in the main, simple. There was an incantation. She brushed the water over the sheet of paper, lightly. That was the way one worked with watercolours, he thought, not that Jeremy had ever done that himself. As Eda moved the brush down the page, the colours sprang up in the wake of the brush, deepening. And far brighter than they were on the tapestry themselves. When she stood back after the first, immediately putting the brush in a jar of clean water, he waited.

"Question?" Her voice was a little odd.

"The colours?" Jeremy waved. "Is that as they were?"

"It is. I'd have done this before we did illusion work, of course. The thread— the thread remembers. And I showed you the back. The colours are closer to what they were on the back. The repairs are, too, but I suppose you can't see as much of that. Where there's black and brown, where I've been working, it faded less. Ready for the next one?"

She didn't really make it a question. Jeremy nodded. From there, they went on without a pause, until they'd done all the tapestries, even the two over the doors. When she finished the last of those, she wobbled, and Jeremy immediately moved to pluck the brush out of her hands, putting it in the jar. "Chair?" Eda was leaning hard on the table, which was more than sturdy enough for the purpose.

"I—" She might have argued, but then suddenly she didn't. "Chair. Please."

There was one, over in the corner, and he brought it

over right away. It was not the best chair for this, maybe; it was one of the older easy chairs, a bit faded itself. Eda sat as soon as it was behind her, closing her eyes.

"May I fetch food? Tea? Clear up the materials?"

"The last one." She rubbed her nose, then grimaced. "I'll be fine in a minute."

"You said running water, plenty of it. Is there anything else I should know? One at a time?" Jeremy asked, trying not to hurry her.

"Pour each one out, one at a time. Leave the tap running between and rinse the bowls. Then rinse the flask and the water we were using the same and let the water run at least thirty seconds. It's the ordinary sterilising charms after that."

"I'll see to that." Jeremy took a deep breath, and then went off to do that. It took him quite a while, including finding Mrs Summers and confirming that she could do the last stage of the charmwork to the desired standard. He also suggested that a tray in Eda's room might be a good idea. Twenty minutes, maybe thirty. By the time he came back, Eda had leaned her head back against the chair. "May I offer you an arm upstairs? Mrs Summers is seeing to the various containers, and she'll have a tray for you."

"Oh." Something in it startled her. "Thank you. Bring the paper up, would you, so I can look at them?"

Jeremy had not expected that, but he carefully rolled them up, handing them to Eda, and offering his arm. He felt he was not a talented escort here, but at least the staircase to her rooms wasn't far. When she was settled in one of the chairs there, he offered to take the papers just as there was a knock on the door. Sorting out where the tray went and pulling over a table for the papers took rather longer than

Jeremy wanted, but then they were alone again. "Are you certain you're all right?"

"Nothing sleep and food won't fix. Not in that order. Oh, this looks good." The meal wasn't anything complicated, just sandwiches, in fact, but several varieties. Jeremy stood up, tentatively. "Please, stay. I'll make more sense in a few minutes."

He sat again, folding his hands in his lap and waiting. Jeremy glanced around, then focused on Eda again. He hadn't paid too much attention to the room when they were making sure it was ready for her, but it now looked like a space someone lived in. There was a loom of some kind, at least he thought it was a loom, a small one, on the table. She was tidy, her things were neatly arranged or put away, but there was a book on the table. Two books, neatly aligned. And a bouquet of cheerful flowers, those had come out of the garden at some point.

When she'd eaten about half the sandwiches, she looked up. "Can you— um. How do we do this? The table, let me move the loom."

Eda stood, and she didn't wobble as much, and it still wasn't Jeremy's place to fuss over her. Instead, he stayed back while she moved the loom gently to the floor, out of the way, and they had the table to work with. "Now it's a bit like putting a jigsaw puzzle together. Look for where the wear marks are the same, or other things match. Any sign that they'd been hung together."

It took some moving around, but it was, after all, a puzzle with a limited number of pieces. And each of the tapestries could only be in a few places. It was rather like the logic puzzles that had been popular when he was at Dunwich, choosing and discarding pieces that didn't fit with the stated parameters. In the end, they had them laid out, and then Jeremy saw something he hadn't expected.

"Do they— do they fit going all the way around? From the side of the door to the other side?" Gaudium had people dancing out in the open, the manor in the background, like some village celebration. The land trailed down to a road, where the rider of Alacritas galloped off into the next wide panel. That was a crowd scene, Tolerantia, like a great mass of people in some public place or palace, it was hard to tell from the architecture. A city, at least. A wall at the end of that turned into something like a church. That was Ethicus, that made sense, and the wall on the other side opened into a glorious archway of a garden, for Honoria. The two would frame one entry into the room, and they balanced each other rather wonderfully.

Then there was a court, what he thought might be a Tudor court. There was the Tudor rose, with a monarch on a throne, though the face and features were indistinct, not a direct portrait. Obedientia, indeed. The last of the wide tapestries circled back to fields and gardens, echoing the garden of Honoria, but this time overflowing with the abundance of grains, fruits and orchards, cows and sheep. Goats and pigs and oxen were visible here and there. The wear patterns had suggested this, but seeing it all together, he could see how the colours blended and shifted, no jarring changes.

"You think it was made for that?" Jeremy glanced at Eda, who was tracing a line of it with her fingers.

"The way the design goes, the colours, the elements— the walls, here and here? Or these details. See the stonework here, it matches." She nodded. "I don't know why they were moved, though."

"This makes me think of the gatehouse stairs." Jeremy

said, gesturing at the image on Stabilitas. "I wonder if— I wonder how much they match. No." Eda turned as if to go. "Not tonight. For one thing, we'll want good light and time. Take your ease. We can look properly tomorrow."

It looked for a moment as if she were going to argue, but then she nodded. "Fair. I suppose you want your own supper."

He was, in fact, hungry. It was rather late. "I should check in with Mrs Summers. Can I send anything else up? Do you have a book to read?"

"Thank you, yes." Now she looked a little faded, like the tapestries themselves. Beautiful, but lacking the vibrancy that suited better. "Tomorrow. After breakfast?"

"I'll make sure there's something filling, then. See you in the morning." He stood, awkwardly, made a slight bow, and then decided that if he didn't go now, no matter how abrupt, they'd be standing there making polite noises at each other for three hours. It was enough to get him to turn and walk away, to find out where Mrs Summers was and his own meal.

CHAPTER 25
JUNE 30TH

"You're right. It really looks like the stairs." Eda was standing in the archway under the gatehouse, at the entrance to the courtyard. She kept looking from the paper in her hands to the open door in front of her, the stairs curving upward in a spiral. "That sort of spiral staircase often looks the same. But I can see the stonework here. And this line." She took a step forward, laying a hand on a line of masonry work that ran between the bricks. "This isn't what you see everywhere, is it?"

"I am not an expert," Jeremy said tentatively. "You've seen more houses like this than I have. Shall we go up and see if there's anything that seems relevant?"

"This is the staircase where you saw the ghost, too? This one, I mean, and not the other side." Eda gestured. "The tapestry has this as a rose, ambiguous colour, and on the other stair, it's a shield."

Jeremy turned around, peered at the other door, then nodded. "This one." He glanced up, and Eda couldn't tell if he was nervous, curious, both, or something else. "I'll go first, shall I? It's my house."

"Here, I think I appreciate you not insisting on ladies first, yes," Eda said. He began going up the stairs, and Eda followed him, five or six steps behind. She let her fingers trail along the stone, on the off-chance that she'd feel something in the stone or wood that her eyes didn't notice.

The upstairs did not seem any different from the first time Jeremy had brought her up here. He took his time walking around it, though, going along all four walls, ducking into the smaller room to the side, before coming back. "I have no idea what I'm looking for. Would you come this way, see if you see anything that matches the tapestries?"

She followed him through the door, into the smaller chamber. This one felt more intimate, somehow, as if the larger room were for show. Eda turned around slowly, then shook her head. "No. I think I don't know enough. Is there anywhere else in the tapestries that looked like it might be this place?"

Jeremy considered. "Can I see them again, out by the big windows?" They retreated to the main room, and Eda was caught again by the name 'The Lady's Room'. She set the pages out, and Jeremy thumbed through them. "The gardens, maybe. The walls, at least, and that's the place I notice the walls outside. And this, Abertas, it keeps catching my eye. Maybe also Gaudium." He frowned. "I seem to remember the library was redone, perhaps a hundred and fifty years ago. They moved a fair bit of the shelving around. Maybe that's why it doesn't catch the memory."

"And also, those two tapestries are over the doors. You wouldn't expect to inspect the details as closely. If there is some clue hidden there, anyway." Eda pursed her lips. "Library later. It'll be easier to look at the gardens now."

Jeremy nodded, gathering the papers, then going down

ahead of her. At the bottom, he stood to keep the door open, offering a hand as she came down the last couple of steps. She put her fingers in his, a little startled at the gesture, but appreciating it. The last few had worn oddly and she'd almost tripped. Together, they turned to walk out toward the garden, side by side.

The brick and mortar walls in the kitchen garden, mostly along the back, weren't all decorative. And while this might be the optimal place for an image of abundance, at least of food, none of the proportions seemed quite right. It was possible, of course, that there had been changes here, too. Certainly, over centuries, it was more likely something had been changed than that it hadn't.

Eda stared at the charm drawings again, squinting against the angle of the light. "I just don't see it. The general colour, yes, and those. What's the name for something on the top of a pillar?"

"A finial, I believe, though I'm not actually sure if that applies to garden walls," Jeremy said. "The walled garden, then?"

"We can at least be thorough." Eda agreed. Then, as they began walking, she whistled, as she usually did, to be kind to the gardening young men. Once she'd gone through a verse and chorus, she asked, "I know why I'm curious about the tapestries. And I'm baffled about how they were hung. Now you see how they connect. But what do you think about it?"

Jeremy walked in silence, both of them angling around toward the far corner and the arched doorway. Jeremy stopped, turning back to look at the entrance and the walls. "This was a prosperous estate for a long time." He gestured at the paper. "Abundance. Abertas. I don't know what that looks like now, what it could look like. The world keeps changing, doesn't it?"

"But people still need some of the same things. Food, though you're not really set up for some of it here. Too far to market for anything heavy." Eda tilted her head. "Fibre is lightweight. Sheep, most likely, in these parts. Dyed, you have the garden space for a wide range of dye plants." He turned toward her, and she smiled. "Those, I know about."

"Do you think we might make a go of that? I only know about materia when it's ready to be used. Even so much as what you did with the charms, I do very little of that." Jeremy said, frowning.

"You live in rooms, right? No kitchen access. So you don't even do your own household cleaning or that sort of thing. A little mint or basil in the cleaning water, a charm to keep things bright and gleaming."

"Nothing like that. And we had a cook-housekeeper when I was growing up, living with my parents." He said it as if whatever life that had been had been a long time ago.

Before Eda could ask more about it, there was a sound from the archway, words spoken quickly, but muffled, so Eda couldn't make out what was going on. The only bit she made sense of came last. "No, I'm going to." Then there was a more plaintive, "Henry."

One of the young men stumbled out of the archway. This was the blond one, the gold of his hair peeping out under a hat. He was dressed in faded working clothes, heavy twill in a brownish green, his shirtsleeves gartered up out of the way. That would be Ernie, which meant Henry was just out of sight. Eda reached out to put a hand on Jeremy's forearm, when he looked like he might start forward. She did not know what had brought either of them out of hiding, but she had some idea how to deal with skittish apprentices.

Jeremy glanced at her sharply, but then took half a step back. Eda cleared her throat. "You're Ernie Harrow, yes? I'm Eda, this is Jeremy." It was not the right mode, but she still didn't understand the terms for staff and all that.

"Mistress Fellowes." The young man stopped about eight feet away, well out of arm's reach. Not that either Eda or Jeremy were likely to fling themselves precipitously at anyone. "Do you mean it?"

Eda blinked at him. The young man wasn't actually terribly young. Though that made sense. If he'd fought in the War, he'd have been eighteen then, so at least twenty-six now. He seemed a few years older than that, perhaps thirty-two or thirty-five. A man who, without the War, would have done an apprenticeship and been well-estab-lished. Here, he shifted from foot to foot, as if ready to bolt like a startled deer if given any cause. Or a rabbit.

"About thinking there is hope for the property? About growing dye plants?" Eda tried to pitch her voice gently. "Yes. You've done a wonderful job with the gardens. Did Waters tell you about the foxglove? We used that to help us figure something out."

"Oh." Ernie took a step to one side, then back, a particu-larly recursive dance. Or maybe a bit like the shuttle going back and forth across the loom, where the picture only appeared after many repetitions. "Sir?"

Jeremy took a breath, and Eda was relieved he wasn't rushing to some answer. "I'd like to make sure the estate can support itself. And I know a bit about materia on the other end, making sure it is evaluated and rated for quality, and all that. If there are plants you think might grow here, all— all three of you, I would be glad to discuss. You know the land. And gardens. Much better than I do. But I know about the business and enough about the bureaucracy to know who to ask."

Ernie went back and forth several more times before he said. "You were talking?" It was as if he'd jumped back to an earlier part of the conversation without caring.

Jeremy nodded. "We were looking at the garden. We think that the tapestries inside might show places here. But it's hard to match them up." He turned, gesturing, and Eda saw Ernie flinch, before he went entirely still for perhaps twenty seconds. Then the shifting back and forth began again. Jeremy didn't move, he didn't speak, he just waited.

"In the house, too?" Now Ernie's voice was near enough a whisper, conspiratorial.

"In the house as well," Eda agreed. "There are old family stories about something being hidden. Jeremy has told me a little about them." As soon as she said it, she wondered if she'd overstepped. When she glanced to look at Jeremy, she couldn't figure out what he felt.

"I knew people up at Baddesley Clinton. Warwickshire. They've gardens. Or Harvington Hall. You could ask to see?" Ernie wove back and forth more, as if there were an additional layer of agitation. "Don't tell them where I am, though. Secret."

As if that didn't open up about twenty more questions. Eda swallowed them down. "Why there?" She didn't think it was one of the magical estates.

"History. Not too different." Ernie glanced back over his shoulder, toward the archway and presumably his friend, still hidden behind the wall. "I have to go."

There was a silence. Neither of them knew what to say. Then Jeremy managed, "Thank you, Ernie. Would you ask

Waters to talk with me about what we might do along the lines of cultivating materia for sale?"

"Sir." There was a tug at the cap. Ernie didn't bolt for the archway, but he took long strides, almost floating over the ground, before he disappeared from view behind the arch.

"That was unexpected." Jeremy cleared his throat. "Shall we make plans to go to Warwickshire?" He then took a step back. "What am I saying? You don't want to go to Warwickshire."

"I am actually rather curious now," Eda said. "Look, I have a journal. Do you have a map? Can we figure out if there's a portal near, or what the options might be?"

"But they won't be magical," Jeremy said. "You can't just invite yourself over. Not to some grand estate."

"No, but I have a journal, a number of connections, and chances are decent that someone knows someone who knows someone. And we can say we mostly want to see the gardens, but we're curious about the house."

Jeremy sighed. "Let us consult the library, then. There are some books that might be a help."

The library was surprisingly informative. It took them several hours, each of them alternating going through the shelves and the books they found. Baddesely Clinton had a number of connections to Catholic recusants. It had been a grand estate for a long time. Harvington Hall was smaller, and now it was rather run down, far more than Oakburgh, perhaps. What information they could find helped Eda figure out who to write to, who might have a connection. By the time she finished a series of polite notes, it was well past ten and they were both yawning.

Jeremy offered her a hand up from the desk. "You needn't."

"I want to." Eda met his eyes, then looked away. "It's an interesting mystery. And I'm invested in solving it now. So long as you permit me."

"I'm sure I couldn't stop you if I wanted to," Jeremy said. "Please. Continue helping. You've had several ideas I'd never have thought of. And Ernie was willing to talk to you. More than to me."

"We will figure out going to Warwickshire then."

CHAPTER 26
JULY 5TH AT HARVINGTON HALL

They had needed to put off any trip until Tuesday. It had taken a day for Jeremy to send a message. Then it turned out the place they particularly wanted, Harvington Hall, was currently owned by the Catholic archdiocese. That meant the archbishop resident there was occupied on Saturday and Sunday. And being on the elderly side, recovering on the Monday. It had at least given Jeremy time to make arrangements, and Eda had gone off to Trellech for several days to catch up on business at home. And to do some research, she'd implied.

Jeremy found he missed her. Certainly, it was more pleasant to share a meal with someone else, but it wasn't just that. He rather enjoyed knowing that she was working away, but that she'd pause in the middle of the day and walk in the gardens and enjoy the space. That after supper, they might well chat, and it would be enjoyable, about a conversation unfolding. It wasn't something where he needed to be on guard.

On the other hand, she had an entire life that had nothing to do with him, and she would go back to it in due course. Within the month, if he didn't figure out funding for the other tapestries, maybe a little longer. And she'd worked late, and through several weekend days, he certainly would not begrudge her the time. He came back into Trellech on Monday, when it was convenient for Douglas and the cart.

When he met Eda at Portal Square on Tuesday morning, she looked cheerful. And also utterly appropriate for a visit. She was dressed in a tidy navy dress. He had no idea how to describe it, but it near shouted propriety. It was absolutely the sort of clothing worn by a respectable woman for a visit to a house owned by an archbishop. It had a neat lace collar and clean white cuffs on the sleeves, and shoes to match. For all that it was proper, the equivalent to his summer weight suit and hat, he thought it didn't suit her near as well as the clothing she wore while working or relaxing. Those had a bright colour or two accented by embroidered bands at the cuffs or a cloth around her hair to keep the dust out.

Thankfully, the portal traffic was flowing well enough. Jeremy had arranged for a cart and driver from the portal at Kidderminster, and it was only about four miles from there to the hall. The driver was a local farming lad, one of those who was glad to pick up a little extra coin while the crops were busy growing. Jeremy had made similar arrangements dozens of times when he'd needed to go to some place or another to examine the growing records for a particular bit of materia. The Carter's Guild kept a list, sorted by who was handy to particular portals and their general availability.

Here, they rolled along smoothly enough, the last bit along a dirt road. Eda cleared her throat once they weren't near anyone. "We should make our story consistent."

"Story?" Jeremy blinked. "I'd assumed we were telling

most of the truth. Not the magic, of course, not with an archbishop."

There was a snort from the carter. Eda smiled. At least she wasn't offended. "Am I consulting with you on the house, then, do you want to mention the tapestries? What I could find in the library wasn't much; the house was in rather a state, no particular magical history. I don't know what Ernie thought we'd find here."

"Ernie, sir?" The carter asked from the front of the cart.

"Ernie Harrow. He suggested we come out, but we're not sure why." Jeremy saw no reason not to answer.

The carter made an entirely different sound, as if he were muffling himself with his hand. Then he cleared his throat. "We're coming up the road, sir. Ma'am." He was in the first half of his twenties, too young to have fought in the War, but he absolutely was discouraging further questions. The cart pulled up, and Jeremy got out, holding out his hand to let Eda get down.

As they were arranging themselves, an older woman came out, looking from one to the other. "Mr Royston, and this is?"

"This is Mrs Fellowes, who is assisting me with some restoration in the home I inherited in Norfolk. She deals with tapestries and wall-hangings. You'd be Mrs Mary Harris, then?" Jeremy added to Eda. "Mrs Harris keeps house for her brother, the archbishop."

"I'm afraid John is feeling poorly today. He may not make it out of his study. But he's agreed I should show you some of the rooms. I'm afraid the house is in rather a state still. It was gifted to the archdiocese in 1923, and of course, there are so many other calls for what money we have. A beautiful house, and a rich history." The woman chattered along amiably, showing them across a little bridge over the moat, that part was exceedingly like Oakburgh. However, instead of a central courtyard, it opened up into a house.

The initial portion of the tour took them through the kitchen, along one wing, then up the stairs. Mrs Harris paused halfway up. "Now, you asked about any unusual features. Your house, it's about the same era. You mentioned in your letter?"

"Built in the mid-15th century. A bit later than this, yes?" It was a relief to Jeremy to see that this house was in worse shape. There were a couple of uncomfortably fresh stains on the wall. And another had a sign of leaks. The creaking of the wood in the wind that would have made him nervous to spend a night in the place, honestly.

"Then you'll want to see the priest's hides." She sounded triumphant and then turned to blink at them. "You don't know about priest's hides? Well, I suppose there aren't so many of them in some places. When good queen Mary died, and her sister Elizabeth became queen, there were all sorts of persecutions of Catholics. People had to go to the Church of England services, or pay a fine, but those who held Mass could be taken, even executed. Now, there were men who built spaces into houses for a priest to hide if the house were searched. We've found seven, over the years, or known about them, but honestly, no one's at all sure if there are more."

"Seven!" Eda said, sounding startled. "Is that a lot?"

"More than anywhere else in England, so far as we know. Now, of course, the trick with a priest's hole is that they're meant to be well hidden. John's done a bit of research here and there, and other people as well. The man who made the ones here was almost certainly Nicholas Owen, though he's best known for Baddesley Clinton. I believe it's just Edward Ferrers now. Not that I know the family well, of course. We've only been here since '23."

"And of course it takes rather longer to know and be known in the area, even with your brother's prominent role." Jeremy said. "I understand. I'm trying to learn that myself."

Mrs Harris beamed at him, but then she turned. "This is one of the easier hides to see. See, the stairs fold up. The thinking was, this was where the altar items and such would be hidden. Someone could hide in there, but it would be more uncomfortable than the other hides."

"Are the others larger, then?" Eda asked.

"Oh, yes." That got them taken on a flurry of a tour. There was one tucked up over a bread oven, one under a corridor, and one up in the roof. The cleverest, though, involved Eda and Jeremy moving a chest of books. Mrs Harris leaned to loosen a single large beam set into the wall that pivoted out. It opened to make a narrow entrance that ran along for perhaps ten feet. It was comfortably large enough for someone to lie down fully, and the air was not nearly as stuffy as Jeremy had suspected.

"Originally, this entire platform was a cabinet, so you'd need to know the entrance was here at all to investigate it. Easy enough for someone to move a box or three of books in front of it if needed, for a little more protection." Mrs Harris sounded delighted by it, as if she'd invented the thing herself, but then she went on. "Nicholas Owen was ever so clever. He was a lay Jesuit brother, so committed to what he was doing."

It was a particular sort of courage and cleverness to plot to keep people safe in that day and age, Jeremy thought. Certainly, he couldn't have done it. He couldn't have kept calm with a house being searched around him.

The last hide was near as clever. What was called The Marble Room had a false fireplace. The stones blackened. There were handholds to climb up into the attic, where there were two more hides. Jeremy did not venture into that one, but Eda peered up into it, looking thoughtful. "I suppose some useful Victorian gentleman scholar, or perhaps earlier, has written a book or two about it? Do you know? Or would it be better to write to the archbishop at his convenience?"

"Oh, there's something in the library. I can go along and look, if you don't mind waiting. There's a little knot garden out here, mind the twist." Jeremy had got entirely turned around, but Mrs Harris deposited them in a small garden with a pleasant tree. Eda tilted her head, but Jeremy shook his slightly. He didn't know what sound might or might not carry.

A few minutes later, Mrs Harris came out, bringing a couple of books, then bustled them back to have a cup of tea in the kitchen. Eda copied down the titles of the books while making calm conversation. By the time they'd left, with a few scones for the trip, the two had heard all about the local Anglican fete, the tragedies and joys of several local farm families, a promising boy who might get an exam place at university, and several bits of folklore. Probably less usefully, they also got the full history of every saint associated with the archdiocese nearby, particularly St Chad, whose relics were in the Birmingham cathedral. It wasn't an ancient building, that one, but it held the distinction of being the first Catholic cathedral built since the Reformation, finished in 1841.

By the time Mrs Harris led them out to the front, and the waiting cart and driver, Jeremy's head was spinning. He helped Eda up into the cart, to her seat, and took his own, waving properly as the cart horse plodded down the road. Perhaps half a mile, well out of sight of the house, the carter pulled the horse to one side, and got her to stop. "Pardon, sir. Mistress?"

"Yes?" Jeremy was suddenly wary. They were well away from anyone else. If the man meant them any ill, there wasn't a great deal either of them could do. Not that he really expected that, but he hadn't expected this at all.

"Pardon, sir." That was a repetition. "You said Ernie Harrow. About so tall, bright gold hair?"

Eda cleared her throat. "May I ask why you're asking?"

"His family had some fields near here. They'd do odd jobs for the house. But no one's seen him since the War. Not here." The carter rubbed his chin. "I was eight, m'be nine, when the War started."

"Old enough to look up to him," Eda said, her voice suddenly very gentle. "He told us we might find something useful here. Should I let him know you asked after him? He's got steady work." Then she closed her mouth, like saying anything more might tell someone else's secret.

"Yes'm. Only, he had a row, the kind people heard over the fields, with his da. Then no one saw him, and I didn't know why, and..." The carter's voice trailed off. "If you'd tell him Jack Morse was asking after him. And if he wants to send a letter, he can reach me at the address you used to make the arrangements, sir." There was something defeated in the man's voice, but also just a glimpse of hope.

"I'll make no promises for him," Eda said. "But we'll tell him, all right? One way or another." She considered. "He's skittish. The head of the gardens, he takes good care of his staff. He's made sure Ernie's got a good place, skilled work, and steady."

"That's, that's good. Didn't like to think of him a beggar

or scraping by in some factory or nothing." Then Jack coughed. "Suppose you want to get back. And sir, I'd appreciate if you'd not mention my asking. We're not really supposed to talk to people, this kind of job."

Jeremy felt at least he could match Eda in this. "Of course you'd want to know a little more. And I won't tell. Just between us."

"Ta." Jack set the cart horse off at a good walk again, and was quiet the entire way back. So was Eda.

CHAPTER 27
JULY 7TH IN OAKBURGH'S LIBRARY

Eda was fidgeting. That was entirely unlike her. She was better trained than that. There was always something a weaver could do with her hands. If she wasn't weaving, and she wasn't eating or asleep or reading, her fingers were almost always busy either knitting or spinning. Sometimes when she was eating or reading, honestly. And she wouldn't entirely make assumptions about what she did in her sleep except that it didn't actually make progress on any physical project.

Now, though, the spindle was propped on the table in front of her, and she was peering at the book next to it. They had not got back to Oakburgh Hall until late on the Tuesday. Yesterday, there'd been no chance of talking to any of the gardeners, as they were all away from the hall for something unspecified. The same had apparently been true today.

Jeremy was across the room from her, peering through his own stack of books. He stood, crossing to a set of bookshelves, then turned over his shoulder. "Come see if any of these look promising?"

CELIA LAKE

Certainly, standing seemed like a better choice than fidgeting more, so Eda stood, brushing out her skirt and leaving the spindle where it was. She came over, leaning over his elbow. "Did you find something?"

"I'm not sure why this book is here." Jeremy reached out to touch it, his fingers running down the leather of the spine, then reaching to pull it out slightly from the shelf. Before he could say anything more, there was a rush of something— magic, tumbling, the floor disappearing or the shelf— and Eda found herself on the ground. She felt very much like she'd been a bobbin in a basket of them someone had upended. Marginally padded by her clothing, like a bobbin was with thread, but not nearly enough.

It was utterly dark, something heavy was on top of her shoulder. It was only because whatever she was on was rather bumpy that she knew which way was likely down. This was not what happened to weavers. Other people had stories that involved mysterious circumstances. Weavers made order out of thread, in good lighting and reasonable comfort. Well, for some values of comfort.

Now she knew she was in trouble, if her mind made that kind of tangle. She tried moving slightly— the weight on her shoulder didn't allow much— then lifted her head and regretted it. She couldn't see anything, and she was certain the room was spinning.

There was a groan from next to her, then the weight moved a little. Then suddenly, there was a voice very close to her ear. "Eda? I am so terribly sorry." The weight shifted, and she fumbled to grip the shoulder against hers.

"Don't rush. Are you hurt?"

That at least stopped him moving and incidentally pushing her further into the floor. "Honestly, I don't know. I

204

feel tossed about." Something in his voice smoothed out a little. "Are you all right?"

"I'm not sure either." Eda took a breath. "I think you're on my shoulder, but please be careful where you move? My head feels odd."

"Oh. Oh, dear." It was the entirely proper exclamation of a man of middle age in an unexpected difficulty, and it almost made her break into hysterical laughter. However, then he set about figuring out how to sit up. He managed it without more than a momentary weight anywhere. Then there was a hand tapping against hers. "Is this your hand? May I help you sit up?"

She wondered for just an instant what he'd have done if it had been her ankle or her knee, or some more intimate part of her body. And then, right on its heels, she realised she wouldn't have minded that. His touch was steady, not demanding something. Jeremy's desire to help came through his fingers, even though she still couldn't see anything in the dark. She cleared her throat. "That's my wrist, yes. Um. Give me a moment? Do you know where we are?"

"Sitting first. I certainly can't have a sensible conversation sprawled on the ground." Jeremy cleared his throat. "May I help you?"

Eda considered. She didn't feel like anything was actually broken, just possibly bruised. Sitting up shouldn't make anything worse. And Jeremy was entirely correct. It was much easier to be sensible sitting up. "Take it slowly, but yes. Here." She opened her hand, then found it taken by his hand around her wrist for more stability.

"On three. One, two, three." When he said the last word, he pulled, and she pushed with her other hand, coming to more or less upright. She felt dizzy, still, and she'd have to figure that out, but perhaps it was only momentary and would pass. The hand in hers didn't remove itself. "I think there might be a wall behind me. May I see if there's anything behind you? How do you feel?"

It was the last question that almost undid her again. He was worrying. She could hear that. Her workshop would have worried over her like this, but not many other people. Not Bert, really. He'd have expected her to make do. He got a bit battered in the course of his work, as he'd said often enough. "If you don't mind. I still feel a little dizzy. Something to lean against and see if it passes would be good."

"Right." The hand disappeared. There was a sense of movement near her, then Jeremy's voice sounded pleased. "There's a wall here. Six inches behind you, if you want to scoot back a little at a time?"

She did that, moving an inch or two, then another, then feeling behind her for the wall and closing the distance. It also let her rearrange her skirt to be far more comfortable. Eda could feel her hair coming down a little, but that didn't matter right now. The cool stone at her back was reassuringly sturdy. She leaned her head back, then said into the darkness, "Where are you?"

"May I sit next to you?" Jeremy didn't sound too far away. "How do you feel?"

"Still shaken. Would you—" She cut off what she was about to say, that was far too much to ask.

"Yes? Would I do something? What can I do? I got us in here, you may certainly ask." It came out of him in a flurry, like he was worried she was upset at him.

Eda took a breath. "Would you sit next to me? Where I can, um. Feel where you are?"

"Oh." There was a rustle of clothing and movement, a shift of air, and then she felt him settle next to her. A few inches to one side, and then he moved so that his hip was just barely touching hers. "Not too close?"

The fact it was dark changed things. She swallowed hard. "Your hand, maybe? I feel like I might float away. Your hand helped."

"If you say so." Now Jeremy sounded entirely dubious, as if he couldn't possibly have any quality useful to that problem. Then he moved, his wrist settling against hers. Then she twisted her own wrist so she could put her fingers in his. "I haven't been much help so far."

"You haven't panicked. You haven't made things worse." Eda hesitated for just a second. "If I must be stuck in a dark room of unknown origin, I can't think of anyone better to be with."

That just made for a very long and increasingly awkward silence. Then Jeremy cleared his throat. "Surely there are people in the world, in Albion, who would actually be a help. One of the Penelopes, for example. The gossip around the Ministry is that they train themselves on this sort of thing. Or some of the Guard."

"Do you get to hear the interesting stories, then?" Eda asked. "We sometimes get commissions from them, of course. Wool and silk weaving for protective charms, that sort of thing. But they don't usually tell stories."

"Well, if you go out to get lunch from somewhere near the Ministry, you sometimes catch them about. The Guard has their own refectory, of course, but everyone likes a change. And a few times, when we're going through the materia distribution, that's an all day meeting four times a year, there will be a tale or two in the tea break. I think one of them figured out it keeps us more likely to be agreeable in the negotiations?"

"Does it work? Or are you insistent on the proper

process and only the proper process?" Eda was curious now, because she'd had the impression of a rather rigid propriety from Jeremy when it came to matters of business.

He squeezed her hand, instinctively, then coughed. "The thing the stories do to me is they make the need real. They used the phlox to deal with an ongoing conflict or they needed a tremendous amount of vervain to stop the spread of some magical blight. It's very easy to think about what I do as being all numbers and letters on a page. But the numbers and letters mean real things to people out in Albion, and it can be the difference between a problem ending well or poorly." He hesitated. "Well, like now."

Eda tilted her head, listening to him. "That's a lot more sensible than many people are." She considered their options. "My head's easing. I don't think I hit it in falling, so maybe it was some effect of the magic. You touched the book, we tumbled in here...."

"Some sort of secret passage. Like we saw at Harvington Hall, but magical." Jeremy took a breath, and now he sounded more steady himself. "Yes. When I pulled the book out. We might be in the wall between the library and the drawing room? I'd assume that, anyway, from the layout."

"The question, then, is how we get out," Eda thought through. "Let me try a charmlight?"

There was another squeeze of her hand. "You're certain? It's not too much, if you were dizzy?" Immediately. Jeremy went on. "No, you're a grown woman. You can decide yourself. Just, you sounded, when, right after." Now his voice trailed off.

"Jeremy." Eda tried for the voice she used when settling down nervous apprentices, or at least something of the kind. "It's been a long time since someone other than Henny or one of the others in the workshop worried about me like that. I really do appreciate it. Let me try the light. If it doesn't work, we'll think through what to do. But light would make it much easier to figure out where we are, if there's a convenient door out, or whatever else might be worth knowing."

He snorted, and that was a wonderful sound. "Right. Yes. When you're ready, then?" He hesitated, and then he carefully removed his hand from hers, though he didn't move away from her otherwise.

Eda cupped her hands in her lap and willed the light into existence. It came up a bit slowly and softly, but then the glow strengthened, until they could see a good few feet in each direction. They were sitting in a stone hallway. There were stone spiral stairs to one side, in the darker area at the end of the space. Where they were showed no signs of a door or entrance at all.

"I suppose there might be something hidden. Touch the right stone or the right pattern, and it opens. But I can't say I much fancy puzzles right now. Shall we try the stairs?" Eda kept her voice light.

CHAPTER 28
IN THE HIDDEN PASSAGE

"Here, let me give you a hand up?" Jeremy pushed himself away from the wall, though he didn't move terribly fast. For one thing, he was not suited to quick movement, nor to coming up with ideas in a new situation like this. What Eda had said made sense. There was no door visible here. They should at least consider the stairs.

Now, she was looking up at him, apparently unworried. The charmlight had a warm and golden glow. It made a silver thread or two in her hair gleam beautifully, like a single strand in some of her weaving. He wasn't supposed to be noticing that, not right now. He braced himself, then offered his hand. Hers gripped his wrist. He was sure she was stronger than he was, but she used her hands for hours every day, and not just for writing. Then he was pulling her up, and Eda was standing, brushing out her skirt with her other hand.

Then she was blinking at him. "Are you all right?" The concern there, the way she leaned forward, almost undid him.

Jeremy nodded once, more sharply than he meant to, but she didn't push at him. He liked that too, but now he turned away, gesturing toward the stairs. "I'm all right. Shall we try the stairs? Or perhaps once to the end and back, just in case there's something more to be seen in better light?"

Eda nodded. She went first, a step or two ahead of him, moving the light around. They both looked closely, but Jeremy certainly couldn't see any variation. All of it looked like stone. He tapped a few places here and there, but it wasn't as if stone echoed like a hollow wood panel might. And besides, if someone had created a permanent illusion for the eye, doing it for sound as well wasn't too unlikely.

When neither of them found anything worth more than a tiny pause, Eda lifted the light. "The stairs? It's my light. I should go first."

"It's my house." Jeremy closed his mouth abruptly.

Eda turned to him, one hand on his forearm. "Does that bother you?"

He let out a hard breath. "I trust you to judge, to judge what's going on. At least as well as I might. Probably better. Unless it's a stack of orderly jars of materia, properly labelled, with a set of calibrated scales next to it."

That, at least, made her first smile and then laugh, as if he'd said the right thing. Or a right thing, at least. And she left her hand on his arm, and he liked that. "As soon as I'm up the stairs, we'll go forward together, all right?"

"Fair." The stairs themselves looked ordinary. She went up carefully, always testing a step with one foot before putting her weight on it, then repeating for the next step. It made the going slow, but Jeremy appreciated the caution. Once she was four or five steps up, he followed her.

They came out in another closed-in hallway, much like

the one below. As she'd promised, Eda had moved to one side, but Jeremy couldn't see the end of the space, shrouded in darkness. "Do we go forward and look?"

"I do like to be thorough. And who knows?" Eda tilted her head. "It's rather tidy in here. I would have expected signs of mice or something."

"Oh, Great-Uncle Dennis was always rather insistent about that. It's one place he spared no expense. I gather Cousin Hieronymus tried to change it, and Mrs Summers just found the money elsewhere. Quite right, too, and of course I sorted that out."

"Skimping on the pest control is nearly always false savings," Eda agreed. "Though, mind, moths are worse for me. All right. Shall we go forward?"

Jeremy nodded, and they took steps down the little hallway space. Somewhat to his surprise, there was a door, framed in wood, with a latch on this side. He contemplated. "Do we think the staircase is purely physical? I mean, we're not coming out on the other side of the building?"

"I'm honestly not sure how I'd tell? Not if it were sensibly made. I know of places like that, the Whitbury place, or there are a couple of others. But it's also the door we have. Try it and go carefully?"

Jeremy nodded. Eda hesitated in front of the door, then lifted the latch and the door swung toward them. At first, it looked like there was more blackness beyond, then Eda nudged it with one finger, and said, as if entirely reassured, "It's a hanging of some kind. Wasn't there one in one of the bedrooms? Nothing at all like the tapestries. I remember it was modern. Well, more modern than the 18th century, I didn't look at it terribly closely?"

"So, no problem with pulling it aside, we won't damage

anything?" Jeremy was willing to move it, in service to getting back into somewhere he knew, but this was in fact something Eda knew far better than he did.

"Let me try something." She set the charmlight hovering in the air, then pulled her hands together, chanting something under her breath until they glowed faintly. Then she ran them over the entire exposed space of the doorway, steadily, standing on tiptoe to get the top of the door. Nothing changed in the light from her hands, and he wondered if that was good.

Then she brushed her hands together. "All sturdy enough to be moved. Shall we?"

He nodded, and then she was holding back a fold of the fabric, enough for him to go first, then for Eda herself to follow. They came out in the bedroom he'd expected but not been sure he could hope for. He turned and there was the hanging, more or less as he'd remembered. Not that he'd paid a tremendous amount of attention to the details.

Eda let it fall down behind them, but she was peering at it. "Much more modern. Second half of the 19th century. I'm certain those are aniline dyes." She raised an eyebrow. "May I?"

Jeremy wasn't sure what she was asking, but he was confident she wasn't going to cause deliberate damage. Even if he wasn't quite clear what aniline dyes were. There was another softly spoken charm, a different glow on her hands; this one had a mauve shade to it, curiously, not one he thought one saw in magic very often. Then she was running her hands, held flat, an inch from the hanging.

"Definitely aniline." He must have looked baffled because Eda added, "Those are recent chemical dyes, developed in the 1850s. Mauve was the first. It's a dead giveaway.

We couldn't dye that colour at all reliably before they were invented."'

"Chemical and not materia? Does that mean it's not a magical tapestry, then?"'

"Not much magic in it. It's had preservation charms on it, I think, but nothing woven in the same way as downstairs. I'd have to look a lot more closely to be sure of that, though. And that's not for now."

"No." Jeremy reminded himself there were, in fact, other problems. "Can we see the door from here?"

"I didn't close it behind me. Can you hold this aside, and I'll see?" Jeremy held the hanging, folded over gently, as Eda leaned to pull the door closed. When the latch clicked into place, it was still a door. It had not disappeared into the wall. She stepped back and Jeremy let the hanging smooth out again. Then he took a few steps back into the centre of the room. When the room didn't change, he peered out the door to the hallway to check it was the hallway he expected.

When he turned back, the wall looked as it had last time he'd been in the room. "You'd never know anything was there unless you knew or looked. Do people look behind every hanging or tapestry?"

"Six-year-olds playing hide and seek." Eda said, in a tone of voice that made him sure there were stories there. "Are you all right? Now we're out."

Jeremy stared at his hands for a minute. "Yes. Though I'm also not sure of some things." He glanced up at her. "Did you mean it, about rather being with me?"

Eda took a step or two closer to him. "Yes. Why would I say it if I didn't mean it?"

Jeremy rubbed his face. "People don't say that sort of thing. Not to me. I don't offend them, I'm pretty sure I don't. But no one really wants to spend time with me. Would choose it. Lunch at work, but just lunch. A chat at a lecture or a concert, but only until it starts. Not drinks after."

"Oh." Eda tilted her head. "I've always had the workshop. Mine, my training. We don't always get on, but the people who rub sharp edges, well, they go different directions." She took a breath, then took a step closer. "You're not telling me no, though? About, um. Being a friend? Or whatever else we sort out."

"No?" His voice cracked in the middle, even in such a short word. It hadn't done that since he was about to go up to Dunwich.

"You're different from—" Her voice cut off, and he assumed that was about her late husband. That was certainly a topic for some other time, if she ever wanted to speak about it. "You never walked out with anyone, anything like that?"

Jeremy shook his head. "I was expecting to be a confirmed bachelor. Not that kind, the way people mean when they say it. Few people want someone who's fussy and precise." Then he glanced at her face, before looking away again towards the window. "You don't need to pretend."

That, somehow, provoked her. She took two steps forward, reaching up a hand to touch his cheek, but not quite connecting. "I am not pretending. Don't you think that. If something you do bothers me, I will tell you." Then her hand dropped to her side. "Besides. I like how you go about things. You think about the details, the consequences. That's rare."

Jeremy met her eyes, and all he could find there, not that he was that skilled at reading people, and all he could find there was sincerity. "Oh." He looked down at her hands. "You meant it, that you liked me being there." This time it wasn't a question, it was trying out the sentence, weighing and measuring it properly.

"I did. I liked that I wasn't alone. But I also liked that it was you. That you'd go at the problem the same way you've gone at everything else. Steadily. If you panic at something, I'm pretty sure you do it slowly. And later. I like that you care about doing the thing right, whatever's in front of you." She hesitated, and then her hand came up, this time resting on his shoulder. "And I particularly like, though it startles me every time right now, that you assume I know what I'm doing when it's something I know about."

"Oh." Jeremy looked back at her face, then at the arm. "It seems rude to argue. Also, a waste of time. Especially when I absolutely don't know even half as much." He gestured with his free hand at the wall hanging. "Like what aniline dyes are."

"Perhaps if we are in Trellech at the same time, and not needing to tend to other errands, I could walk you through the museum and show you some specific things?" Eda said. "Or one of the Weavers' Guild display days."

"I'd like that, very much." Then Jeremy blinked. "Is that the sort of thing people do when they're walking out?"

"Yes. If you like to think of it that way." Eda hesitated for just a second. "I'd like it if you would. To be clear. No commitments, just finding out what it's like. I kept thinking that at the Midsummer Faire, actually. That it would have been more fun going around with you, talking about each part."

Jeremy swallowed hard. "Oh. I had no idea." Then he heard a sound coming out in the hallway. "We might talk more later? I'm sure you want to wash up after all the dust? Maybe Mrs Summers knows more about the shelf."

"Of course." Eda lowered her hand. "Later. I'll see you at supper?"

"Supper." Then he took a breath, stepped back, and turned to go out the door and catch his housekeeper before she disappeared down a different staircase entirely.

CHAPTER 29
LATER THAT AFTERNOON

Eda couldn't stop staring at the tapestries. Perhaps it was just wanting something ordinary— ordinary to her, at least. The afternoon's adventures had shaken her up more than a little. So had the conversation with Jeremy, though she regretted nothing she'd said. Eda had wondered what it would be like to walk through the Faire with him. Or somewhere else. Perhaps sharing her favourite bakery in Trellech and finding out what his was. They'd both lived in the city more than long enough to have their own particular haunts.

The word 'haunt' though, got her back to thinking about the tales of the ghost, and Jeremy's own experience. And to the puzzle of the tapestries, and whether it meant anything to have them in a different order. A ghost often suggested hidden treasure or something of importance. Not necessarily money, that was the thing. So what was the ghost doing, and why was she— probably she— only seen near that side of the building?

Staring at the tapestries did not help as much as she wanted. Working on the repairs might have. But she had to admit her shoulders were complaining a little from the tumble into the hidden hallway earlier. Her fingers were not exactly at their most deft and confident. She'd foul up whatever she touched right now.

That wasn't like her at all, and Eda didn't like this feeling one bit. She wished she could go chat with Henny, sit down in her comfortable kitchen. In any kitchen, the one here was decidedly off-limits. With some reason, it was where other people worked. She couldn't go barging in whenever she wanted. But she wanted a mug of tea, a solid one, her favourite shades of blue and green glaze. She wanted Henny's hearty common sense, and the sound of the looms going steadily upstairs.

None of that was on offer, so here she was with her uncertain feelings, her fumbling fingers, and no idea what to do with herself until supper. That, though, apparently distracted her enough that she near jumped out of her skin when there was a rap on the door. "Eda? Are you—"

She twitched around, staring at Jeremy, her mouth open before she pulled herself together. "Sorry. You startled me."

"I didn't mean— should I go away?" He'd changed; he'd got the worse of the dust earlier, she thought. He had put on a jumper instead of a suit coat. It was made of a deep rust and brown pattern that brought out his eyes and hair rather nicely. Though perhaps he'd got the thing when he'd had a tad less grey coming in his hair. The jumper was distracting enough that she stared at him for a moment.

Then she shook her head. "No, please stay. I wasn't. It's been hard to settle. Your jumper's lovely. Hand-knit by someone?" Oh, it likely was by someone specific, but she was curious who.

"My mum, I've had it for ages. Since my twenties. She'd knit me at least one a year, though some of them have become too friendly with moths. I think she hoped I'd find a wife and there'd be a child or two she could knit adorable things for. Even when it became obvious I wouldn't..." He shrugged. "Now, well. There's the estate to think of, and that's a different problem with not having children."

Eda nodded. "I've something of the same with the workshop. And you don't have anyone, no cousins you're fond of or whatever?"

"You have met my rather awful aunt. One of them. There are a few cousins, a couple in their twenties. I suppose I could pass it on to one of them. I'll have to, somehow, but I don't know any of them very well. You know, the sort of thing, letters at Christmas or Solstice or whatever each year. They say a lot of virtuous congratulatory things. It's not obvious how much is papering over problems."

"Debt, infidelity, bad choices in other ways. Falling into a bottle." She looked up. "No direct experience of those. If you were worrying." Then she was caught again by the colour on him. She couldn't get herself to look away.

Jeremy glanced at his arms, then back at her. "Is there a problem with me? My jumper?"

"No! I was thinking the colour rather suited you. Not one I'd have expected you to wear, maybe, but—" Now the sentence had got awkward again. She swallowed. "I like how you look in it, personally."

"Oh." Jeremy looked back at her, a little uncertainly. "I, um. Thank you? Is that what one says in this case? Given I didn't choose the colour."

"You chose to put it on," Eda said, feeling on more solid ground now. "You chose to keep it, and take good care of it. Those things count." She took a step or two closer to him, then she admitted, "I feel a little like I should have put on something more interesting."

"Do you have a range of interesting frocks in your trunk? Not that you don't look lovely." Jeremy got that out far more quickly. Flattering her was apparently much easier than her complimenting him. She'd changed, but she'd just put on a different skirt, a green that went rather well with the rust, and a blouse. She'd also put her hair back up, so at least it was pinned in a coil around her head rather than wisps twining down the back of her collar.

"Some. Though you're right, most of the nicer ones aren't very practical." Eda hesitated for a second, but so much about this situation was unusual. Talking about how she did things wasn't out of line. "I like a skirt and blouse. Easy to pick something that's easier to work a loom with. Even if I'm not the one doing most of the weaving. Every so often, it makes sense for me to do a few minutes to settle the tension better or figure out what's going wrong."

"So a skirt, more, um." Jeremy blushed, rather charmingly.

"More fabric." Eda said.

"And you like colours. You've that green, there's the blue one, and the flowered one, and the one with the pattern, I don't know what to call it."

"Paisley. But properly woven, not printed. Someone in the guild does it. That's where most of my fabric comes from. Then my dressmaker makes it up. I could, I know how to sew, but…"

"But you're busy doing many other things with your hands." Jeremy considered. "I— may I say something more personal?"

Eda tilted her head. Again, she had that feeling of being sure he couldn't actually manage to be insulting even if he tried. "Please ask."

"You like colour, don't you? The hanging you showed

me, the way you, um. Touch it?" He waved his fingers at the tapestry on the frame. "The way you talk about it."

"I do." She didn't quite turn away. She knew he'd assume it was because of him, and no, it was because of her. "I grew up north, well up near Yorkshire. A lot of beige and lichen and not that many bright colours. A lot of the bright and deep ones, they're expensive to get, or it takes more dye to get the deeper colour. And we didn't always have a lot to spare. And then my husband, he didn't care for it. He wanted all of that kept in the workshop, not brought home."

"You said you had a workshop somewhere else." Jeremy hesitated, then took a step closer to her. "And now you make things with colour. For yourself. Your clothes, the hanging." Then, as if he were being exceedingly daring, which he was. "Your bedroom furnishings?"

It took a moment for Eda to react, then she blushed. "Yes. All bright jewel tones, a whole range of them." Then she asked, trying to keep her voice even. "And you?"

"My bedroom?" His blush got deeper.

"Oh. No! I mean, I wasn't trying to pry." She hadn't been, though now she was curious. He'd be tidy, of course. She couldn't imagine him leaving socks or pants or undershirts around, or whatever bit of newspaper he'd been reading. But muted colours. "I meant colours."

"My mother, she liked knitting with colours. Most of the jumpers I have are like this. This, um. What's the word?"

"Saturation." Eda supplied.

"Blue and green and shades of brown, and dark red. She didn't like me in orange or yellow or bright red, though she used a little in jumpers with more complicated patterns." Jeremy looked up at Eda again, meeting her eyes. "If you don't think it's, it's too informal, I'll wear more of them."

"Not at all. And you're at home, and who else is there to see?" Before Eda could say anything further, there was a cautious knock on the door. They both turned, at nearly the same time. Eda blinked, not sure what to make of what she saw. That was Ernie; she was fairly sure she could see his cap and hair peeking out over a large bouquet.

"Pardon, ma'am. Sir. I wanted to bring these in. A bit of pretty?" He sounded like he was insisting everything was completely normal. Eda knew that tone of voice from apprentices, usually when everything was about to collapse.

"Those are gorgeous." They were. It was no problem for Eda to say it. "Please, put them down on the table here." Ernie did, then stepped back, looking like a deer about to bolt with a great leap, but not quite running, yet.

Jeremy said, his voice quiet, "Thank you. And thank you for the pointer to Harvington Hall. I'm not sure of what to make of some of it, but I think it was a help. Worth doing." Then, before Ernie could say anything, he added. "Jack Morse asked to be remembered to you. And if you wanted to write, I've an address where you can send it, private. A good young lad."

Eda heard that. Jeremy had, she thought, learned it at his office, getting new young men and women sorted in their work. He had a no-nonsense tone in his voice, as if he were following an expected script, but it would all work out fine.

"Jack?" Ernie coughed. "Oh." Again, there was the shift of weight, and again Ernie didn't quite bolt. "He— he asked after me?"

Eda nodded. "We mentioned that someone had said we

should have a look, and your name. When we were on the way back, he asked after you. He looked up to you a fair bit. We didn't tell him where you were, just that you had a good place."

"Ah, not much to look up to now, ma'am. Did he say anything else?"

"He hoped you'd write, and he said—" Eda put this carefully. "There'd been a row. That your family worked the estate, back when? And you'd gone away. During the War, maybe?"

"I was on leave, yeah." Ernie swallowed. "I'll think about it."

He turned, Jeremy calling out, "I'll give Mrs Summers the address to pass on." But the young man didn't look back.

"How odd," Eda said, looking after him, down the hallway. "I hope we didn't upset him too much. But he's the one who said we should go. He must have realised we might run into someone." Then she realised Jeremy had turned to look at something - the flowers - and he was staring. "What is it?"

"That's phlox. I'm fairly sure it's Eirene's Phlox. One of the magical varieties, particularly potent." Jeremy gestured. "I didn't know we were growing it. It's not on any of the lists I've seen."

"Are you sure that's what it is?" Eda had seen it in gardens, of course. The Temple of Healing, she was sure it was there. All the phloxes were good for peace and restorative quiet. But she wasn't good enough with plants, well, any plant that didn't make the dyes she used, to be sure.

"About the variety? Not entirely. That it's phlox? Oh, yes. Where on earth is it growing? And why is it here? It does grow wild. Maybe there's a patch of it."

It was clear that Jeremy was going to be chewing on that particular puzzle for a little. Eda offered after a moment. "Books in the library? Carefully avoiding that particular set?"

That broke the spell of it a little. Jeremy snorted. "Fair. I'll be able to set it aside, at least for a bit, once I'm sure what it is. I'm sure we've got a proper botanical around that's been published in the last half-century. Shall we?" He gestured, not quite offering his arm, but encouraging her to join him, and she did.

CHAPTER 30
THAT EVENING

J eremy knew he was distracted that evening. There had been a great deal to the day, between the finding of a secret hallway and Ernie's flowers. The books in the library, and a close examination of the bouquet, had confirmed what Jeremy had thought. The phlox was definitely a magical variety, difficult to cultivate, but much in demand.

What he didn't know was what to do about it. Or what to do about anything else. Supper had been complex. Not exactly awkward, as if Eda refused to permit it to be awkward. But there were dozens of things he wanted to say and didn't know how to talk about. When they finished the pudding course, fresh fruit and cream, she looked up. "Perhaps I might come up to your rooms for a nightcap? Or if you prefer, you could come to mine?"

Jeremy blinked at her, owlishly, for a good ten seconds. But then he nodded. It would let them talk more privately. The staff were scrupulous about respecting those two spaces outside the necessary cleaning. And it was tricky to eavesdrop in either anyway, both had empty and locked rooms on either side. "I'd like that. You've not seen mine, of course." Part of him worried he'd left things untidy, but then he took a breath. He hadn't been untidy since he'd gone to school. It wasn't in him.

They finished the meal, and after a slight hesitation, he offered her his arm. That was the sort of thing people did when they were walking out, wasn't it? Or walking up. At least the staircase on this side was broad enough that two people walking together was comfortable, not cramped. Once they got to his rooms, he pressed his hand to the panel beside the door. Jeremy heard the little click of the lock and pulse of the warding, and then opened it.

His rooms were, not unreasonably, larger than hers. He had a sitting room, a dressing room, a bedroom, a bathing room, and a separate water closet, all rather sensibly arranged. He suspected Great-Uncle Dennis had planned it all thoroughly. It had a beauty of utility behind the design that echoed what Jeremy had known at Dunwich, and that also felt like the better arranged portions of the Ministry quarter. He'd brought a few things with him, or taken a few out of storage that had been his mother's. But honestly, Eda had made the place more her own, in her own rooms.

Now he took a step back, waiting to see what she said, trying not to show his anxiety. She looked around, from the landscape over the fireplace to the books on the table by the sofa, then tilted her head. "These aren't the colours you'd pick?"

He shook his head. "No. We haven't redecorated. It didn't seem, I didn't feel right doing it. Yet. I suppose that's a sign of something." He gestured. "I think this was cousin Gervase. Mrs Summers said my great-uncle liked the earthy tones, greens and browns. I'd like to bring it back to that, I suppose, but I don't know how to make everything go together."

Eda tilted her head. "Have you ever tried anything with watercolours? Even just for fun?"

"No?" Jeremy felt entirely unmoored now. "Why?"

"We could get a sketchbook and a tray of paints, good for mixing. We could go to the garden, into the woods. The view of the house from across the moat, wherever made sense or caught the eye. And then you could match those colours. Bring them back and put them here. Greens and browns, mostly, but also splashes of pink and white and red and yellow, like the flowers. You could do each room with a different scene."

He blinked at her, his mouth open. "Did you just come up with that?"

"Well, I do look at scenery and translate it into thread on the regular." Eda beamed at him. "I could make you a tapestry, too. Your very own. That's easier. I know the dyes I want, mostly. Well, I will when you pick a specific scene."

"You'd make me...." Jeremy stopped. "How long would it take?"

Eda shrugged. "Working on it on my own time? Three years, maybe, for something three foot by four. An hour or two a day." She didn't seem bothered by that at all.

"You'd— you'd want to do that for me?" Jeremy looked down. "You're offering?"

She took a step toward him, then a breath and another step until she was picking up his hands in hers. He could feel the callouses there, or whatever he ought to call the changes in her fingers, where thread and movement had worn habits. "I'm offering."

"I don't, I mean. I'm not much." He got it out without looking at her, but he was watching her hands, how they were holding his. She squeezed once, and it got him to look at her face.

"You're steady. You know what you like and what you don't. I like that. I like that you care about this house. That your first reaction with that phlox wasn't to go get angry at Ernie and demand answers. It was to go look in the library and make sure your guess was right. And you still haven't shouted at him."

"That's not, that's not enough for a tapestry." It came out sounding rather pitiful. "I mean, your work is, it's so much time and skill and what little I've seen is beautiful. The way you take care with each thread, with each detail. All the trouble you went to match the shades." He twitched his chin. "What if you decide in a year that you're done with me?"

"People talk about that, with knitting. Any big project like this. I'm thinking I'd like to take the risk. If we end up going our own ways, we can sort it out then." She tilted her head. "I could probably design it to include the seasons. That's an interesting challenge, actually. A band at a time, so that if something happened, bringing it to a state I could finish would be... that's actually a fascinating problem." She then laughed, her eyes gleaming. "I'm going to do that, just for the fun of it. I'd need to get the low-warp loom set up. We usually use the high-warp." Then she tilted her head. "I've just lost you."

"Yes?" This was absolutely plaintive. "It's not a problem doing it that way?"

"Oh, no. I just haven't for a while. And I haven't designed something that would work like that, not all one piece. But it's a lovely challenge." Then Eda took one of her hands, almost drew it back. "May I touch you? Your face?"

Jeremy swallowed hard. "Why?"

"Because I would like to. I don't think you've had much of that at all? I haven't. Not for ages." There was a ghost there, and he suspected things had, at one point, been kinder and sweeter with her late husband than they had been further on in their marriage.

"Not much. I walked out with a few people before the War, but it never went, well. Hands. Arms. Not faces?"

"Ah. Then may I touch your face?" She repeated it deliberately, before going on. "And in a little, I am going to ask you if you would like to touch me, or whether you would like to kiss. So you can think about that in advance. May I?"

"My face, yes." Jeremy took a breath, trying to steady himself, shifting his feet so he felt better balanced. Eda pulled her fingers away from his, then he watched her bring her hand up to hover just beside his cheek. She met his eyes, briefly, and he nodded, then she focused on where her hand was. Or was about to be. A second later, he could feel her touch, her fingers just resting on his skin. He closed his eyes, looking at anything was overwhelming. Then he felt her thumb stroke as her hand pressed to cup his cheek, and he couldn't help leaning into it a little.

"There. Will you, with me?" Her voice was entirely calm, but he wondered how she was managing it. This felt like magic, the purest kind, distilled down into warmth and connection and something he couldn't name.

Jeremy felt like he couldn't breathe for a moment. His heart was pounding. Then he made himself open his eyes and lifted his own fingers, matching what she did. He knew how to use his hands. He'd used them all his life. That helped, and it didn't, because this was a new sort of touch and skill. But then he could feel her skin under his fingers. "Like that?" He coughed. "Do you like that?"

"Oh, yes." She rubbed against his fingers, much like a

cat might. They could get a cat here, actually. There was plenty of space to keep a room with looms and thread closed, and space for a cat or cats. Besides whatever felines lived in the outbuildings and caught mice, he knew there were some of those. He tucked the thought aside for later, because she said, "You can move your hand, if you like." Her free hand dropped his, and came up to undo a button of her blouse, then another. It bared a little skin. "Here, do you want to?"

It was an absurdly intimate gesture, and yet the throat was a place that he saw, day in and day out. She was not exposing her, well, any of the rest of her. Certainly, women wore rather less, men too, when bathing at a lake or the seashore. Or in a wide range of current sporting attire. He glanced at her, meeting her eyes for just a second, and she nodded, encouragingly. Her own hand stayed where it was, like she was making a stable tripod, somehow.

Again, he took a breath, deliberately, then he let his hand drop. It was a few inches. It felt like forever. First the back of his fingers brushed against her skin, then he rearranged his touch so it was the fingertips. He just let his hand rest there, breathing as evenly as he could, taking it all in.

"I like this very much indeed." Now Eda sounded content, a cat in cream. "That it is special to you, that you're — you're not assuming. You're savouring. I like being savoured, it turns out."

It should have been silly, or at least a line from a melo-drama, but it wasn't at all. Each word was like a stone in a still pond, ripples shimmering out. He just managed to nod once, because he certainly couldn't form words.

She didn't say more, then. Instead, she just reached to touch his hand, encouraging him to explore a little more.

Her fingers guided his, as he began to learn the shape of her. He supposed she had learned how to make sense of this long ago, at least in other forms, but each touch, each angle, felt new to him. It would take him forever to feel confident with it, but she seemed to be enjoying it.

Finally, slowly, his shoulder began to ache, and Jeremy blinked several times. "I, may I— this." He stopped and tried again. "This— you— are wonderful. I'd like to, um, that was a lot of new things."

"And your head is full now." Eda nodded once. "I am used to teaching apprentices. Will you apprentice to me, in this, for so long as it amuses us both? Or delights, encourages, or arouses us both?"

He was nodding along until that 'arouses'. Jeremy had explored a little of her throat and chest, the back of her neck, fingers brushing at her ear, but nothing more than that. Not lower than her collarbone. Certainly not any of the other mysteries of a woman. "I, erm. Arouse?"

"If you are done tonight, I will go back to my room and do something about that on my own. Does that— oh, yes. It does." Her eyes widened. "You're going to think about that now, wonder what I'm doing. Grand. Consider that incentive to continue learning, then." Eda looked joyous, in a way Jeremy hadn't been sure about before, younger and with the weight of the world gone. Then she cocked her head again. "Do you, ever? On your own?"

He flushed. He could feel his cheeks turning scarlet. "Sometimes. Mostly, I suppose you'd say for mechanical reasons? Like shaving." Then he coughed. "Tonight, maybe more of the thinking, though."

"Good. A bit of fantasy's a fine thing. Fantasy that we might do something about when you're ready, even better. And we can talk about that too. Not tonight. No sense being entirely too much." Eda rocked slightly, then grimaced. "Also, my knee is complaining now. Best I go lie down. May I kiss your cheek?"

The last question startled him, but not too terribly much. Jeremy nodded, and then there was a kiss on his cheek, lingering. Not like Mother's, it promised other things, later, brief as it was. "Good night. A wonderful night. I should..." He gestured with his free hand. "Shall I see you back to your room?"

"Oh, I can manage. And besides, I rather like the idea of walking away, letting you watch me and think about the future." Eda grinned at him, a flash of pleasure, then she turned.

He did, in fact, enjoy watching her walk. There was a little sway to her step. Just when she got halfway down the hall, she turned and looked back at him. Then she disappeared down toward her own rooms at the far end of the house.

Jeremy sighed, closed and locked the door, and then went into the bedroom, falling onto the bed on his back, entirely sure he'd dreamed the whole thing. He hadn't. He'd come to grips with that in a few moments, and then, yes, explore.

CHAPTER 31
THE NEXT DAY

Eda found herself in a yearning sort of mood the next day. The time with Jeremy had been delightful. She hadn't known that she had that streak of boldness in her, not like that. But she'd loved watching him try a new thing, something that was right on the edge between delight and terror, that came out in awe.

It wasn't awe of her, not directly, or at least she didn't think it was. She was no Aphrodite, to descend and ask mortals to worship her. But there was something she found compelling in the way he'd treated every moment of it like something to be treasured, even when he was visibly nervous. She had come back to her room, and put up a good sound charm. Then she'd spent quite a bit of time letting herself drift with those memories while she touched herself.

After, when she was full of glorious lassitude, she'd permitted herself to wonder what he was doing. And what he'd look like if, she hoped when, she was the one to bring him to some kind of overwhelming pleasure. Eda couldn't avoid thinking of Bert. But Bert had been a little older.

While he hadn't had much more experience than she had when they married, he'd certainly heard more commentary from his guildmates about what sex within a marriage ought to be.

She thought, her nightgown still rucked up and her hand on her thigh, that it would have been a lot easier if there'd actually been a problem with the sex they'd had. He hadn't begrudged her finding her own pleasure. He'd encouraged it, though in modes that he also enjoyed. At the time, she'd felt that fair. There was no reason they couldn't find somewhere in the middle they both wanted. But when things had got less pleasant, the sex had faded out, until it was occasional. When he felt they ought to, and she felt she ought to oblige. She'd wanted it. But she'd also wanted it to feel different, and she hadn't known how to ask for what she wanted. Eda had mostly wanted to chase that memory of what they'd had, knowing each other.

She didn't know Jeremy. And she wanted to know all those things. The way his eyes might widen at a touch, or how his breath caught when she was right on the line between pleasure and overwhelming sensation. Eda certainly hoped for more of that to come. There was so much more they might try together. And she thought Jeremy might actually be far more inventive, over time. He seemed likely to be willing to try things beyond the ordinary sorts of sex that people talked about at least a little with their friends.

Or at least whatever Bert had talked about with his friends. Weavers could in fact be very lusty. The whole process of inserting one thing into another did lead to a lot of jokes. But the women she'd talked about it with had a range of preferences. It made talking sometimes easier, and sometimes trickier, so as not to make people feel hurt.

She went to sleep rather pleased with things, even though she had no idea where whatever she and Jeremy were exploring would actually lead. He wasn't the sort— Eda wasn't either— for a brief fling. Jeremy had this estate, which he was growing to care more about every day. Eda had a life and workshop and looms and friends in Trellech. But that was a problem she did not need to solve immediately. There were rather larger ones to tackle first. The phlox, the hidden passage, the tapestries, to start with. She was sure they might add to the list, still.

Eda spent the morning working on the repairs to the Gaudium tapestry. It needed doing, and she found the detailed repetitive work soothing, as always. Well, perhaps not entirely soothing to her neck, but she was used to that. She finished up with the patch she was working on around eleven, and by the time she paused for lunch at noon, she'd reset the frame so she could work on the next spot comfortably.

Jeremy had left her alone for the morning, but when she joined him in the dining room, he smiled, standing to pull out the chair for her. It wasn't at all necessary, but it made it clear he wasn't afraid to be close to her. She reached to touch his arm, lightly. "I hope the rest of your evening was pleasant? Mine certainly was, if with some aspirations for other things at some point."

He blushed, nodding. "Me as well." Then he swallowed as Mrs Summers brought in the luncheon. Jeremy then cleared his throat. "Eda, would you be free for a little after luncheon?"

Eda blinked. "If you like, certainly."

"In that case, Mrs Summers, would you check and see if Waters could talk to me for a few minutes in the garden? There's no trouble, but I'd like to ask him a question about something. Eda, your eye might be helpful, if you don't mind." There was something more determined about Jeremy now, as if he'd gathered up his self-confidence. Eda found that rather attractive.

It wasn't just the self-confidence itself; it was seeing the process of it, moment to moment or day to day. She realised with a start it was like seeing a loom strung for work, and then seeing the design build. There was always a moment where it went from a plan and a hope to something real, and she was seeing that now, in Jeremy, in motion. Certainly, she wanted to see the next steps.

Once Mrs Summers had retreated, Jeremy spoke, his voice low. "I was thinking, among other things, about what you'd said about not getting upset, and doing research. I'd love you there, in case you hear something in his answer I miss. But I'd like to ask Waters about the phlox, if there's a way to grow it deliberately, and explain the materia needs. That should be the right mode, shouldn't it? This is something the estate might do well, is it possible?"

"And if it already is growing, well, there's a chance for him to share that, without being tangled up in, I don't know." Eda beamed. "Oh, that is clever."

"I am glad you think so," Jeremy offered her a smile. "And I do mean that you might spot something I miss. But I don't want to force him. Waters is an excellent gardener. And he's taking care of the two younger men. Protective. I like that, even if I worry about what else might be hiding."

Eda nodded. "Me too. I wish I knew if Ernie had meant to leave the phlox as a hint or not. I suppose we might find out, if we ask right. Or give it a little time after the asking. Both."

"Both, and probably several other things." From there, Jeremy turned the conversation to something simpler, a few stories of people he knew in the Ministry in different departments. Eda shared a few from her own guild. The combination carried them through lunch, and at the end Mrs Summers let them know Waters would be glad to talk to them at half one.

"Let me show you the tapestry work, then." That occupied them agreeably for forty-five minutes. Eda could give Jeremy an estimate of the remaining work now, with more confidence in the timeframe. She had another two weeks, probably, to finish Gaudium's repairs. Then they'd have to decide what to do next.

Somewhat to her delight, Jeremy stood close beside her. Then, tentatively, at first, he let his hand rest on her arm, when she was showing a detail. He didn't lean. He was obviously prepared to step back if Eda gave the slightest hint it was unwelcome. Instead, once she'd finished her actual sentence, about the shades of golden yellow and the dyes used to achieve it, she added, "I quite like you standing like that. To be sure I've been clear."

"Ah. Good." It flustered him just the right amount, given that he'd been the one to make the move in the first place. But it was delightful to just linger in this space where a simple touch had a growing trust and comfort implied. Eda almost didn't realise how much time had passed until she looked at the clock. "Shall we?"

"Let's." Now, Jeremy offered her his arm, and they strolled together through the courtyard, round the path through the gardens, and over toward the walled garden. Waters was waiting there, hands behind his back, straw hat pushed back enough they could see his face. He took in the way they were walking, but Eda, for one, was sure the gossip from the house would have reached him by now, anyway. Not that the staff knew details, but they could certainly guess at a development or three.

"Waters." Jeremy cleared his throat. "I wanted to talk to you about an idea I had. You might need to go away and think about it, perhaps discuss with Henry and Ernie. That's quite all right. If you need more details, we can talk about that whenever you're ready."

"Sir." Waters shifted his weight, his voice wary.

"Ernie was kind enough to bring a bouquet. I am not a gardener. Gods know I'm not good at growing things. But I do know phlox. I perhaps hadn't explained my work at the Ministry. It has involved evaluating materia, anything grown and used for magic, so it can be ranked for quality and amount, and so that the necessary Ministry departments can request what they need for their work. There's good money in some of it. There are some plants that are always in high demand. Eirene's Phlox is one of them."

"Ah. Sir." Waters spoke, then rumbled to a silence again.

"Now, I'm not asking you right now where this came from. What I want to know is if we can grow more. Or if there's a way to grow other plants that might be in demand. I have a list of some of them. Others I'd have to check with the Ministry. And of course, I've not the slightest idea what might grow well right here. Some of it, yes, the region, all of that. But I know some of it's down to the specifics of a particular meadow or greenhouse or what have you."

"So, what you're wanting, sir..." Waters sounded cautious now, but Eda thought that caution had a bit more optimism in it. "Is to know if we can grow specific plants. How much of them?"

"Well, that's what I'd want to know, too. The right plants, and the estate could more than support itself.

Enough to do the restoration work, fix the roof. Maybe make it easier to get in and out of town. A second cart and horse, for example, and someone to drive it. It would depend on the specifics. And, of course, the harvest. I expect it would take some time to establish the plants."

"Aye." Waters looked down. "How about I have a chat with the boys? A few days, m'be, to sort out what space we have, what we might grow. Do you have a list with you now, sir?"

"I do." Jeremy sounded triumphant, and he produced a list from inside his jacket. "Can you read my handwriting there? That's the common name, that's the Latin, and then there are notes about a few of them. If you know about plants of similar sort, perhaps a patch in the woodland? I'd love to know that, too."

"We'll be having a look. And a talk. Sir." Waters tugged at his hat brim and took a step back. "If I may, sir?"

"I don't mean to keep you. Eda, shall we continue our walk before you get back to work? And before I do the same. Accounts don't keep themselves." Jeremy sounded delighted, honestly. Eda was going to wait until they were back on the open side of the manor and could be fairly sure no one was within hearing range before asking, though.

Once they were there, she stopped and turned to face him. "How do you feel?" Eda met his eyes briefly, and she could see he was full of some emotion, but not one she could name at all.

"Nervous. Delighted. I think that went well, don't you? Giving him some time to figure out what to say? I don't think he'll destroy anything. There's no reason for him to. And we're not going to pry, of course. But I hope…" Jeremy let out a breath. "Even just a steady supply of the phlox would be tremendous. Both for the finances and for people who need it. So I hope this comes out right."

"Not the sort of thing you can force." Eda tilted her head. "Depends where I put the emphasis in that sentence, doesn't it? It's not the sort of thing anyone can force, growing delicate plants. But it's also not something you, Jeremy, could force. It's not in you to get things done that way. And yet, just laying it out might have spooked him entirely. You are clever."

"I am glad you think so." Jeremy hesitated for just a second, then reached to cup her cheek in his hand. "As a reward, do you think we might look forward to a little more time together this evening?"

"Oh, yes." Eda found herself beaming, so much her cheeks might ache. "Decidedly. More of what we've done so far, or something new?"

"I think I am full up on new experiences for the day, but I would enjoy more practice with the ones I have already tried. If that doesn't disappoint?"

"Oh, no." It came out breathy, enough to make her flush now. "I'll look forward to it. Let me get back to the tapestry, then, for a few hours."

"Of course." Jeremy offered his arm again, and they walked back inside together. He left her in the great hall, going off to his own tasks, but she heard him whistling as he disappeared down the hall.

CHAPTER 32
JULY 11TH

July 11th

Jeremy spent the Saturday and Sunday quietly. Eda did a fair bit of work on the tapestry. For some of the time, he brought his book and sat in the corner of the great hall, reading to the quiet sound of her work and her humming. He found it rather soothing, actually. When she took a break, she'd show him the next piece she'd done. The more she showed him, the more impressed he was at the delicacy of touch and vision that she brought to her work. And by her utter commitment to doing the thing right.

They'd gone for two long walks, both of them avoiding the gardens and going out away from the house to the other end of the grounds. This time, he'd had the good sense to bring a birder's guide with him. They spent a pleasant half hour trying, and usually failing, to differentiate the birds they saw. Last night, they had progressed so far as exploring a little more touch while sitting down, taking their time at it, but Jeremy was still nervous about kissing.

Kissing, for one thing, seemed to involve a number of

aspects all at once. There was the angle of the head. He had heard the jokes about people bumping nose into nose. There was the difference in their heights, though sitting helped a bit with that. He did not know what to do with his hands, what Eda would enjoy, and what she would find inappropriate. Though that one, he could ask about. At some point soon. He didn't think Eda was impatient, exactly. But she'd been clear, with words, rather than making him guess, that when he was ready, she was as well.

On Monday, he'd set all of that aside, going back to his office and the muniments room to keep trying to make sense of the accounts. He was back well into Great-Uncle Dennis's accounts, where things mostly made sense, but the handwriting was not always legible. When he felt a headache coming on from trying to read where it had faded or splotched, he gave up for the afternoon, and went back to the library. Carefully avoiding the shelves with the hidden door, he worked his way through the titles, drawing out a couple to look at.

One had engravings of some of the local houses. It wasn't exactly a regional history, but it focused on a dozen or so of the magical estates in Norfolk, or at least those areas of them that the owners had been willing to let the author document. He set it down on the table, flicking through the pages until it was time to suggest Eda take a break and a walk. There might be a bit of sun, even, in an hour or so.

Jeremy was thumbing through the pages of one of the estates he didn't know at all, when he was caught by something. The book was talking about architectural details that encoded symbols or meaning in various ways. He'd been about to turn the page, but one of the illustrations, of a square mounted on a pillar, reminded him of something in one of the tapestries. Jeremy read through the chapter, which had an annoying lack of firm details. It made him think, though, rather more about the details in the tapestries themselves.

When it was about half three, a reasonable time for Eda to take a break, he went along to the Great Hall. He brought the book with him and waited until she tidily set her needle and tools aside and stood up. "Afternoon. Not a lot of progress, I'm afraid. I ended up having to take out half of it. Bad colour match."

Jeremy nodded. "I was reading this, and I got to thinking. Do you have the sketches of the two tapestries over the doors? I'm wondering about the specific books there, if they mean anything."

Eda blinked at him, and Jeremy set out the book, holding the pages and doing his best to explain what he was thinking. This was not a subject he knew nearly enough about. He felt like he was looking at someone else's records, in a field he barely knew. He could do the sums well enough, but he didn't know what they actually meant, if there were discrepancies that a trained eye would spot immediately.

Once Eda has read the chapter as well, she pursed her lips. "I don't know. It's hard to read, that might be the ageing, of course. Let me get them out." She laid the two sheets out, side by side. Eda leaned over to peer at them, then turned to go and fetch her magnifying glass from her working tray. She brought it back. "They look like they ought to be legible. My Latin's also not really anything."

"Mine either. It is not," Jeremy offered, managing a joke, "generally useful in Dunwich's education, except as it relates to materia names. And these aren't those. I'd know those, or enough of them. We could bring a copy to the Trellech library, though. They must be able to read it, or know someone who could."

"Any of the Schola ritualists?" Eda said. "And I know a couple I could ask. But it would also be— I mean, if there's something hidden here, do you want other people knowing about it?"

Jeremy had no answer for that at all, not in the moment. He let out a breath. "Let me think about that. Does any of this make sense to you?"

She stood back a little from the drawings and then looked up at the tapestry hanging on the wall. "Do you mind steadying the ladder while I look at it better? I'm wondering if there's something in the colour."

"It's my house. Shouldn't I be the one on the ladder?" Jeremy said, warily. "But certainly, if you want."

Eda snorted, but he was fairly sure she was amused, not annoyed. "I am smaller, lighter, and also know what I'm looking at." She turned to glance at him, and added, as if she were testing something. "Also, it gives you an opportunity to admire my lower limbs. I am told they are still shapely."

Jeremy blinked several times, then laughed. "By whom, please?"

"Usually Henny, and she's mostly teasing. I think. But I am rather proud of my legs. Floor looms do wonderful things for the leg, actually." Eda gestured. "Ladder?"

It was still standing in the corner, and moving it over to one of the doorways didn't take very long. Jeremy tested it to make sure it was actually steady, then held it as Eda climbed. The position did give him an excellent view of her lower body, from the hips down, and he couldn't decide whether to look at her or what she was doing.

She had climbed up there with the magnifying glass in her apron pocket, and now she moved a little, shifting her weight to look at different aspects. "Ha! I was right. Do you have pencil and paper on you?"

"Um. Yes. Don't move too much, please. I can't hold the ladder and write."

For the sake of his nerves, he was glad she stayed still. "Ready?"

"Yes." Jeremy had got the paper and pencil, balancing it awkwardly on one of the steps of the ladder nearest him. "When you are."

"There are several letters that look like they've a metallic thread running through them. Or maybe a charm. It's hard to tell. It's the first letter of the titles. G. E. H. Not every book, um...." She listed off the colours, then. A moment later, she added the relative height and width of the books with the letters picked out, and Jeremy scribbled down what she said. He was using the shorthand the Ministry of Materia used for such things as size and shape. Then she said, "All right, coming down now?"

"Ready." He held the ladder steady, until both her feet were on the ground, then moved it out of the way. "Those don't seem like they fit together. Unless there's an anagram? I'm terribly bad at those, honestly."

"Me too. Look, let me get out all the copies, and we'll see if anything seems like it matches up." That took another few minutes to clear space to have them all out. In the end, they put them on the floor, so they could have them in what Eda had decided was the proper order. Jeremy agreed with her, mind, but she'd been the one to sort it out.

Now, they stood in the middle of them, and Jeremy kept looking down. He started at one end, looking at the Latin words. "Honour. Obedientia. Abertas. Stabilitas. Eloquentia." Then he went to look at the tapestries themselves, peering at the A of Aʒertas. "Eda, is this the same thread as on the books?"

She came over behind him, resting one hand on his arm as she leaned down to look at the woven flag with the name of the tapestry. "The same. And just the first letter."

"H. O. A. S. Maybe E." Then Jeremy went back to the circle of paper. "The other four are G, for Gaudium. A, for Alacritas. T for Tolerantia. And E for Ethicus."

"Gate!" Eda got it a moment after Jeremy did. "Could— this is where I want better Latin again. They're all virtues. Maybe they had to make do?" She turned around in a circle. "Gatehouse? Given the stairs, we already figured out the stairs."

Jeremy nodded. "But where, though?" He let out a breath. "There's a surprising amount of space up there."

"Let's bring the copies up with us. Maybe we'll figure something out. Does that book you brought have images of this house, anything that shows it like it was?"

"There are some engravings, yes. I suppose that might be a help. And it's not as if there are terribly many places a door or a hiding place could be. It's windows on two sides, after all, so it's something tucked under the stairs, or in the interior rooms."

"Or between the floors, there is that odd way they take up more space thar. the rest of the house. But that's what investigation is for. Look, let's explore for ourselves, carefully. If we don't find anything, maybe we can find an architectural expert?"

"Wanted, one architectural expert suited to find hidden spaces." Jeremy shook his head. "Where you find one of those, I have no idea."

"I'd get Ferry to ask his lordship. There must be people

in the country who have secret spots in their houses, and people who make or maintain them. Not our sort of people. Well, you have a house like that now."

"Yes, but I'd like to know where the hidden places are." It came out sounding rather frustrated. "I'm sorry, Eda." Jeremy offered the apology immediately. "You've been a tremendous help trying to figure this out."

She came over, looked at him, then touched his arm again. The way she did when she wanted to be closer, he'd noticed that about her. "Understandable. Look, let's go into this better prepared. Do you have some chalk or something we can use to make markings that will wash off? I'll go fetch some of my sturdier thread, I can make a charmlight. Is there a lantern for one? A bottle or two of lemonade and some snacks? We should tell Mrs Summers what we're doing in case we don't reappear."

"Now, that is an excellent idea. And plan." Jeremy would probably have thought of it in a few minutes. "Why don't you go find what you want to bring? I'll find Mrs Summers and some chalk and snacks and rope." He tilted his head. "A sturdy bag, too. And paper and pencil and something to write on." It was getting to be quite a list. "Meet you in the courtyard in a few minutes."

"Excellent." Eda bent to pick up the copies of the tapestries. That certainly gave Jeremy a chance to admire her shape from a different angle, and he waited until she stood to turn away to his own tasks. She winked at him, and he went off, blushing slightly.

CHAPTER 33
THAT AFTERNOON

Eda had given some thought to what to bring with her, including a plumb bob and a few other of her small tools. Sewing chalk, two strong spools of thread meant for heavy cloth, a range of needles, two small pairs of scissors, and a notebook and pencil. She added the long measuring tape, the one they used for tapestries, too, that ran a full seven yards. Eda also found a lantern that should hold a charmlight down in the bottom of the working trunk. She must have left it there from one of her consulting trips.

When she met Jeremy back in the courtyard, he had a satchel over his shoulder. "Mrs Summers gave me some supplies, and she'll come look for us if we don't come down in two hours. Time for tea. She asked if we'd leave a note with where we were when in each room and what we're doing next."

"Ah, now, that's sensible," Eda said. "I found some chalk, too, and I have two spools of thread, one blue and one red, in case we each want one. Let's. The more we delay, um. The more I might try to find an excuse. And I do actually want to figure out if there's anything there."

Together, they went to the gatehouse stairs, then up to the first floor. Eda considered. "We should be systematic. There are some places we know there can't be a hidden room, anywhere there's a window. Though we should, I suppose, open them and wave an arm around to make sure it's not an illusion."

"If there are illusions, there's no hope of us finding anything." Jeremy said. "Surely?"

Eda rocked back on her heels a little. "It's an interesting question. If there was a serious search, they'd bring in someone who could dispel illusions. But then there's the door in the library. That doesn't look tricksy, but it is." She frowned. "Some of the Guard can find and remove illusions, and I'm fairly sure the Penelopes too. It's the sort of thing they'd need to do sometimes. Though I'm sure it's a complex bit of magic. The kind that there are rows of books about, and it still only works about one time in two the way you expected." Then she tapped her finger on her other hand. "Do you have records of specialists here? Or visitors?"

"Oh, yes, that's quite complete. Especially with people having to come and go from the portal." Jeremy blinked at her. "Oh, I see what you mean. It's not as if they'd list a secret purpose, would they? But all the visits, back as far as I've skimmed, the purpose made sense. I was trying to see if there were seasonal or cyclical patterns." He stammered for a second. "Is that odd?"

"It's very sensible." Eda said, firmly. "How far back did you get?"

"Into the previous generation, maybe a decade before Great-Uncle Dennis took over? So if there had been some-one, either they had another reason listed for visiting, or it was before that. And you said illusions needed to be renewed regularly, didn't you? When we were talking about the tapestries." Jeremy peered at it.

"Generally, yes. By someone. Once they're set, someone in the household might be able to, if they knew how. A few places with tapestries, the butler or housekeeper learns the knack, or the lord or lady of the demesne. But you still need an illusionist out for a touch-up. Just less often. Still, every decade or so, if you didn't want something to fade oddly." Eda shrugged, slightly.

"In that case, we can have a working theory and see what we find. We'll work from the idea that whatever illusions there might have been hadn't been renewed." Jeremy looked at her cautiously.

"And didn't you say this was mostly locked up for ages? And your cousins didn't do much with it." Eda considered the room, which certainly didn't look as if it had had much recent attention.

"No. The stairs are awkward for getting anything up. Far too much bother, when there's so much other house." Jeremy looked around the room. "All right. This room, we have the large windows here. The bed there." It was on the wall facing the courtyard, which had no windows. "There are two— do you know what those are called— towers sticking out with windows. Here is a chimney. There may be a room or rooms on either side connected to the main house. Is that about right?"

"Does your book say?" Eda considered the towers. They matched the two with the staircases on the courtyard side. That was practical and symmetrical, but it made for many places something might be hidden. "And there was the hidden space where you got into it from the fireplace. We can't discount a fireplace, apparently, though that seems terribly awkward if you needed to hide in winter."

"Magic helps, I presume? Though you'd not want to light it again, either. Huh." Jeremy put the satchel on the table, took out a book, then strung the satchel over his shoulder again, opening to the pages about Oakburgh. "Oriel windows, apparently. See, here's a sketch. And there's a floor plan, which at least gives us a sense of what we're looking at, perhaps?"

That occupied them for a few minutes, figuring out what they could match to the plan, and what they couldn't; there was a new wooden wall, it looked like. "I think we're just going to have to be steady and meticulous." Eda said finally. "And measure things. There are some measurements there, and proportions. We can quickly check the wall with the windows, and the oriel windows, and then focus on other things."

"Do we start here, or do we start upstairs?" Jeremy glanced around. "This would seem to be the more likely. Easier to get to if you were elsewhere in the courtyard, possibly even multiple entrances? It would be tricky to scramble all the way up quickly, without risking being seen in one of the windows."

Eda hadn't considered that part, actually. "There's also less upstairs, so trying there might let us work out the process better?" In the end, that was where they began. The initial measurements fit with the floor plan sketches, and they went around peering at and knocking on every bit of brick that wasn't absolutely an outside wall.

"This staircase feels odd." Eda was standing on the east side, on the second floor. "But I don't know why." Jeremy was a few steps below her, and blinked up at her. "But the walls aren't thick enough to have something there. It's only a few inches."

"Can we figure out where it matches downstairs? We probably can." Eda nodded, and went about making a few more chalk markings. From there, she moved about, running thread as a measure from where the interior wall met the exterior wall on both sides. Then, carefully, they went down a floor to the far side of the Lady's Chamber from where they'd started. Eda came around to stand in the oriel window on the west side.

Jeremy had been taking down numbers, but now he looked at her. "What's the matter?"

"Can you help me come and look here? Or would that offend your systematic preferences?" She watched him carefully, not sure how much it was all right to press. Jeremy got up immediately and came over to where she was standing.

"Here?" He gestured at the wall. It angled behind where the fireplace was. It was just large enough for a narrow door. The whole thing was brick, though, not a piece of wood that could pivot. She didn't know much about architecture, but she assumed that a large amount of brick needed more space or design to move. "Here, you try pressing along that side. I'll watch closely."

Eda took a deep breath, and pressed her hands as high as she could reach, then worked down, brick by brick, covering half the narrow wall on her side. Tracing her fingers along each line of mortar, she couldn't find any particular differences. As she bent over, she went all the way down to the floor. Nothing shifted, nothing seemed different.

"Let me try. Can you hold the book and the light?"

Jeremy offered them to her, one in each hand. Eda juggled them so she could hold the book where she could see the floor plan. Jeremy did as she had, just on the left side, closer to the opening to the main room. He got perhaps halfway down, about where a door handle would be in an ordinary door, when he frowned. "It feels like there's something here. But it's not moving. Here, you try."

He took her fingers in one hand, holding her hand in his, and tracing it. "See? Or feel, I suppose."

Eda grimaced. "I do. But it's not moving. It doesn't feel like it moves." She bent over to look at it. "Just moving would be easy for someone else to find, wouldn't it? What if there's some particular cue? A charm. We probably can't figure out a charm ourselves." Then she blinked. "Wait. Catholic house. The Lady's room. Mary, mother of god."

Nothing quite moved, but there was a different feeling under her fingers, an anticipation. Now Eda was casting her mind back over the various lore and tales and literature she knew. Quite a lot of it, because a lot of that had gone into tapestries, especially some of the older ones. "Stella Maris." Nothing changed. "Regina caeli?" It came out tentatively, and again there was that slight quiver.

Jeremy, softly, offered a simple, "Domina?"

At that, the brick Eda was touching sank into the wall a quarter inch or so, and then the wall shifted sideways, filling some of the opening to the main room and revealing a dark space. When the wall finished moving, it was perhaps two feet wide at most, and Eda could see stairs. "Write a note." Eda said. "Leave it here. In case—"

"You think we should both go?" Jeremy was eyeing the dark warily, but with some obvious curiosity.

"I think better two of us if there's something odd there.

And Mrs Summers knows to come find us. Leave a note. And we'll stretch out the thread as well and the chalk marks. Here, I'll draw an arrow or two while you write." Eda set to work doing so. She sketched out an arrow pointing to the brick, the word written below it, and then an arrow to where the space opened. The mechanism was entirely curious and cunning. On the other side, a bit of wood panelling hid some of the joins. Once Jeremy had finished a note, leaving it prominently in place, he took a breath. "Shall we?"

"Yes." Eda took the lantern and went first, unspooling a length of red thread as she went. She'd tied it off to a table leg in the little tower space. A set of narrow stairs went up into that space between the two floors. It opened into a room that must run along the front of the gatehouse, tucked between the two sets of windows. It was perhaps ten feet long, four or so feet wide. Eda could touch both sides with her arms not fully stretched. And the roof slanted from three feet at one side to nearer six. Jeremy came in behind her, and then he gasped over Eda's shoulder.

Sitting there, in the middle of the floor, a tidy pile of boxes, were a dozen or so crates and chests. They were all sorts of shapes and sizes. They looked old, and Eda was honestly nervous about touching them. Who knew what they held, or if it was even safe to handle?

Before she could find words for it, Jeremy's hand was on her back. "I am thinking I would like to cheer. And kiss you. May I kiss you? Before we think of anything else?"

That, at least, she had some idea about. She turned, automatically tucking the spool of thread into her pocket, and held out her hands to him. He took each one in his own, kissing the top, then pulling her closer. Eda stood a little on tip-toe— he was enough taller she needed to— and then realised she'd have to begin. One breath, and then she was kissing him, her arms going around his shoulders, and his, after a brief hesitation, around her waist.

CHAPTER 34
LATER THAT AFTERNOON

J eremy had not expected quite such a response to his request. One moment he was asking if he might kiss her, the next Eda was in his arms. He dropped the spool of thread in his surprise. The thing he hadn't yet begun to get used to, in what they'd done so far, was what it was like having a warm human person so close. Someone who wasn't Mother, at least, and Mother had never particularly tended to the physically affectionate.

He'd thought, for a long time, that he didn't care for it. Certainly he hadn't known enough to miss it. But Eda— Eda was warm, and she smelled like lavender and other herbs. And it seemed like whatever she wore felt good under the fingers. The wool she chose wasn't scratchy, the cotton or linen was washed and smooth, draping rather than catching. The whole experience of it, even before he got to the touch itself, pulled him in. It was like dipping a hand into lavender buds or dried nettle, any of the materia where he could handle it without damaging it, the sense of it.

It was no problem letting her guide the kiss. She

certainly had a better idea what she was doing. Jeremy was startled, though, when he felt her tongue press against his lips, then gently inside. It seemed absurdly intimate, so close to teeth, so easy to move the wrong way. He did his best not to jerk or startle, opening his mouth a little but unsure how to respond.

She pulled back when he was almost out of breath, leaning her cheek on his shoulder rather than looking him straight in the eyes. "I would like more of that. In due course." Jeremy also appreciated, very much, that she was straightforward about saying that sort of thing. Unambiguous about what she wanted, without actually expecting it of him. He didn't have to guess, and he was terrible at guessing about other people.

He took a breath, not moving otherwise. "I expect I'm not very good at it."

"Yet." Eda sounded amused. "Your first time, or first in a long time? Of course you're not a master of the art yet. Good thing I'm used to teaching people."

Jeremy ventured a joke, then. "I thought you mostly taught people to do things with their hands, not their mouths?"

It made Eda laugh, so that was a good sign. "I shall make an exception for you. Though also, teach your hands a few things when you're ready." She lifted her head, then, to peer at him. "More than a few, I hope."

"Erm." The thought of that made him flush again, and he didn't know what to do with his hands now. He kissed the top of her head, where it was within easy reach. "What do we do now?"

"I don't much want to disturb the boxes." Eda said, cautiously. "I think we want an expert. But I also think whatever expert we— you— invite out is going to want a little more information than 'we found an elderly pile of boxes'. So perhaps we should take at least some notes? See if anything is open or easy to open?"

"We." Jeremy was sure of that part. "Both of us. I would much rather see this through with you, if you're willing."

"Also," Eda said, considering. "I have one of the magical journals. In my room, it's how I've been checking with Henny. I can write to Ferry. Lord Carillon has a tremendous fondness for old books. I am certain he has a list of suitable experts handy. Or maybe even more importantly, can tell us who to avoid."

"If you trust her. And him." Jeremy certainly didn't have a better sorting mechanism other than figuring out who was on the approved lists for the Ministry. And while that told one something about general competence and standard of work, it wasn't much help in other dimensions, like what someone was like to work with. He'd stumbled on Eda from a combination of the lists and checking with the Guild. And the fact there were probably fewer tapestry restorers than there were antiquarians. Almost certainly fewer. "I can't think of a better place to start."

"Right. Let's get down a few notes. Working together." Eda took a step or two back, then circled the boxes carefully. "It looks like there's writing on the one here."

There was. It was an old form of secretary hand. Eda pointed. "Can you read that?"

"I can, yes. Give me a minute. And the charmlight, here?" Jeremy indicated where it would be most useful to him, and then he pulled his glasses out of his jacket pocket and peered at it, reading it out. It took saying the words out loud to make sense of them, but it was, apparently, a high level inventory. There was no date, however, nor any real information on how long the items had been there.

"You can't guess?" Eda said.

"There's a word for reading old handwriting." Jeremy said, frowning and searching his memory. "Paleography. We talk about it at Dunwich, especially anyone who's doing the classes related to banking or treaties. Old documents come up. Or family holdings. But it's not something I ever did much with, beyond the basics we all got."

"One of these days, I want to sit down and compare our respective training at the two schools," Eda said. "No idea?"

Jeremy shook his head. "If you forced me to suggest one, I'd say the late 1600s. The Restoration, maybe. But I don't know how the family would have been tied up in that. Or maybe they weren't, maybe something happened and no one knew this was hidden here. Or how to find it. Shall we go back now? Take the list and— that's rather a good sketch of what it looks like."

Jeremy was actually startled by it. It was a properly artistic sketch of the boxes, from all four sides.

"Oh, good. I wanted the details, as well as the count. I'm not a very good artist, but I'm a decent copyist? If you see the difference." Eda shrugged. "I can put a copy of this in the journals. It'll give a sense of the size."

They retreated up the stairs to the original passage. The door had not closed behind them. Jeremy glanced at the wall. "I suspect there's some trigger, but let's not worry about that. I'd rather lock the doors, for the moment. The gatehouse is already warded."

"Let's." It wasn't until they were coming back down into the courtyard that they saw Mrs Summers crossing.

"Oh, sir. There you are. I was just beginning to worry." She took a step back. "Is everything all right?"

"We found something interesting, but I want to keep everything locked up until we can get an expert or two out.

Can you see about having at least one of the guest rooms made up? Eda knows someone who might recommend the right sort of people, but I don't know how quickly we might schedule anything."

Eda took that as her cue. "I'll go see about writing. Supper at the usual time?" Jeremy nodded at her. He couldn't write the note, and he certainly didn't want to hover over her shoulder while she did. Or rather, he wanted to, and he wouldn't permit himself. It wasn't useful.

He was, however, prompt in getting to the supper table. He'd spent the hour or so in between washing up, and then lingering in the library, wondering if any of the books might have more about the relevant history. Jeremy hadn't dared go near the shelf that had triggered the hidden door, and the other books that looked promising weren't easy to skim.

Eda had also changed. She was wearing a bright green summer frock, her hair had been put up differently, and she looked lovely. Jeremy fumbled for what to say inside his head for far too long and finally managed to say just that. "You look lovely. The frock is a gorgeous colour on you." She had beamed like he'd come up with some flowery compliment, so perhaps he hadn't failed too badly.

By what he thought was mutual agreement, they avoided the topic of the hidden space over supper. Mrs Summers was in and out. Eda let her know that she'd written about an expert or two, and she'd know more within a day. To Jeremy, she added, "Ferry's checking with his lordship over supper. She expects someone will present her with a tidy list by lunch tomorrow. Possibly sooner. It's handy to know useful people who know even more specifically useful people."

"I'm glad we will not be sitting here in suspense for too

long." He'd worry about fees at some later point. But an initial consultation probably wouldn't be too expensive. He hoped. They had to start somewhere, and if whoever was initially recommended was too expensive, perhaps they knew someone less so. He would worry about that later, when he had actual specifics to work with.

After supper was over, and the plates cleared, he offered his hand. "Will you come up to my rooms for a chat?"

"I'd love to." Eda put her hand in hers, squeezing her fingers once. "I like how you invite me. How it feels like a treat."

It made him smile more than he expected. "A treat. Well. Something we both enjoy, certainly?" They walked up, hand in hand, until he was fumbling a little for the door.

Once they were inside, the door closed, the warding keeping it quiet. Eda turned to put her hand on his forearm. "I think you might be worried you won't be good at this. Whatever it is we're doing together."

"I'm fairly sure I'm not." Jeremy said. "I understand accounts and ledgers. This is nothing like that."

Eda tilted her head. "You know how to learn a new skill. You're careful about your movements. I've noticed that about you. If you wanted to learn to weave, I bet you'd be the sort who wove tight, but an even tight, not with bumps and bobbles. That's a skill other people have a hard time learning." Then she glanced down, a bit shy. "I like you learning. I like you not assuming you already know what to do."

Jeremy hesitated, then reached out to touch her face with his fingers. "Your husband was like that?" He didn't quite nudge her chin up. He wasn't sure he could cope with her looking at him like that, but he wanted the touch. She nodded once, skin moving against his fingers. "That history's there." He gestured with his other hand. "Like the house. All this history I don't know and don't understand, and might never grasp. And maybe that's all right. Maybe we decide what we're doing now. Together?"

"Together." Eda said. "As much as we can. I'd like to. I mean, I haven't figured out some of it. What together might mean if I'm not working on the tapestries here? And I don't want to think about it tonight."

It was indeed certainly a massive tangle for her. And Jeremy wasn't remotely in a position to figure out what he could even offer her, beyond what she already knew of the house. Maybe when he'd talked more to Waters and to whatever expert made sense of the hidden room and its contents. "Not tonight." They could put it off, even as reasonable, sensible people with structured lives and other obligations, for another week at least. And still have a fortnight to make actual plans once his leave ended. "Will you come - um. Somewhere more comfortable than standing here?"

She looked up at him then. "Your bed? We needn't do anything new, but it would be more comfortable. More options. Less horsehair sofa being itchy."

"Was that a problem? My." Jeremy took a deep breath. "My bedroom, then. This way." He led her through the door. The bedroom was not out of place in a house like this, and there were no hangings around the bed. But it was a massive four-poster, all carved wood. She stopped in the doorway, then laughed. "Do you feel like a lord lying there? Or out of place."

"Definitely out of place. On the other hand, it is definitely a bed with room for company. Can you sit, or there's a stepstool somewhere, it tucks under, I can find it?"

"Oh, I can manage. A little undignified clambering." Eda turned to glance over her shoulder at him. "More of a chance to admire my legs? I'll take my shoes and stockings off, though."

"I would not turn that down, no," Jeremy agreed, mock-seriously, before he smiled at her. "I find your legs attractive, though this is perhaps mostly because I've seen your face, your hands and arms, and your legs. The rest of it might well match up."

"We will see what you think when you have the opportunity." Eda left her shoes and stockings in a neat pair to one side of the door. She crossed to the bed, taking a little hop to twist and land on the bed. "There. Please, join me?"

Jeremy did.

CHAPTER 35
JULY 12TH

In the end, Eda had not made it back to her own room. It had been a long time— she could count the days if she chose to— since she'd shared a bed with someone. She was out of practice. Jeremy had never learned the skill. On the other hand, it was a decidedly enormous bed. It turned out there was more than enough room for them to curl up, space between them, but facing each other. In the night, she'd woken to find his hand had covered hers, and she hadn't wanted to move. It might have made Jeremy take his hand away, and she didn't want that.

Though she also really hadn't been capable of a conversation at the time. The depths of the night were not a time for good sense, or talking as delicately as Jeremy might need. And she could be patient. They didn't have to sort out whatever this was all in one go.

By the next time she woke, Jeremy had curled on his side, his front away from her, and when she looked properly, he was reading a book. "Morning." She made a point of moving a little before she spoke and was pleased he didn't startle badly.

Slowly, he twisted back. "Morning." Then Jeremy made the face she had come to realise was him being embarrassed. "Did you sleep well?"

"Very." Eda said, cheerfully. And then she set about making the morning easier. "How about I go off to my room, and we can both get ready for the day the way we're used to? I want to check my journal and see if Ferry had anything further. See you for breakfast?"

"I, erm. Yes. That seems an excellent idea. Do I—" Jeremy pushed himself up on one elbow, nearly losing where his finger was holding his place in his book.

"I am quite capable of finding the door on my own. You needn't rush getting up. Unless there's warding on the way out?" Eda asked it gently, making it into a little tease. He shook his head. "Then I'll put my dress on, and hope I don't run into anyone in the hall." She glanced at the clock beside his bed. "Probably not. They should all still be downstairs. Much easier to keep my dignity."

Jeremy sat up at that and lost his place in the book. Eda bent over to pick up her discarded dress. She'd slept in her combinations, which she'd done before and which had been the sensible choice between clothing and a bit more progression in whatever they were doing. A progression far more comfortable to sleep in. She slipped the dress over her head, doing up the buttons, and waited to see if Jeremy was going to ask a question or not.

"Have you done that before? Walked back from, what are we calling this?"

"From a gentleman's bedroom?" She turned to face him. "Not for a long time. If they see me, it's no bother. We're grown adults. Certainly no one's going to say anything to you about it, and not to me, either." Eda shrugged. "Mostly I'm amused that at my age, I'm doing this."

Jeremy nodded once, then held out his hand. She slipped her shoes back on, not bothering with the stockings, tucked them in her pocket, and came back to the other side of the bed. "Might you be willing again, then?"

"Oh, yes." Eda took his hand, curling her fingers through it. They had not done anything that had made her scream in pleasure. But she was, in fact, an older woman than she had been, and she'd actually preferred the quieter pleasures. She'd persuaded him to touch her a bit more, while she touched herself more intimately than he was ready for yet. "More like that. More beyond that, when you like. And your bed is excellent, even if it needs a ladder."

He smiled at that. "More chances to admire your legs. And other parts of you." Then he brought her hand to his lips, kissing the knuckles. "I'll see you at breakfast."

Eda made short work of running a bath, washing up, and pinning her hair up for the day as soon as it was dry. She spent rather longer fussing over which frock to put on. In the end, she picked a blouse and a skirt with cheerful flowers. When she looked at her journal, however, she was startled to see a much longer message than she'd expected, and not from Ferry. She read it twice, then brought the journal down to breakfast with her.

Jeremy was just about to sit down, and she waved it at him. "Could we go into town tonight? Or first thing tomorrow? Lord Carillon, or someone, has arranged three appointments for you, but I am to check and let him know if the times are manageable."

Jeremy sat down with a soft thump. "Three? Who am I meeting with?"

"I've got that. Here, you can read it yourself." The letter was masterfully written, the sort of flourishes that made it easy to hear Lord Carillon's voice in her head. She'd met him several times, of course, supervising the work Ferry was doing at Ytene. He'd laid out each of the specialists, suggested that the order might suit for these reasons. One had an interest in architecture, one consulted for the banks about recovered objects, and the third had a particular niche that was, in fact, relevant. Also, Lord Carillon had included a note that the third, a man, overcharged if given the chance, and he gave a range of reasonable rates, given the travel involved.

Jeremy took his time reading it before looking up at her over the top of the journal. "You didn't expect this?"

"This is Lord Carillon at his most helpful. I have not had that particular sun focused my direction before, no." She shook her head. "I suppose it would be of interest to him, for his own reasons, as well as helping Ferry. Anyway, shall I say we can be there?"

"Both of us?" Now Jeremy sounded a bit tentative.

"Both. For one thing, I want to know what they tell you, if you don't mind me listening in. And possibly one of us noticed things they'll ask the other didn't. Or can confirm a point, or think of a detail."

"That's true." She'd sat down in the chair next to him, right at the corner of the table. He reached out to cover her hand with his. "Eda, I absolutely want you there. Please. All right. And today, you'll work on the tapestry, and we'll take a walk, and— ah, Mrs Summers. Would it be more convenient for us to have a ride to the portal late this afternoon or first thing in the morning, please?"

"First thing, sir, would be better. Douglas has to go in for the market day, anyway. Will you be coming back that night? Oh, and Waters asked if he could have a word. Around four, if that's convenient for you? They'll be done with the garden work by then." Mrs Summers had brought their plates in, setting one in front of each of them. Eda was famished, she realised, so it was a good day for a hearty breakfast.

"I think so, yes, if that isn't a bother. He can just stay in town for the day. Isn't that what we've done in the past?" That meant they could sort out the rest of the plans. Eda didn't need to worry about packing an overnight bag. Jeremy walked her to the great hall once they were done eating. Eda settled into her work remarkably quickly. The repairs, those were a thing she knew. And by now she'd been working on this piece long enough to have the feel of the thread and the tapestry itself in mind as she worked. When she took breaks, she sorted out the rest of tomorrow.

At quarter to four, Jeremy turned up again, waiting until she found a reasonable stopping point. "Ready? And Mrs Summers says the cart will be ready at half-seven. She's packing a breakfast to bring with us. We'll be in Trellech before ten, plenty of time for the meetings." Those were, at least, all in the same place, the offices of someone Lord and Lady Carillon knew on the edge of Trellech. She'd been glad to lend a room with a little privacy and space.

They walked to the gardens arm in arm, but as soon as they turned into the walled garden, they were surprised to see not only Waters, but Ernie and Henry. The two younger men stood well back, still visibly skittish, but they seemed determined. Jeremy nodded once at each of them. "Waters. Ernie. You must be Henry. Should I ask Eda to wait a little further away?"

"Ah, no, sir. Not if you'd prefer not." Waters glanced from one to the other. "You'd asked Mr Haldane about the income on the estate, sir, some days ago. And he'd put you off until after harvest is in."

"I did, yes." Jeremy was frowning, pursing his lips. "And you wanted to speak to me about the phlox."

"Yessir." Waters took a deep breath. "You see, sir, Ernie's a right hand with growing plants. He learned it from a boy. His father was head gardener several places. And Henry's picked it up. I've always had a green thumb and good training, and we were already doing somewhat."

The man was not getting to anything like a point, but then Eda realised where he must be leading. "Are you saying that you've been growing— cultivating, deliberately — plants that Jeremy didn't know were here?"

Waters looked terribly relieved. "Yes'm. We harvest them proper, sir, and sell them on. They go through someone in Trellech."

Jeremy rocked back on his heels. "But they're not labelled with the estate, I'd have noticed that." The three men in front of Eda looked entirely confused. "Oh. I— did anyone explain what I normally do? Beyond work in the Ministry?"

"Not so much as you'd notice, sir," Waters said. "It's not the sort of thing we'd ask questions about. Better not to ask questions, sometimes."

"I work with the Ministry of Materia. There are a number of plants— well, take Eirene's Phlox— that grow wild. But if they are cultivated, and the circumstances can be documented, they can be properly registered. That provides some protections— people who know about them can't reveal it outside the proper circumstances. It protects the plants. They may have made you do that for what you've done so far."

Waters nodded hesitantly.

"But it's also a higher fee, per quantity, when the harvesting conditions and circumstances are known. But as it is, that money's been going back to the estate?" Jeremy stopped, and this was the moment where Eda knew she'd fallen in love with him and that it wouldn't be a problem, because he immediately went on. "Please tell me you've been properly paid for your work in this? Before whatever came into the estate coffers?"

Waters broke into a smile. "Ah, we might be interested in talking about what you mean by that, sir. But Mr Haldane was careful; we got a fair half, split three ways between us, of the profit."

Jeremy said absentmindedly. "Well, we will see about that. Make sure it's fair." Then he looked up, his eyes gleaming. "Please. Will you show me your greenhouses?"

That smile got bigger. "Aye, sir. Ernie, would you?" He turned back to the younger men, and Ernie nodded. He patted Henry on the arm, gently, and then said, "This way?"

Going behind the arch of the walled garden was a revelation. Eda wanted to bring a sketchbook out here, immediately, into the greenhouses. They were full of green and white and golden yellow, and every shade of pink and red imaginable, along with shades of purple and a touch of blue. Everything was well-tended. And as Ernie talked them through each plant, Jeremy wrote down note after note. Ernie's confidence grew with each question. Jeremy might not know how to grow any of them. But he certainly understood what they were, why they mattered, at least enough to have some comment about each.

By the time they made it down to the far end of the greenhouses, Jeremy turned. "This explains a great deal, and I'm very glad you trusted me enough to tell me. It means I'll need to have some discussions with my work, there's a question of conflict of interest. There's a process for it. I've just never been on this end of it. But keep growing things, and I'll sort that out. And..." Jeremy's smile widened. "Make some people happy, knowing provenance is something we'll be able to verify."

"Sir. Perhaps when you're back from Trellech, then?" Waters glanced at the younger men, but they had nothing to add, so Jeremy and Eda made their farewells and retreated to the house.

CHAPTER 36
THE NEXT DAY AT THE MINISTRY

J eremy waited, perched on the visitor's seat. Somehow, he'd managed to get an appointment with Master Fulbrook on almost nil notice, largely thanks to Eda offering to make the arrangements by journal. He had given her the proper language. She'd written to Mistress Norris, and Jeremy had an appointment confirmed for half three.

The other appointments of the day had gone smoothly enough, though not remotely as Jeremy had expected. The space had been nothing like what Jeremy had expected. It was a little house tucked into the eastern edge of Trellech, right before the meadows that helped anchor the illusions that hid the city from the river. The room they'd used had been elegantly done up in shades of green and purple, though the building's owner was apparently not nearby. It was her assistant who'd let them in and kept them stocked with tea.

The first appointment had begun with things Jeremy understood, but rapidly got out of his depth. Out of Eda's too, though she followed it for longer than he did. The woman in question had at least stopped, backed up, and asked more informative questions. The long and short of it was that hidden rooms in a magical estate were always fascinating. She would be glad to come and examine them at his earliest convenience.

After that, the second appointment was a little easier. It had been with one of the Scali women, who'd identified herself as a specialist in art and forgery. But also, she said, in the odd problem that sometimes turned up like this, when the provenance was unknown. She'd mentioned there were other specialists in the family she could consult. Jeremy had agreed that she might also come out and look. It had been an easy decision, after she'd laid out a decidedly practical approach for dealing with the containers.

It hadn't hurt that she'd promised to bring several young, strapping men, trained in handling delicate items, for the actual process. Or that she'd offered, before anyone could figure out how to ask, to have the lot of them under formal oath. That included not sharing any details without direct and written permission. Her fees were high, but Jeremy felt it would be money well spent. The Scali built their reputation on trustworthiness. While they weren't the bank Jeremy had used, he understood why many of the Great Families preferred them. If this were the kind of attention they provided as a general rule, they were absolutely a resource he wanted on his side.

The last appointment had been difficult. Master Lambert had largely ignored Eda. Jeremy hadn't been able to figure out if that was because Jeremy was the owner of the home. Or whether he ignored women— or at least women who hadn't gone to Schola, like he had— on principle. On the other hand, Lord Carillon had been correct that his expertise might be relevant. The man was a historian and researcher, familiar with the history of the Roystons in the period, though he'd never focused on it. He was perfectly positioned to make sense out of the family records. And also to figure out when the treasure, if that was what it was, had been hidden, and who might have done so. Those were all things Jeremy decidedly wanted to know.

In the end, Eda had judiciously invoked the name of Joanna Scali and said she was scheduled to have a look. Master Lambert had immediately minded his manners better, and agreed that he would wait to hear when the new materials were in a fit state to be reviewed. Jeremy suspected setting up space for that would take Mrs Summers and the staff a few days, at least. Beyond whatever time it took to remove things from the hiding places.

All of this was satisfactory in several ways, but it had not made Jeremy less nervous about his appointment with Master Fulbrook. Especially since he'd been kept waiting longer than expected. When the door to the office finally opened, Mistress Norris rose from her desk, slipped inside, and then came back out a minute later. "Master Fulbrook will see you now." Then she added, judiciously, "Master Kendrick is with him." Kendrick was Jeremy's direct superior, one of the seniors in the department.

Jeremy did not have time to decide whether that was a good thing or a bad one. He nodded politely. "Thank you, Mistress Norris." Then he took a breath and walked in, unsure what he'd find.

The two senior men were in chairs near the window, a third one set out for him, on the right. "Have a seat, Royston, please." Master Fulbrook looked up, Kendrick nodded, and Jeremy did as he'd been bid. "I gathered from your correspondence that you had a matter relevant to your department?"

"Yes, sir. Sirs." Jeremy cleared his throat, then he reached into his satchel and pulled out the notes he'd made. "As you know, I've been on leave to tend to an estate left to me by the family. It comes down through my great-uncle's side, then two cousins, both sadly deceased now." He'd say the right words. Though the more he'd learned about what Gervase and Hieronymus had had in mind for the estate, the more he found it hard to keep sorrow front and centre. "It turns out that the gardens on the estate are unusually productive, including several plants I know are highly sought after."

Master Fulbrook's eyes lit, and Jeremy knew that look. "You can confirm provenance? Why the... oh, yes."

"Conflict of interest, sir," Jeremy agreed. "I only learned the scope of the details yesterday. I have a complete list, though of course I didn't have the proper forms to fill out."

"Quite, quite. Not exactly what one packs for a stay in the country. Even for us," Master Fulbrook considered. "You intend to keep the estate?"

"Yes, sir. There's no one else in the family line to pass it down to, certainly no one who could properly steward the materia. There are a few young cousins who might be trained up in that, perhaps, but I don't know any of them very well. One recently out of Dunwich, one recently out of Schola, both with at least some experience in Flora or Materia."

"Both Roystons?" Master Fulbrook asked it almost idly.

"Yes, sir. Um. Both are still in apprenticeships, but I'm afraid I don't recollect the years they left school off the top of my head." Jeremy should have looked it up. He knew he'd missed something. Not that this was obvious. He was trying not to flinch and shrink into his jacket when Kendrick spoke.

"If you intend to keep on, hmm. May I have permission, Daniel?" That was to Fulbrook, obviously. Jeremy had, of course, at one point or another come across the first name, but never heard it used.

"I certainly think that is the sensible choice here, yes," Master Fulbrook agreed. "The list, please, Royston, while you talk?"

Jeremy handed over the list, glad he'd recopied it neatly and properly, all the species names properly included. Kendrick cleared his throat. "You are right to have reported this promptly, both because we could very much use new sources and because of the position it puts you in. And it is a good thing you've been on leave. What I would propose is something that's been done before, though now I think on it, perhaps not while you've been senior enough in the department to know."

"Sir?" Jeremy frowned, confused.

"We do have an option for consultants. Men and women who are familiar with our standards, but who for whatever reason do not wish to be employed by the Ministry directly. In your case, you'd be able to manage your own estate, but you would also spend some time tending to evaluation and the necessary documentation for others. How much would be up to you and your need for income. A fair bit of it can be done by post, but there would be some visits needed. Most of the places we could use someone right now are not as remote as you are, and the travel would be a week or two each season. Much of the time, you'd go from portal to portal, a few hours at each place, two or three in a day, for a full list of properties."

Jeremy knew that such a thing existed, but he'd never

focused on the details. "And that would mean a steady, or at least reasonably predictable income. And a chance to make sure the estate was managed properly."

"Just so. Particularly with an eye to expansion. You are not a Flora specialist, you're not expected to be. But you have a good eye for what needs to be a priority, and what can wait for a quieter season. And of course, we have no doubts about your ability to do the documentation to standard."

Jeremy wanted desperately to consult Eda, and he couldn't. However, he could hope she might like the idea of him being about more, with the same relatively flexible schedule he'd had the past fortnight or two. Or, no, that was a thought. "And I could do some of it from other locations, sir? Trellech, though obviously not out of the Ministry offices?"

"Certainly. You might be familiar with Agathine Broomethorpe?" She was one of the notable Flora experts. Of course he'd heard of her. Jeremy nodded, and Kendrick went right on. "She spends the Trellech season in town, then retires to the country. A matter of making sure she gets correspondence promptly, but other than the visits to the various sites, the work can travel."

"Indeed." Jeremy nodded. "I'd prefer to see the details, sir, before I make a formal agreement, but the general terms are certainly suitable. And I understand the difficulty for the department."

"Not just doing the right thing, but being seen to do so. None of us needs to be called up in the Courts for a hint of impropriety. Such a bother to have to prove it false." Kendrick nodded, then went quiet as Master Fulbrook handed the list to him.

"I appreciate the notes on how long they've been growing. Some of the rhizomes should be suitable for harvest, yes?" Master Fulbrook leaned forward.

Jeremy nodded. "From what I went through with the gardener, yes. We didn't have time yesterday to get all the details down. But he's been working that ground on his own since just before the War. And with his nephew and a friend of the nephew's since they came back. I'll be glad to make sure they all have a steady income. They've done wonders with not much in the way of resources."

"And your cousins had no idea?" Master Fulbrook leaned back now, and Jeremy was fairly sure that was a deliberate choice, making the question seem almost idle.

"Waters only told me yesterday, and I'm fairly certain it's because I had a guess or two. One of the young men put a bit of Eirene's Phlox in a bouquet. I haven't figured out if he meant us to spot it or not. Honestly, I don't know how much he knew about what I did, other than work at the Ministry. Both of them are skittish, and there's a strong divide between staff and, well, me."

"And the rest of the house isn't too much?" This was a more idle question.

"Apparently excellent tapestries— we're renovating one, and we'll see after that. And the house is in decent repair. A few interesting discoveries. I was talking to a few people to consult about that."

"Right. Hmm." Master Fulbrook tapped his fingers. "I think we can see our way to having you keep the original terms of your leave. I expect we'll want you back to do a bit of formal training and handover for whoever takes on your role, but that can wait for August. A week or two, with oaths to make sure anything relevant to your own harvests is handled aboveboard, we can manage that on a temporary basis. I'll put in the request for someone from the Courts as soon as we're done here. No more than a month, then we'll release you to your consultancy. That would let you spend the winter sorting things out, and let us look forward to a well-managed new supplier in the spring."

Put like that, it almost seemed easy. Jeremy wanted to leap at the idea, but again, he didn't know what Eda would think about it. He'd have to ask her. It was the sensible way forward for him, professionally. He couldn't keep on as he had, not without divesting himself entirely of the estate. And he didn't want to do that.

"Just so. Right. If you'd tell Mistress Norris to come in, then. We'll let you get on with things. Daniel, you can stay another half hour, yes?"

"Of course." Jeremy got a nod from Kendrick as he stood. "I'll write with the details, but if you plan to be back for August first, we'll take it from there."

"Sir. Sir." Jeremy nodded and then went to make his own escape. Mistress Norris looked like she wanted him to linger, but as soon as Jeremy made it clear she was wanted in the office, there was no time for that.

Left on his own, he saw himself out, and began the walk back toward Eda's workshop.

CHAPTER 37
THAT AFTERNOON AT EDA'S WORKSHOP

July 13th

"Here." Henny put the mug down in front of Eda. "Talk. The rest of them are gone for the afternoon."

The rest of the workshop was spending an hour or two at the Guild, and then would be free for the rest of the day. Eda hadn't complained when Henny made that clear it was her plan. For one thing, if she left Henny in charge, it was a bad idea to interfere. And second, arguing with Henny usually didn't go well for whoever was doing it.

Eda peered up, cupping her hands around the mug. "About what?"

"You've got a look to you." Henny sat down, her skirt billowing out as she tugged the chair in. "You're smiling more."

That made Eda blush. "Am I?"

"That is a question. Questions are not talking. Not the way I mean. Why are you smiling?"

It wasn't as if Henny were going to let her get away with it. "I've been really enjoying myself." That was entirely true, if also an insufficient sort of comment. Eda went on, covering the easy bits first. "The house is fascinating. More so because well, we found something."

"You said that's why you were in town for the meetings. And why I had to run notes to three different places." Henny held up her hand. "Don't you apologise. I could have sent one of the others, but it was a lovely day, and excuses to stop at three bakeries I rarely make it to besides."

Eda snorted. "I don't suppose you have any of Lana's scones left?" She asked it hopefully, because it was one chance in two they were all gone.

"I, as your loyal second, seeing to all things in your absence, made sure that one got hidden away in the cupboard only we have the key to. And I nobly did not eat it this morning, even though it was sitting there tempting me." Henny got up and went to fetch it. The cupboard in question was used for the actual cashbox, as much as they did any work in cash. But they were often upstairs, and it was always slightly possible someone might come in. They needed a place for the copies of things like the workshop's registration and taxes, or the apprenticeship agreements.

That it was also a useful cupboard for protecting hoarded pastries was simply a pleasant extra. Henny rummaged, unlocking it, then brought out the plate with two scones. "Also, one more for me."

"Figured." Eda reached out as soon as Henny put the plate down. This one was cherry and orange, one of those combinations that needed this point in the summer, really. She savoured the taste, taking two bites before setting down the rest for the moment. "We found boxes. We think it must have papers, but possibly items, too. That's why we were talking to experts. Entirely out of my line of things, except for being able to make the connections."

"Ferry said, yesterday." Henny nodded, amused. "All right. And you're not going to say more about what's in them."

"No. Mostly because I don't know yet. We knew enough not to try to move them. Who knows what might fall apart? But there are some family tales about a hidden treasure. Maybe it's something in the papers." Then Eda said, carefully, "I really like it there."

"Because of the building? Or because of Master Royston?"

"Jeremy." Eda felt herself blushing again as she said it. "And not just as my employer."

Henny leaned back, setting her scone down and tapping her index fingers together. "Is he the reason you've been smiling like that?"

Eda nodded, just once.

"Well, good thing that's not against guild standards, per se." It wasn't. There were protections, of course, but those were part of the contracts, and if need be, they could go to the Courts and have it confirmed under the truth magics. Not that Eda expected to need that, but it resolved concerns about whether work was done or if there was some sort of undue influence. Then Henny tilted her head. "What does that mean, you'll want to do more work for him? If he's got the money?"

Eda looked at her hands. She'd want to do it even if he couldn't pay her, though obviously, there was only so much of that she could do. "I don't know. He had to talk to people in his office. There's something else he had to ask about. That has to do with regulations, there. I'd like more time with him, but I don't know. Maybe he has to be here, in Trellech, for the Ministry. Maybe he ends up spending time at the estate, but what would I do if he did that?

Maybe it's both, but that's a lot of back and forth. It's a bother."

Henny frowned. "What do you want to do? Or, wait, no. What do you know about where he lives in town?"

Eda shrugged again. "Rooms with a landlady. And it's not as if there's really space here. The looms are where the bedrooms were. Mine is tiny, barely enough room for my bed and the wardrobe as is. I'm sure he wouldn't want people tracking through all the time."

"Which we do. We could probably be trained out of it again, but it might take a bit." Henny wrinkled her nose. "You could get a different workshop space again. There are a couple coming open in the Crafter's Quarter proper. But I don't know about the light or the floors."

"Never do unless you see the place. I suppose that's an idea. I'm not saying no out of hand. I'm just not sure how it'd work." She shrugged once. "I'm fairly sure he's enjoyed the time we've been together, but that doesn't mean he wants to uproot everything he's done." Eda turned her hand palm up. "It doesn't mean I do either."

Henny leaned forward, elbow on the table, and peered at her. "You sure about that?"

It was no use hiding. "I want him to want something new. I don't know if he's going to. And I don't want to get my hopes up."

"Right. We can start there. You could also try something out, three or six months, and see what you think. You don't have to make only one decision, do you?" Henny shrugged, then circled back to the larger question. "It's like the weaving. Draw the cartoon, set up the warps, go from there. You can make changes as you work."

It reminded Eda. "Oh, I— um. I might want to get the

low warp loom out of storage. For a project." No, that was no good. She was blushing again.

"For— oh, for him. Eda, love, that's a commitment." Henny tsked, but it was her amused and only slightly worried tsk.

"I had an idea. A series of seasonal images. If anything happened, I could work one season at a time. Less commitment. I thought, oh, three foot tall? To go by a table or there's a stretch in the room he's been using as an office?"

"And you don't have hopes." Henny shook her head. "All right. I see why you want the low warp. Any thoughts on yarns? I saw there's a good batch of undyed woolen silk, and the prices were better than I expected. Or someone was saying they're hoping for a nice batch of Leicester Longwool to come in. It's still with the spinners."

"Let me know if you hear more? Or a blend with Suffolk, I suppose. I hadn't heard if Agatha was doing that again this year. And I suppose I'd be interested in hearing about any of the Romney. I don't even know who the wool producers are near Oakburgh. It's so isolated in some ways. But there have to be some. It is England." Wool was not quite eternal, but it had certainly held a firm place in the economic wellbeing of the land for centuries. And even these days, with industrial spinning and weaving and even new-fangled fibres, wool still had a place.

"Of course." Henny pulled out her notepad, making a few quick notes. "Maybe more next week. I'll write. Usual price range if I need to leap on a batch? I'll do the maths for quantity."

Eda nodded, without even thinking about it for a second.

"You do have it bad." Henny sighed. "All right. What

would make you happy, then? And how's that different from now?"

"It's just, I like being around him. We're neither of us twenty or even thirty. More time sitting in the library, both of us working. Or he's brought whatever he's reading into the Great Hall and sat there. He doesn't interrupt, he doesn't hover. He certainly doesn't say what I'm doing is boring to watch."

"So, rather different from Bert, then?" Henny had the right to poke at that. She'd known Bert, and she'd been around long enough to see some of how it was before things got less pleasant.

The question made Eda pause. "Bert never much liked any of that. Even when he was making a point of wanting to be around. He'd get bored, he'd touch the yarn and put it out of sequence." He'd make noise, in a particularly annoying way. It was never enough she could say something about it, but more than enough to irritate. "Jeremy's different. And he's got his own interests, too. The house, right now, but the gardens and materia. I think given half a chance, he'd like to learn a lot more about the actual plants." That was a new idea. She'd have to put it to him.

"Well." Henny was about to say something else. Then there was a knock at the door. "Is that him? It's probably him."

"Likely. I can get it." She made to get up.

Henny shook her head. "I'll let him in. And then I'll get out of your way."

Eda sensibly didn't fight. She leaned on her elbows, the mug resting on the table. It wasn't as if she couldn't hear what Henny said.

"Master Royston! Eda's in the kitchen. But just a moment." And then, still audible, but soft and fierce. "If you make her cry, I'll make your life miserable. See if I don't." As threats went, it was rather ambiguous, but well-meant. Then she heard Henny grabbing her things.

Jeremy stammered for a moment, then he got out, "I hope never to do that, except in joy. If that's permitted?"

Henny tilted her head, thinking, then Eda could see her nod. The angle from where she was sitting was just right. She was pretty sure Henny had done that deliberately. "Fair. Go on through."

There was the sound of the front door opening, then closing, and then about ten seconds later, Jeremy walking toward the kitchen. He bobbed his head in the door. "May I?"

"Please. There's some tea in the pot, still, if you'd like. And mugs there - the ones on that end aren't anyone's in particular." Each of the people here regularly had their own hook for their particular favourite, but there were always other people in and out, or some needing washing. "And here, half a scone, from one of our favourite bakeries across town."

Jeremy hesitated, then selected a green mug. "That was Henny." He didn't make it a question.

"The one and only. I'm sorry, I didn't realise she'd be quite that fierce." Eda offered, uncertain now.

When Jeremy looked back at her, he looked baffled. Then he took his time, pouring the tea. Silently, she broke the scone in half and pushed the uneaten bit across to him. "Why wouldn't I want your friend to worry about you? Though, er— it might be nice to know what she might be worrying about?"

"Ah, well. That's a part we have to talk about, isn't it? Do you want to do that now, or wait?"

"Oh. I'd like to do it back at the house. I need to think

through some of my day. I've some choices to make, no matter what, but it's been rather a long day and a lot of meetings."

"Tea. Scone. And then we'll make it to the portal in good time to meet Douglas." Eda could be decisive about that much. It turned out. And she was just as glad to have a night to sleep on the next conversation, too.

CHAPTER 38
JULY 14TH AT OAKBURGH HALL

"Do you have—"

"Can I ask—"

The two of them collided, sentences running over each other, before Jeremy stopped and gestured at Eda. They'd got back the night before. But Eda had been yawning even before they finished supper. Jeremy had walked her to her room and wished her restful sleep.

Now he gestured at her again, offering a helpful "You first?"

"Is now a good time to talk? About um, Henny and yesterday?" Eda looked nervous, and Jeremy immediately stood up, coming to take her hand and guide her back to the sofa. She sat, rather automatically, and he did too, close enough together they weren't quite touching, except for that hand, but close enough.

"Please." Jeremy added almost immediately. "I've something I'd like to ask you, too."

"Oh." That almost stalled her. Then she went on, ducking her chin. She hoped he'd understand she was uncertain, but doing this anyway. "Talking to Henny, yesterday, I realised how much I enjoy your company. You being around. Even when it's the two of us doing things quietly. You didn't come and read today, while I was working, were you— were you avoiding that?"

"You were very focused, and I didn't want to interrupt," Jeremy said, promptly. "I missed it too, but I was working on something. The thing I wanted to tell you about. Before, um." He coughed. "What does that mean, what you said?"

"Henny pointed out I could, if you wanted, if it was something we both wanted." Eda stalled again. "That we could try whatever it was we were doing for a while, and see how it worked. That what we decide now doesn't need to be the only choice."

Jeremy looked down at his hand holding Eda's. "And what does that mean? I— look, my meeting was a little complicated. Do you need to be in Trellech, then? Is that what you're saying?"

"I, no?" Everything felt stuck all of a sudden and strained. "I was trying to say, if you're willing, maybe here. I don't know all of how to make that work, though."

"Here?" Suddenly he squeezed her hand, reached for the other. "You mean that?"

"Yes?" It ended almost in a squeak. Jeremy almost dropped her hand. Then he was taking a breath. Eda went on, at least a bit reassured. "Apparently we should talk about that?"

"I was assuming that you wouldn't be able to. There's no portal. You have your workshop. You love your workshop and your house."

"Well, I'm not proposing giving it up. Either of them. But Henny was clear she can manage quite well. And it's not as if we're on the other end of the world. I could plan on a regular trip, work out whatever made sense for Douglas or whoever was driving the cart. Go in on one trip, for the market, come back on the other. With a little planning, it wouldn't be a huge bother." She'd been thinking about that today while she worked, how to make the back and forth not a bother. Wednesday midday to Saturday would give her time in Trellech during business hours, and to see to things. And while the apprentices were under her supervision, they could come to the estate, or she could nudge Henny to fully qualify as mistress of weaving in her own right. And it wouldn't need to be every week. Every fortnight, maybe.

"And you'd really want here?" Then he met her eyes. "Me?"

"Here. You. I suppose— wait. How did your meeting go?" She hadn't asked, had she, and she'd meant to, only she'd been so lost in thought today. And he hadn't been around much. She hadn't been sure where he'd gone.

"Ah." Jeremy took a breath, then took both her hands in his. "If we go on with the materia growing here, I can't keep my current position. I suspected that. But honestly, it's more important to have the materia than to have me. If circumstances change, and we weren't growing here, or I weren't in charge, I could go back. All the proper notes in my file, about it not being the quality of my work. But if I leave the Ministry, there are options as a consultant. Helping document provenance and harvesting. It would mean some travel, a week or two a quarter, most likely, and a lot of paperwork and documentation between times."

"But you like the documentation." Eda said. "And you could do that here?" She was trying to figure out what he felt about it. "You'd like that?"

"Exactly. And I would, I think. It's different from what I've been doing, but not very? And," He hesitated but then

291

went on before she could ask why he'd stopped. "I did rather like your idea of having people come and learn weaving, or maybe other skills? Come for a week or a fortnight, holidays? Good country air? Or maybe there are children from London, the magical bits, who could use an outing in supervised numbers?" Jeremy shrugged, a little weakly.

Eda leaned to kiss his cheek. "We can talk about all the options and decide which you like. And tolerate. Maybe not starting with hordes of young people. I'm fine with apprentices, but much younger than that and I'm not sure either."

"You never wanted your own?" Jeremy said it, and then he looked completely miserable. "I'm sorry, that's prying. You needn't answer."

Eda tugged his hands around hers better into her lap. "If we're talking about time together, for months or years to come, I think you get to ask. Especially if it's all right if I don't answer, or not right then. A few things I might need to work myself up to talking about." Like how finding out Bert had died had been full of grief. But it was more grief for what they'd had that had been good, than any hope that the good parts were going to be frequent after he came home. She was sorry he hadn't been able to prove her wrong there. That was a decidedly awkward feeling to have, never mind to talk about.

Now, though, she swallowed. "We'd talked about it. It was never the right time. He wasn't making enough. Then I was, but we were relying more and more on what I made. And while you can weave, pregnant, the kind of work I do is more awkward. Bending and twisting and such. And we just kept on like that. I enjoy having apprentices. They're all different, even though they all like weaving well enough. Different personalities, different skills. I suppose that happens with children you have yourself, but maybe not the range I get. You? I mean, besides..."

"Beside not having anyone at all interested?" Jeremy shook his head. "I thought about it in the abstract. But much as I cared for my parents, I never really had the impulse. Not more than as a hypothetical sort of thing." He looked off toward the window and Eda couldn't read his expression. "There are a couple of younger cousins. I'd want to find someone who could take the place on, manage it properly. Two of them are in the right sorts of apprenticeships. Maybe we might have them out, one at a time, anyone else who seems likely that we come across?"

"It's not as if this is a demesne estate, and the bloodline is important. And there are ways to do a proper magical adoption and keep the entail. I've heard about that." Eda wasn't actually clear on the details, but she knew on the demesne estates, some magics came down through a blood connection more clearly. Not that people didn't get adopted in, or in a few tales she'd told, have a child outside the marriage raised within it. "I'm good with apprentice age. Seeing what people want to be good at and do with themselves. And you must have cousins who are less awful than your aunt. It's not like that's hard."

Jeremy made such a face at that, grimacing, letting her see it, that she was delighted. "We can find out. And it would be here. We'd set the expectations. All right. When we get ourselves a little better sorted, I'll get a little more background and see about writing. We can frame it as setting up the place as we are, and would they like to come visit and see if they had any ideas?"

"There." Eda leaned back a little. Her shoulder was beginning to twinge. "Can I ask where you were all day?

Not that I left the great hall or that hallway, mind, but you weren't around much."

"Staring at the boxes in the hide. I suppose that's what we call it. Probably a priest's hide. I didn't unbox anything, but you remember what the specialists all said, that having any idea what was in them would help? I just took the lids off the top boxes, and one of them had a complete inventory. Good paper, better preservation charms, it turned out. I made a copy. Can you send it through on your journal?" Then he hesitated. "And can you tell me how to get one, please?"

Eda laughed. "Trellech. They're not cheap, you know that. But it's worth every penny. And if you're consulting, it will make things easier, I'm sure. Or the times when you're away or I am." Then she tilted her head. "Anything obvious on the lists? That you want to talk about?"

"Some things that will make the historians grab for them. Carefully. With protective gloves and such. Papers. Some silver and jewelled pieces, what I think are some talismans. And some documentation of funds held by a bank. Not one of the ones I know, in Trellech. But if that still exists, it might be a tidy sum. There's no real sign of what happened. Which means, I think, a mystery for the historians, of the interesting sort."

"Enough to make it worth pursuing, then." Eda considered. "And enough money from the gardens, we hope, not to mean you'd have to give up the place, or turn it into some sort of, I don't know."

"Not an aerodrome, or all the trees cut for lumber, certainly. If we can work out people to be here, in a way that suits, I think I'd like that. More people who won't bother the gardens. But we needn't rush. And if things go well, if the papers have some meaning, maybe not. Even just having items to loan to museums might bring interest in the materia, and so on." Jeremy retrieved one of his hands, finally. "It seems like we have a decision? I can't offer you riches beyond your wildest dreams. But I can offer you an interesting home with as yet forgotten history, and beautiful gardens, and plenty of space for as many looms as you want?"

Eda found herself smiling - and actually, a little misty-eyed - by the last of that. "Well, and I'm me. Callouses on my fingers, creak in the winter, certainly not as lithe as I was."

"But still," Jeremy offered, deadpan, "With excellent and shapely legs."

She laughed. "As you say. But I would be glad to be here, legs and all, with you, and see what we make of it. For as long as it's good for us both."

"That's a good hope." Jeremy twisted now, almost ready to kiss her. "May I hope that is a very long time to come?"

"Please. Yes."

EPILOGUE
JUNE 24TH, 1928 AT THE MIDSUMMER FAIRE

"There, see? Isn't that the carriage maker you wanted to talk to?" Eda leaned over and pointed, just before a number of cows crossed between them and the long display barn, with the carts and carriages outside.

"It is. Let's see. You had an idea of what you wanted to see. And what order?" Jeremy glanced around. "Oscar's set for the day. He said he'd meet us by the portal in Swaffham."

Eda considered that. Oscar, Jeremy's younger cousin, had been settling in well. He wasn't living at the hall, but he'd made arrangements to spend his holidays there, including the week of the Faire. He was quiet, but that was fine. It was Jeremy's sort of quiet.

When he'd first visited last autumn, he'd had several excellent suggestions. Since January, they'd had several sets of apprentices visiting with their apprentice mistresses or masters. They'd stay for a week or three, with space away from the everyday to focus on some particular skill or project. Mrs Summers and the staff kept everyone well-fed and comfortably housed. It wasn't the sort of thing that would support the estate entirely, but it helped quite a bit, especially while the gardens were a work in progress.

At any rate, Oscar was still getting to know them. And they were getting to know him. But it seemed at least plausible that they'd have good results there, as well. Certainly he'd shown a fondness for the hall and the history, and he'd been working on writing up notes about the history of the hall into a longer work. Granted, he'd only got ten years into it. There was a lot more to do, but that was the way of something so built up from individual choices and the world around them.

Eda considered the options now. "If the carriage maker isn't terribly busy right now, let's start there. I should go admire a fair amount of fibre, and possibly also some sheep, but you don't need to be with me for that. And then we wanted to look at the garden supplies and the household goods."

"Mrs Summers had a few things she wanted us to look at, yes. I've the list..." He patted his jacket pocket, then pulled out the notes. "Here we are. And I'm glad to come look at fibre with you, so long as no one expects me to have clever things to say about it."

"You now reliably know your silk from your wool from your linen." Eda was amused. He'd picked it up rather quickly, actually, though he was still finding blends of fibre something of a challenge. Or breeds of sheep and the staple length differences. "And you're getting quite good at the dyes. That's some of what I want to look at. There are some new combinations on offer, and it's more fun to look here. And perhaps bring some home." Not that she needed more yarn. Need was the wrong verb there. She almost certainly had enough to keep her occupied for decades.

On the other hand, she now had an entire room in the hall devoted to storing her fibre, and that was glorious. There was still space left, nearly a third of the cubby holes they'd built into the shelving. She'd found that knitting shawls was comfortable when talking to people who were staying. Having a number of shawls lying around the place against the chill went over very well. "You could help me pick the colours for another shawl? Or maybe some gloves for the young men."

Ernie and Henry - and Waters - had been thriving this summer. Near as much as the plants they were tending. Jeremy had got all the paperwork in good order before last winter, and it had meant they could go into the spring with dozens of plans. Not all of them had come out as well as hoped. That was the trick with living things.

But more of them had been successful than the average for materia growers, that was what Jeremy had said. And even better, the ones that had particularly thrived had been some of the trickier plants to nurture, so Jeremy's former colleagues at the Ministry were delighted. It was still too soon to be certain, but if the summer and autumn went as well, they'd be in an excellent position to build on going forward. Grow from. Eda wasn't certain of the best metaphor.

Jeremy made an agreeable sound at that, and so they wandered off, arm in arm. The carriage maker was not terribly busy, and they had enough of a chance to talk through some options. Jeremy had wanted a lighter pony cart, suitable for three or four people to take to Swaffham, as well as the larger cart. It would be easier to stable a smaller horse, and to find somewhere for the cart in the stable yard for a day trip. They had a look at the options on offer, and agreed to talk more through the journals in the coming days, with hopes for the cart itself before September.

From there, they wandered through the kitchen and household goods, and Jeremy ordered near enough everything that Mrs Summers had wanted. The one exception, Eda cleared her throat and had a thorough chat with not just the saleswoman but the owner and maker of the pots in question. She determined that there were other sets that might suit better. And be cheaper, besides, but just as sturdy. Eda promised to check with Mrs Summers and make arrangements for one or the other by post, leaving the bank information.

Eda stopped, as they turned away from the stall, and Jeremy paused beside her. "Something you remembered needs doing?"

"Nothing like that. I just wanted to take a moment to stop and enjoy being here. With you."

He leaned in, kissing her cheek, he was getting much more comfortable with that much public show of his steady affection. "Everything in its time, yes? Take as long as you like. I've no plans for the rest of the day besides enjoying the faire with you. Fibre next?"

"Fibre next." Eda was entirely contented at that.

If you enjoyed *Weaving Hope* and would like to read more of this series, please sign up for my mailing list to get all the latest news and fun extras.

Your reviews (on whatever review site you use) are much appreciated, too!

Read on for some historical notes about weaving, Catholic recusants, and other details behind the book.

AUTHOR NOTE

Hello, and thank you so much for this quiet little story of buildings and gardens and tapestries! As always, tremendous thanks to Kiya Nicoll, my editor and friend. And thanks as well to my early readers, for helping me making sure all of the story (and the central puzzle) worked.

First, some chapter notes, and then - if you're the sort of person who likes having a reference - some additional notes on the tapestries and their original sequence when they appear and the correct sequence.

Weaving in general: There are a great many ways to do weaving, and I've gestured at a number of them here - different kinds of looms, different kinds of processes. What you see Eda doing on the small portable loom she brings with her to Oakburgh Hall is a typical setup for a small home loom. As looms get larger, they can do wider fabric, more complex patterns (depending on the design) or work better for certain kinds of weaving, like the complex illustrative designs of a tapestry. As Eda notes, for larger looms, weavers would often work in pairs. Collaboration is a big part of helping keep things moving in a workshop, because the individual steps can be time-consuming or just need more than one pair of hands.

Thanks to my friend Elise Matthesen for sharing her long-developed knowledge about natural dyeing (and a set of samples for me to pet and admire). I didn't get as much into dye here as I might, but perhaps in some future book we'll revisit it.

Catholic recusants: There's a tremendous amount of history here, but if you're not familiar with the period, the Tudor era under Henry VIII and through Elizabeth I's reign brings in a great deal of back and forth about religion. Catholic recusants were those who remained Catholic (refusing to attend Church of England services) - laws were on the books from 1558 until they were finally removed in 1888. The term these days is usually applied to members of the aristocracy and their families. Various of these notable families created spaces for mass to be said in their homes, or to provide a secure place to hide itinerant priests (travelling around the country).

Priest holes or priest hides would be the term for those hidden spaces. I'm delighted to have finally written a book that includes some - they're an architectural aspect of history that's absolutely fascinating.

More about the history of Baddesley Clinton below, but Oakburgh Hall here is based closely on Oxburgh Hall, a real place (moated and with towers and all). I've taken a few liberties with the specific setup of the space, including the inclusion of the priest hole in the chimney, but it's based on similar spaces in other buildings. The hidden passage in the

302

library, however, comes from some historical renovation discoveries.

Chapter 5 : Castile soap is a particularly good choice when working with fabrics that can pick up oils from your hands. The name comes from the fact it was originally principally made in Castile, Spain. It was probably based on soap and recipes brought back from the Crusades around Aleppo.

Chapter 6: The famous Unicorn Tapestries (now at the Cloisters of the Metropolitan Museum of Art in New York City) were bought by John D. Rockefeller in 1922 and given to the museum in 1938. I'm very grateful to the Met for the extensive information they've shared about the tapestries, including things like calculations on how long that weaving would have taken and detailed discussions of plants and animals in the panels.

Chapter 10: One of the more amusing research problems for this book was figuring out the likely edition of the Encyclopaedia Britannica. The 11th edition was published in 1910-1911, in 28 volumes plus an index. That edition is notable because they had solicited significant experts in the field to write the articles, and many of the articles are works of art in themselves. Supplements to this edition came out in 1921 and 1926. Beginning in 1920, Sears Roebuck took over the encyclopaedia, with the next full edition (the 14th) coming out in 1929 and a revised 14th beginning to have rolling revisions starting in 1936.

Chapter 26: First, if you're at all interested in Harvington Hall, they have an excellent set of videos on YouTube showing off various aspects of the house as well as an informative website. As noted here, Harvington Hall was donated to the Archdiocese of Birmingham in 1923. It was rather decrepit then (and the roof did actually collapse in

1929). In the period, it was the home of the Archbishop and his sister.

The priest hides here and the ones at Baddesley Clinton were both the work of now Saint Nicholas Owen, a Jesuit lay brother responsible for a great many clever design ideas. Unfortunately, he was eventually caught and martyred. The hides described here are the ones that were known about in the 1920s, but in all these houses, there's always a chance there are more waiting to be discovered. Harvington Hall is considered to have the finest set of surviving priest hides - and also the largest number found to date in a single home.

TAPESTRY REFERENCES

Finally, a word about the tapestries. Each of them is based on a virtue, named in Latin. Unfortunately, none of the ones on the common lists start with a U, so there's a little bit of fuss to get the idea of the location of the hiding place across. And because these are magical tapestries, the designs were chosen to help anchor enchantments for the benefit of the household.

In the order the tapestries should be hung, they are as follows. Gaudium, Ethicus, Honor, and Stabilitas are narrow, Eloquentia are the two wide but short tapestries that hang above the double doors on each end of the room. The others are wide.

Gaudium or joy, depicting dancing out in the open, some communal celebration.

Alacritas or promptness depicting figure on horseback, as if riding to battle.

Tolerantia or tolerance, a varied scene showing many styles of dress and manner.

Ethicus or ethics, several symbols of particular saints

on a stone wall. (Neither Eda nor Jeremy are skilled at identifying these without more research.)

Honoria or honour, gate opening up into a verdant garden. H can also stand here for herbipotens, the abundance of plants, with echoes of the symbolic associations of plants and particular ideals or virtues.

Obedientia or obedience shows a scene at the Tudor court, around the time the tapestries were made, with various symbols helping anchor the time and place like the Tudor rose.

Stabilitas or stability has an architectural detail of the gatehouse stairs.

Eloquentia or eloquence have rows of books, eloquence put onto pages.

The whole spells out gatehoase (with that second a pretending to be u). And of course, the actual images, especially the S, give additional hints.

When Eda first begins to work on them, they are in order as Ethicus, Obedientia, Alacritas, Honoria, Stabilitas, Tolerantia, Abertas, Gaudium, Eloquentia.

Thank you again for joining me for this journey. The best way to get all my news is by signing up for my mailing list. Check out the contact page on my website at celialake.com for other places to find me and more about my Patreon and Discord.

The next book in the *Mysterious Arts* series will be a romance involving Gemma Smythe-Clive (Cyrus's daughter, for people who have read other books involving him) and a romance where she's around forty years old involving beer brewing, herbs, and a bit of a mystery.

ALSO BY CELIA LAKE

VICTORIAN

Council Mysteries

Claiming the Tower

Mysterious Fields trilogy

Enchanted Net

Silent Circuit

Elemental Truth

Charms of Albion - standalone

Pastiche

Sailor's Jewel

Four Walls and a Heart

1920S

Mysterious Charm

Outcrossing

Goblin Fruit

Magician's Hoard

Wards of the Roses

In The Cards

On The Bias

Seven Sisters

Mysterious Powers

Carry On

The Fossil Door

Eclipse

Fool's Gold

The Hare and the Oak

Point By Point

Mistress of Birds

Mysterious Arts

Bound for Perdition

Shoemaker's Wife

Perfect Accord

Facets of the Bench

Weaving Hope

Harmonic Pleasure

1930S AND 1940S

Land Mysteries

Best Foot Forward

Nocturnal Quarry

Old As The Hills

Upon A Summer's Day

Illusion of a Boar

Three Graces

The Magic of Four

Liminal Mysteries

Grown Wise

Apt to be Suspicious

OTHER STORIES

Complementary

Winter's Charms

Forged in Combat

Learn more about the world of Albion and future books at my website, celialake.com. Additional information linking characters, places, and timelines is available at my authorial wiki at bit.ly/celia-lake-wiki (or get there from my website under the menu that says "more information").

Sign up for my newsletter to be the first to hear about future books and learn about fascinating bits of research. Happy reading!